THE
ALCHEMIST'S
DOOR

THE ALCHEMIST'S DOOR

LISA GOLDSTEIN

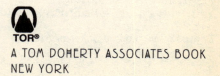

TOR®

A TOM DOHERTY ASSOCIATES BOOK
NEW YORK

THE ALCHEMIST'S DOOR

Copyright © 2002 by Lisa Goldstein

Book design by Heidi Eriksen

Edited by Beth Meacham.

A Tor Book
Published by Tom Doherty Associates, LLC
175 Fifth Avenue
New York, NY 10010

www.tor.com

Tor® is a registered trademark of Tom Doherty Associates, LLC.

Library of Congress Cataloging-in-Publication Data

Goldstein, Lisa.
    The alchemist's door / Lisa Goldstein.
        p. cm.
    "A Tom Doherty Associates book."
    ISBN 0-765-30150-4 (hc)
    ISBN 0-765-30151-2 (pbk)
    1. Dee, John, 1527-1608—Fiction. 2. Judah Loew
ben Bezalel, ca. 1525-1609— Fiction. 3. British—Czech
Republic—Fiction. 4. Prague (Czech Republic)—Fiction
5. Jews—Czech Republic—Fiction. 6. Astrologers—
Fiction. 7. Alchemists—Fiction. 8. Rabbis—Fiction.
9. Golem—Fiction. I.Title.

PS3557.O397 A79 2002
813'.54—dc21   2001059605

First Hardcover Edition: August 2002
First Trade Paperback Edition: April 2003

Printed in the United States of America

0 9 8 7 6 5 4 3 2 1

To my mother, Miriam, and my father, Harry,
with thanks for the stories,
and everything else

THE
ALCHEMIST'S
DOOR

This much is true: That in the 1580s King Rudolf of the Holy Roman Empire summoned astrologers and alchemists and magicians from all over Europe to his capital in Prague. That Doctor John Dee, the famous Elizabethan student of the occult, was one of the men summoned, along with his associate Edward Kelley. That Rabbi Judah Loew, the man who is credited with creating the golem, an artificial being made of clay, was already living in the Jewish Quarter of the city.

It is not recorded that Dee and Loew ever met. But it is not recorded that they didn't. . . .

1 "TELL ME AGAIN," JANE DEE SAID, FOLDING A shirt briskly and setting it in the trunk. "Why are we leaving England in such a hurry?"

"We're not hurrying," John Dee said. "Prince Laski wants us to go with him to Poland, nothing more."

"Then why can't we leave tomorrow, or a week from now? I have to close up the house and send off the servants, and you should arrange for money to be sent after us—"

Dee stopped in the act of folding a pair of hose and looked at his wife, studying her fine reddish blond hair, the small lines at her mouth and eyes that had appeared when their first son, Arthur, was born. Her gray eyes regarded him levelly.

How much could he say to her? He could not tell her the truth, how everything had gone horribly wrong; he could not ask her to share the fear that had weighed on him since that terrible evening.

"I heard something from your study a week ago," she said. "A deep awful voice. And Katherine was in there—she's only two. What did she see?"

She had read his mind, the way partners in a long marriage do. "No harm came to Katherine, I swear," he said, quietly praying that that was true. "Kelley and I take all the precautions necessary—"

"Kelley!" Jane said. She spoke softly; his assistant Edward Kelley had been living in a spare room on the ground floor for over a year. "Why do you listen to that man?"

"We have been over and over this. Because he can hear the angels speak, and I cannot."

"He can hear your money speak, more like. Why should he be the one to hear them, and not you? You are a good, God-fearing man, and he is—he is a man who has had his ears cut off as punishment for some crime. How can you trust him?

You know why the magistrates order a man's ears clipped. For forgery, or coining. Or for necromancy."

"He is no necromancer."

"I hope, for the children's sake, that he is not."

They continued packing, folding and sorting the family's clothes, moving through the house to collect cookpots and books and pewter plates. "Is Kelley coming with us?" Jane asked, adding bits of cedar and sprigs of lavender to a trunk.

"Yes."

To her credit she did not complain about the other man again. "How will we afford all this?" she asked.

"We have money," Dee said shortly. But Jane knew as well as he did that their money would last a few months, if that. They would have to find a patron. Prince Laski might reward him, God willing. . . .

"You should have the moneys from your lands sent after us," she said once more.

He did not reply. Jane was right, but he could not afford to take the time to arrange it. He placed the bag holding the transparent ball of crystal in the last trunk, nestling it carefully within piles of clothing, and then closed the lid. Bells rang outside, tolling three hours after noon. He had hoped to be away much earlier.

Still, he could not resist a last hurried look around. He walked through the house, taking in everything—the beams blackened from countless hearth-fires, the scuffed wooden floors, the battered furniture—as if for the last time. He had grown up in this house just outside of London; it fit him like a familiar piece of clothing. Finally he climbed the stair to his study, a small room perched precariously above the rest of the house, and looked at his beloved library: the orrery, the astrolabe, the books he had amassed with so much trouble.

He went downstairs and found his wife in the children's room, holding Rowland, the baby. He took Arthur and

Katherine by the hands and called for their servants to carry the trunks and bundles. Kelley joined them silently on the ground floor, a small sack slung over his shoulder.

A servant led the way down to the Thames. At the dock they met Prince Adalbert Laski and his retinue. Dee's heart sank at the sight of Laski's escort, which was far too large to travel as quickly as he wanted.

They boarded a boat for Greenwich, which they reached in the dead of night. "We take rooms and wait for morning, yes?" Laski said in his peculiarly-accented English.

"Let's go now," Dee said.

"Why?"

"Because—because the time is auspicious for traveling."

"It is middle of night now."

"Let's wait," Jane said. "The children have to sleep."

Katherine and Rowland were already asleep, but Arthur was bright-eyed and awake. "Where are we going?" Arthur asked, pleased with the sudden notice being taken of him. "What is happening?"

Dee gave in, knowing that Jane was right, and they found rooms at an inn frequented by travelers and sailors. When everyone was asleep he opened his diary and wrote carefully, "21 Sept., 1583. Saturday." And how long, he wondered, before we get to our destination? But he wrote about the day's events with a light tone, in case anyone read what he had written.

The next day they boarded a grander ship that would take them to the continent. A gale blew up almost immediately, returning them to shore. The bad weather continued into the night, forcing them back to the inn. Dee cursed the delay and paced in the confined space; they had taken a small room to save money and he was hemmed in by Jane and the children and Kelley and all their luggage. Rain beat irregularly on the roof, adding to his frustration.

Jane bade him to be patient; they would leave when the weather permitted. He could not tell her what he feared: that the thing he tried to escape from would not let them go.

Four days later the storm finally cleared and they were able to cross the channel. On the continent they boarded yet another ship and navigated through the oppressively flat country of the Lowlands on a roundabout route to Poland. They followed the filigree and tracery of rivers and canals and tributaries so small they didn't even have names; they saw windmills in the distance, and foul-smelling marshes; strange birds shrieked to them as they passed. A chilling wind came off the water, and sometimes an unhealthy mist rose about them, obscuring the river. They passed no one but farmers and an occasional low barge carrying trade goods.

Their ship moved slowly, so slowly. And while they sailed he was forced to be idle, and his mind—used to teasing out puzzles and studying philosophical questions—began to plague him with unwelcome thoughts. He remembered a story he had once heard a Yorkshireman tell, about a kind of mischievous fairy called a Boggart. For years the Boggart had tormented a Yorkshire farmer and his family, had curdled their butter and snarled their knitting and blighted their crops and thrown their things about, until finally the family packed their possessions and made ready to move away. "So you're leaving the old house at last?" a neighbor said, and the head of the family replied, "Heigh, Johnny, I'm forced to it, for that damned Boggart torments us so." He had scarce uttered the words when a voice came from the butter churn, packed with the rest of the household goods in the cart—"Aye, aye, here I am." "Oh, damn thee," the farmer said. "It's no use." And he pulled on the reins of his cart-horse and said to his wife, "We may as well turn back to the old house as be tormented in another that's not so convenient."

Odd how the story came back to him. He even remembered the Yorkshireman's broad dialect—"t'ould hoose," he had said. Not so odd, really. But he had left the—the thing, whatever it was—behind him.

He and Kelley dealt with kindly angels only. That was what he believed, and what he held to despite everything. Kelley saw them in the crystal, and Dee asked them questions. The unkindly angels, the evil angels, that is to say the demons . . .

No. He had left it behind. It could not come to torment him in another house. If it did, he had uprooted his family and sent them on a mad chase through Europe, all for nothing.

"Why we go this way?" Prince Laski asked once. "Travel over land is better, yes?"

"This way is just as good," Dee said. He did not mention to Laski his forlorn hope, the tale the old wives told, that demons could not pass running water.

Unlike Jane and Laski, Kelley did not question him at all. Kelley argued, as he always did, his speech a continuous litany of complaints: they should never have left England, he should not be forced to use the scrying glass so often, they should continue their search for the Philosopher's Stone instead.

Dee knew, of course, of Kelley's obsession with the Philosopher's Stone. The Stone, the goal of every alchemist, was made by the forging of opposites to create something whole, something perfect and incorruptible. Whatever the Stone touched would become perfect as well: mortal men would become immortal, impure metals would change to gold. It was for gold that Kelley pursued his experiments with potions and elixirs. He had no time for theories of perfection and imperfection; he wanted, simply and wholeheartedly, to be rich.

From the beginning Kelley had made no secret of his desires. He had first come to Dee over a year ago, in March of 1582, in the company of a friend of Dee's, a Master Clerkson. It was the day after the aurora borealis, and ever since then Dee would wonder, fancifully, if the man had blown in on the unearthly blood red lights.

Kelley called himself Talbot then; Dee never discovered why. He had a down-turned mustache, and although he was young compared to Dee, only thirty, his yellow beard was already turning gray; the streaks made it look as if his beard were rusting. He seemed to have two expressions, one jaded and worldly-wise, with drooping eyelids, and another more forceful and alert.

Yet Kelley could see angels in the ball of crystal, and Dee could not. Dee did not know why this should be so: it seemed grossly unfair, almost—though he shied away from the thought—a mistake on the part of God. Kelley was sometimes recalcitrant or bad-tempered or blasphemous, or all three. But Dee's place, so far, had been only to ask the angels questions and record their answers in the book he called the *Liber Mysteriorum*, or the Book of Mysteries.

At Dee's urging Kelley joined their household. As the months passed, though, Dee noticed oddities about the other man, things that made him uncomfortable. And Jane, who was so level-headed, had been suspicious of Kelley from the first.

For one thing, Kelley always wore a close-fitting black cap, even inside the house. Then one day he came to breakfast without it and Dee saw, shocked, that there were ragged stumps where his ears should be, that his ears had been cropped. And ten months after he moved in with them he mentioned casually, as though it was a detail of not much importance, that his name was really Kelley, not Talbot.

Once Dee opened his diary to see that Kelley had crossed out whole sections, most of them concerning Dee's secret doubts about the other man. Kelley had also added fulsome paragraphs praising his own scrying ability, paragraphs that mimicked Dee's hand perfectly. Dee remembered Kelley's clipped ears—which, as Jane never ceased to remind him, was a punishment meted out to forgers—and he wondered. "This is Mr. Talbot's writing in my book," he wrote, hoping to avoid confusion later, and he began to write in other languages besides English.

By this time, though, he had traveled too far along the road Kelley showed him. Kelley could see more in the glass than anyone Dee had ever known. At every session they had together Dee felt as if he traveled to another world, a wondrous world filled with angels and spirits and color and rare knowledge. Sometimes he thought that he was speaking directly to God, that he was on the verge of learning God's plan for the world. Kelley satisfied his hunger for this knowledge; it did not matter if the man had a hundred names.

On October seventeenth Arthur and Rowland became ill from the cold and they were forced to go ashore in Emden. Laski stopped at an inn that looked far too expensive for Dee's taste, and he and his family continued on until they found something smaller.

The innkeeper led Dee and his family upstairs and through a narrow hallway, then opened a door and ushered them inside. The room beyond was tiny, with peeling whitewash; it smelled of mold and congealed candlewax. Wind rattled the shutters and sent gusts of freezing air through cracks in the windows. The fire in the stone hearth was out and dust eddied in the corners.

The innkeeper showed Dee into the other two rooms, each as small and cold and musty as the first. Both contained a lumpy narrow bed, a chest and a chamberpot. Dee thanked the innkeeper and showed him out.

When the man had gone Dee spoke a few words. A candle on the mantelpiece blazed into light. He used it to build up the fire and kindle the other lamps. As he walked he felt as if he were still moving, still swaying to the motion of the boat.

Jane stripped the filthy linen off the beds, then sorted

through their trunks until she found sheets and blankets. As she drew them out Dee smelled the cedar and lavender she had packed them in, and for a moment he was transported back to their home in England.

They settled the children in bed. Dee studied Arthur and Rowland carefully, feeling their foreheads, lifting their lids to peer into their eyes. "They need a good warm broth," he said to Jane. "And some feverfew, if you can find it."

She nodded doubtfully and left to find the kitchen. Dee went back to the front room and stood before the fire.

A moment later the door opened and he looked up, expecting Jane. Prince Laski stood there. One of the shutters flew open and banged loudly against the wall; Dee jumped at the noise and looked at the window. The forest began a mere few yards from the inn, he saw, the serrated edges of the pine trees cutting at the sky.

"The angels speak to us tonight, yes?" Laski asked in his outlandish Polish accent. Kelley's angels had promised Laski that he would become king of Poland, and the prince was eager to learn more about his fate.

Dee went to the window, staring out at the darkness of the forest. What was he looking for? The thing he feared would not show itself; he almost wished it would, wished he had something tangible to fight. "No," he said slowly. "We must not summon the angels in such a godforsaken place as this."

The minute the words were out of his mouth he wanted to call them back. The place was not godforsaken; surely God would not forsake any of them. One of his children cried from the next room and he excused himself and hurried toward the sound. Dreadful imaginings filled his mind, and he prayed under his breath as he went. Prayed quietly, so Laski would not hear him and guess that anything was wrong.

Nothing is wrong, he told himself fiercely. Their first attempt across the channel, when they had been driven back to shore—that had been perfectly natural and not the action of some supernatural force. The shadows he sometimes saw leap upward when there was no fire to make them dance—that was his imagination. And the children's illness . . . He shook his head. No, they had left the thing behind. He was certain of it.

The child was Katherine, crying in her sleep. He hurried toward her and held her. Poor Katherine, he thought. The scars on her palms had not yet healed. He studied her as she fell back to sleep; she looked peaceful enough.

Jane came into the room. "The innkeeper's wife nearly ordered me out of her kitchen," she said. "I had to beg her, to tell her our children were sick. And then she thought we carried some contagion and wanted us to leave the inn entirely." She woke Arthur gently and lifted the broth to his mouth.

Three days later the children were recovered enough to continue on. At Hamburg, on November sixth, they parted company with Laski and his retinue; Laski needed to attend to some business. Borrowing money, probably, Dee thought. He had learned on the journey that the prince was nearly penniless; it was no wonder he wanted the kingship so badly. They hired wagons and drivers and transferred their household goods, and pushed on by coach to Lübeck.

There were hills now, and villages nestling among them, nearly hidden by the trees. Churches thrust up steeples sharp as daggers. The roads grew more crowded. They passed soldiers, pilgrims, wandering scholars, merchants with packtrains. Peasants dragged their two-wheeled carts to market. Twice they shared the road with a group of monks, and Dee looked at them in wonder; there had been no monks in England since bloody Queen Mary's time.

In the outskirts of Lübeck they passed an orchard, its few leaves flaring gold in the setting sun. "Oh, please, stop the coach!" Jane called out suddenly.

The driver stopped. "What is it?" Dee asked.

"There's an inn behind those trees," she said. "Let's stay there tonight."

Now he could see a spacious whitewashed building sprouting all manner of turrets and chimneys and gables. Roses climbed trellises halfway up the walls. It was the kind of inn, he knew, that would strain his meager budget. But it would be good for the family to stay somewhere pleasant for a change; they all looked pinched, anxious, even the children. He nodded and they stepped down from the coach, then began the laborious task of carrying the trunks and bundles inside.

The innkeeper, a widow, led them upstairs to a group of clean, freshly-aired rooms. Jane unpacked a bit and sat down, looking with satisfaction at the plump featherbeds. But Dee's fears had not left him, not even here. They should be moving, he thought, hurrying without ceasing until they reached their destination.

They went downstairs to a supper of very good fish pie cooked with ginger, pepper, and cinnamon. "May I speak with you?" Kelley whispered to him.

"Certainly," Dee said.

"I'm sorry I was so angry earlier," he said. He was always penitent after an argument; it was as if two angels struggled for his soul, one good and one evil. "I will look in the glass again for you. Tonight might be an auspicious time."

They might be able to risk it, Dee thought. He could not imagine a demon haunting them here, in this place that seemed so ordinary, so good. Perhaps if Kelley was truly repentant the good angels would return. And Laski would expect them to resume the experiments sometime; if they started tonight, with Laski gone, at least the prince would not be there if they failed.

They went up to their rooms after supper, and he saw Jane and the children to bed. Then he took out the red silk cloth embroidered with powerful signs—the Seal of Solomon, the names of angels, some of the hidden names of God—and spread it on the table. On top of that he set the wax tablet, inscribed with stars and pentagrams and the symbols of the planets, and the stand for the showstone. He moved carefully, aware that one misstep might bring disaster on them all.

Finally he reached into the gray velvet bag for the show-stone, a perfect sphere of transparent crystal about the size of a baby's head. He peered into the glass, still hoping after all this time to see something. There was only his reflection, upside-down, as though he had drowned. He looked older than he remembered, older than he felt. Others had found wisdom in his long face, his piercing eyes, and Jane, he knew, thought him handsome. But he saw only the harsh lines scouring his cheeks and forehead, saw that his beard and his neat cap of hair had become almost completely white. He set the ball carefully on its stand.

The two men prayed, and then Kelley bent over the glass. "I see—it is Madimi who comes to me," he said. The child-angel Madimi was one of their most frequent visitors. "She says—she is dancing now, she is very pleased with something."

Kelley raised his head. "Look," he said, pointing to one of the chairs. Dee looked, though he knew he would see nothing. "There she is, dancing on the back of the chair. She is wearing a gown of changeable silk, red and green."

Dee wondered for perhaps the hundredth time what it would be like to see angels everywhere. If it was true that everything in the world had its own angel—every person and clock and book and stone—then whatever you looked at would be incredibly alive, a constant shift and play of colors and motion. And he wondered again why this sight had been given to Kelley and not to him.

Kelley stopped. The silence in the room grew. Something moved in a dark corner. It is the fire, Dee thought. The fire is making the shadows dance.

There is no fire.

His heart kicked at his ribs. He looked quickly at Kelley. Kelley was bent over the crystal once more; he had noticed nothing. Because there is nothing to notice, Dee thought. It is your imagination, it is nothing. . . .

Suddenly he realized how cold he was, how the cold permeated every part of him. A powerful shiver shook him like a seizure. "What—what do you see for me?" he asked, breaking the silence.

"I see eleven noblemen in rich sable," Kelley said. "One man wears a sable cap and sits on a chair inlaid with precious stones. 'Pluck up your heart,' he says to you. 'You will become rich, and you will be able to enrich kings and help those who are needy. Were you not born to use the commodities of this world? Were not all things made for man's use?' "

Dee forced himself to relax. Most of the angels Kelley summoned spoke in convoluted metaphors and parables; this one was far more forthcoming. And he would not mind being wealthy, not for Kelley's reasons but because, with enough money, he would finally be free to pursue his studies without worry.

"What about Laski?" Dee asked. "What do you see for him?"

"He will become king. He will triumph over the Turks. His name will be spoken in every capital in Europe."

Suddenly one of the shadows seemed to detach itself from the rest. A change came over Kelley. He laughed harshly. "All gone," he said. "All gone. No hope."

Dee clutched one hand tightly with the other, only dimly aware that he was hurting himself. "What is gone?"

"Castles, swords, kingdoms, crowns," Kelley said. "His name will be spoken in every capital in Europe."

"I—I don't understand."

"All gone. Your books. Your library. What you value most in this world."

"What happened to my books?"

Kelley laughed gleefully. "Fire, flood, destruction," he said. "Your library is gone."

"Master Kelley!" Dee said desperately. "Master Kelley, stop! Look at me."

"The queen is your enemy," Kelley said. "In England they condemn your doings and say you are a renegade because you left without the queen's permission. They say you despise your prince."

"Edward Kelley!"

Kelley looked up from the glass, his face showing confusion. "All gone," he said softly.

Dee felt hopeless, defeated even before he began. Dread weakened him like an illness. Something was about to go terribly wrong, some force was building that would destroy him and his family as easily as he crushed an insect, and he was powerless to stop it. Worse—it had already happened, had already been set in motion, like a wave building out in the sea. He would find out what it was only when it came to shore, and by then it would be too late. By then his ill fortune would have overtaken him.

He roused himself to glance at Kelley. The other man's face looked normal enough, and his voice had not changed; he had not been taken over by the demon this time. Perhaps it was not here. Perhaps they had outrun it. But what if they hadn't?

"Master Kelley," he said. "What did you mean? Do you remember what you said?"

The confusion cleared slowly from Kelley's face. "Yes," he said. He shook himself, like a dog coming out of the water. "It was—it was a small foolish devil, nothing more."

Dee spent the night in the bedroom, praying and pacing,

sometimes both at once. Jane slept, her face clear and untroubled. Once in a while he stopped to look at her, as if to remind himself that innocence still existed in the world.

His conflicting thoughts whirled like a maelstrom. If Kelley had called up the demon then they should flee now, hurry on and hope it would not follow. But this spirit had harmed no one; it was probably not the demon. But it had taunted him maliciously. Would an angel do that? But what if they were not taunts? What if the angel was telling the truth? But if it was telling the truth that meant that his library had been destroyed.

In the end it was the fact that Kelley's voice had not changed that decided him. Kelley had not been able to summon the good angels, he thought, but this one had not been the demon he feared. "A very foolish devil," Dee wrote with relief in his book. Still, he began to record the angels' speech in Greek to hide their conversations from the malign spirit, though he knew it for a vain hope even as he did it. Angels spoke all the tongues of the world.

They pushed on, slowed by snow and ice. On Christmas morning they came to Stettin. Dee was never more desirous of going to church, but he saw only a Catholic cathedral, its stained-glass windows lit like a vision from another world.

He thought long and hard about worshiping there: in England he would be arrested as a heretic if he were found at a Catholic service. But it hadn't been so long ago that Queen Mary had enforced the Catholic religion, and then everyone had gone to a cathedral like this one. All worship was the same thing, really, he thought suddenly, and then understood to his surprise that he had always thought so, and that it was only away from England that such a foreign idea could become clear.

He led his family into the cathedral. The old sonorous

Latin phrases sounded like a secret language from his child-hood, familiar and mysterious at the same time.

Laski and his retinue rejoined them at the beginning of January. Heavy snowfall turned the road as white as unmarked paper, and the trees to either side were sere and bare; their branches knocked boldly against the coach like spirits seeking entrance.

On February third Laski, who was riding on horseback next to Dee's coach, suddenly called out. "There it is," he said. "That is my tower, over there. My tower, from my castle."

Dee looked out the window, hardly daring to believe it. They had reached their goal, the prince's estate at Lask.

He had hoped that Laski would give them rooms on the estate, but instead the prince directed them to lodgings in town. His first sight of the estate was a confusion of outbuildings and people and a great castle on a hill, all of it covered in a fresh dusting of snow.

A soft dusk had fallen by the time they got to their inn, but enough light remained for Dee to see that it stood near a church. He took that as a good omen. He gave orders for the baggage, helped Jane prepare the children for sleep, and then collapsed on one of the beds with weariness. Safe, he thought as his dreams began to gather around him. We'll be safe here.

As time passed the feeling of safety grew, and over the next few days he began to allow himself to remember that terrible evening, the memories he had forced away for so long. The afternoon session had gone well that day, and Dee, excited by the progress he and Kelley had made, had urged Kelley back upstairs to his study after supper.

He had built up the fire against the chill September air. The cloth, the wax tablet, the showstone, all had been set out that afternoon, and they needed only to pray before beginning. Kelley bent his head over the glass.

"The angel Madimi comes to me," Kelley said. "She is dancing in her frock of changeable colors."

"Why has she come?" Dee asked.

"She wants to see you."

"And I want to see her." Suddenly Dee felt all his loneliness and frustration and desire, and he asked, "Why can't I? Will I ever be able to?"

"She says, 'Your sight is more perfect than his,' " Kelley said.

"More perfect than whose?"

"Mine. She is pointing toward me."

Dee's heart leapt. "But when will I be able to see her?" he asked again.

Kelley ignored him. "Will you, Madimi, lend me a hundred pounds for a fortnight?" he asked.

"Master Kelley!" Dee said, horrified. "You cannot ask the spirits for money. God will give us what is necessary."

Kelley fell silent. "Go on, man," Dee said. "What does she say? What do you see?"

"Nothing. I see nothing."

Dee sighed. Kelley frequently stopped in the middle of his visions, out of weariness or frustration or just sheer stubbornness. "Ask her when I can see her," Dee urged. "Please."

Kelley hesitated a moment and then said, "I know a spell. . . ."

"What?"

"Remember I told you I found an old alchemical manuscript buried in Glastonbury? It contains a spell for summoning angels."

"And this spell—will it allow me to see them?"

In response Kelley began to recite: a gibberish of English and Latin and nonsense syllables. Suddenly the table shook violently. The showstone jerked and rolled toward the edge; Dee made a grab for it and by a miracle managed to catch it before it smashed to the ground.

A smell filled the room, something unpleasant, like a noxious chemical. A loud babel of voices spoke, then stopped, then spoke again.

Then suddenly the room was silent, the table steady. Was it over? "Can I see angels now?" Dee whispered.

"Hush!" Kelley said. "What is the price for knowledge?"

"What do you mean?"

"What is the price for knowledge?" Kelley said again, much louder this time. "How much will you pay? Anything?"

Was this part of Kelley's ritual? Would he pay anything? To know, to finally see the angels. . . .

Another part of his mind told him to stop, to say nothing. There was something wrong with Kelley's question, something he would understand if only he had time to think. . . . But Kelley importuned him again. "What price?"

"Anything," Dee said quickly, before he could change his mind.

"Good," Kelley said. "The angel comes to me. You will see him soon."

Kelley's voice changed, grew deeper. That had never happened before. "It is all useless," he said. "Hopeless. Nothing you do can make any difference. You cannot protect them."

"Protect whom?"

"Anyone. Anyone you love."

"Master Kelley!"

The door to the study opened, and his two-year-old daughter Katherine came in. She took small uncertain steps to the middle of the room. "Katherine, please," Dee said. "You must—"

He never finished. The voice, whatever it was, left Kelley and entered Katherine. She began to laugh, in the same deep tones Kelley had used. It sounded terrible, coming from a child. "You cannot protect, for example, your daughter," she said.

As Dee watched, terrified, she tottered toward the window. She slammed her tiny hands against the glass, over and over, until the window shattered outward. She grasped the windowsill and pulled herself upward, ignoring the shards of glass lacerating her palms.

She was going to jump. They were three floors from the ground. Dee cried out and leapt toward her. "You cannot stop me," Katherine said in the horrible voice. "I will kill your daughter. I cannot be stopped. You can only run away."

He grabbed her by her middle and pulled her back. She laughed again, but now Dee noticed that there was a look of torment on her face, as though she were trying to escape whatever had hold of her. He held her tightly. She slumped in his arms and her eyes closed.

"Katherine," he said. "Katherine, are you all right?"

She opened her eyes and began to cry. Was she still possessed? Her cries, at least, sounded normal. What had that— that thing—been? Not an angel, that much was certain. A demon.

He tried not to shudder, tried not to tear himself away from her. She cried out something in the baby-talk that he could not understand, though Jane could, and he relaxed a little.

In the days that followed, though, he began to think that the demon was still with them. Sometimes he smelled its foul odor, or saw something move out of the corner of his eye. Objects fell to the floor with no one near them, and once, terrifyingly, a pewter mug flew across the room and hit the opposite wall.

After a while he realized that these things only happened when Katherine was present. Sometimes she would jump at the loud noises, or burst into tears, but at other times she did not seem to notice the confusion around her. Dee did not know which would be worse, to know that a demon stalked you or to be taken over by it unaware.

He reread his diary and discovered to his horror a passage he had forgotten, from his very first session with Kelley on March 10, 1582. The angel Uriel had warned him of an evil spirit who, he said, "haunts your house, and seeks the destruction of your daughter." They must exorcize him with brimstone, Uriel said; Dee could not remember if he had done so or not.

Now he filled the house with the dreadful smell. He read books, consulted friends, recited incantations. He brought all his knowledge, all his reading, to bear. Nothing he did helped. He asked Kelley, many times, what he thought had happened in the study, but the other man claimed to know no more than he did.

Then one morning he saw Katherine wander through the house, muttering in an impossibly deep voice. He took her by the arm and shook her. She turned to him, empty-eyed; he had the idea he could see her soul guttering out. "It is over," she said in that eerie voice. "All gone. All gone wrong."

Almost without thinking he had left the house, saddled his horse and ridden as fast as he could toward Prince Laski's lodgings. He would not stand by, powerless, and watch his daughter tormented. The demon had said that they could run away, and finally he realized that that was the only choice left to him.

Prince Adalbert Laski, a Polish nobleman visiting London, had invited Dee to go to Poland with him. Dee had never even considered the offer; he was happy in England, reading his books and doing his experiments. But when he reached the prince's lodgings he blurted out his acceptance, seizing on it as a sinner takes a holy relic.

Now, in Poland, he and Kelley rode out to Laski's estate a good deal, their horses moving stolidly through the flurries of snow. Dee's first, hurried glimpse had not told the whole story; several of the outbuildings stood abandoned and one entire wing of the castle had been closed off and allowed to fall into ruin. There were few servants, and several times Laski had to wander through his hallways, calling out, before he found someone to serve them supper or build up the fire.

But the prince had enough money to agree to become Dee's patron. "Thank God," Jane said when Dee told her the news. She had not complained, but Dee knew that she had been worried at how quickly their money disappeared on the journey.

A month later the angels were still telling Laski that he would be king, but there was no further news for him. The prince grew impatient, even angry, and once or twice he shouted at Kelley when the angels refused to tell them anything more. By this time Dee had discovered he needed certain books for his research, and he decided to move on to Cracow with his family and consult the university there. At the back of his mind was the slightly unworthy thought that in Cracow he and Kelley would not have to see Laski as often.

Cracow was a jumble of buildings old and new: Gothic churches, sculptured Italian facades, the university, a fortress. Dee barely saw the city, barely ventured outside the house they had rented, not even to go to the university as he had planned. For once Kelley was in a good humor, and Dee hastened to take advantage of it, spending hours closeted with the other man, both of them bent over the showstone.

They received only good advice; Dee became certain that they had left the demon behind. The angels assured them once again that Laski would become king, and gave Kelley cryptic instructions for making the Philosopher's Stone, and told Dee what herbs he should take for the winter illnesses that had not yet left him.

In fact there was good news wherever he looked. Jane took him aside and whispered that she was with child again. If the child was a boy he vowed to name him Michael, after one of the angels who appeared to Kelley in the glass.

Spring came, and then summer. Dee hardly noticed. He felt renewed, felt the same excitement as when Kelley had first come to his door. They spoke with the little girl Madimi; Michael, the spirit of wisdom; Nalvage with his curling yellow hair. Then, on a night in late summer, Kelley looked into the glass and told Dee that he saw Jane lying dead, with her face battered in.

"What?" Dee said. "No."

"Yes. Your wife is dead."

"No—don't be foolish. I can hear her downstairs."

"She *will* die, then. And so will your servant Mary, drowned in a pool of water."

"No," Dee said, unable to raise his voice above a whisper.

"Yes." Kelley's voice grew harsher, deeper. He laughed. "And your friend in England, Henry Sidney. Dead, all dead."

"No!" Dee said. "Stop it!"

"And your library burned—"

Dee slapped his hand over the crystal. Kelley wrenched his gaze away. He stared at Dee, his eyes unfocused. After a long time he said, "What? Where—"

"You are with me in Poland," Dee told him.

Kelley nodded slowly. "And I said—oh, my God. I said your wife would die." He looked genuinely shocked.

"We must leave now. Quickly."

"Why?"

"The demon. It's followed us."

"How do you know?"

"Your voice changed. It was horrible. The demon's found us again."

"God. What do we do now?"

"I don't know. Try once more to outrun it."

"Can we? It found us here—"

"That's the only thing I can think of. We must—we must hurry, though—"

"But where can we go?"

Dee hadn't thought. "Prague," he said suddenly. "Emperor Rudolf invited me there once. He invited many people—scientists, astrologers, alchemists, mathematicians. The Alchemical King, they call him."

"Alchemy," Kelley said thoughtfully. "Then he, too, searches for the Philosopher's Stone."

"So they say."

"Good," Kelley said. "Let's go."

Dee went into the bedroom. It was not late, but Jane was sleeping; her pregnancy had begun to tire her. How could she possibly travel now? But there was no help for it.

Jane stirred and looked at him sleepily.

"I must leave again," he said.

She woke fully and sat up, gazing at him with her level gray eyes. "Leave? But I cannot travel quickly in my condition—"

"It has found us again," Dee said.

"*What* has found you? You never told me what happened that night."

"I called something up—"

"You said we were safe—"

"Hush. I said you and the children are safe. I'm the one it wants."

"This is because of Kelley, isn't it? He's the one who summons those things, isn't he? I warned you about him from the start—"

"Listen," Dee said urgently. "You'll be safe here. It wants me—it comes only when I am present. Stay and continue on when you're ready. I will write you from Prague."

"Prague!" Jane said. "Are we going to Prague now?"

Dee looked at his wife. What had Kelley seen? He studied

her features as if memorizing them: the reddish blond hair, the gray eyes. Kelley had said that her face . . .

No. She was fine; nothing had happened to her. Nor ever would, he thought fiercely.

"It seems so," he said.

TWO HUNDRED MILES TO THE WEST, IN PRAGUE, Rabbi Judah Loew thought he heard something. He had been having a late supper with his family; his wife Pearl was talking. But over her another, louder voice spoke a sentence in a foreign language, and he heard the word "Prague."

Another voice answered, this one female, and she also said something about Prague. And somehow Loew understood that these people would be traveling to his city, that he would meet them, that his fate would be entwined with theirs.

Something was about to happen, that much was certain. Those strange signs and portents in his study. . . He looked at Pearl, wanting for perhaps the hundredth time to tell her what he suspected, and for the hundredth time being unable to.

The voices had fallen silent. "Judah?" Pearl said, looking concerned. She was a small woman, her figure rounded from childbearing. Over the years her hair had gone from a lustrous brown to iron-gray and had become coarser, almost wiry; she wore it, like all modest women, tucked up under a kerchief. Her eyes were a deep gray-green—like the sea, Loew had thought when he had first seen her. "Judah, did you hear anything I said?"

He shook his head. "I'm sorry," he said. He gazed out over the table, seeing the three of his six daughters who had come for supper, his son, their spouses and children. The small room had not been enough to contain them all; some of the younger children sat at a makeshift table in the tiny hallway. The tables bowed under the weight of the dishes; the candles shone over the faces of his loved ones, their cheeks shiny with grease after the large meal. Up until two months ago he had thought himself the most fortunate man in the world. But God, apparently, wanted more from him.

Two months ago he had looked at the four books on his desk and had noticed that they were all open to page thirty-six. Engrossed in his studies, he had shrugged this off as coincidence and pulled another book from his shelf. The book had opened, almost of its own volition, to page thirty-six.

Since then he saw the number everywhere he turned. He would be invited somewhere; the address would be thirty-six. He would buy a new book or some trinket for Pearl; it would cost thirty-six pennies, or he would get that amount in change.

In all his studies he had come across only one meaning for the number thirty-six. An old Jewish tradition said that there were thirty-six righteous men who upheld the world. According to the tradition if any of these men should die, or stray from the path of righteousness, the world would come to an end. They were called the *la'med vavniks*, from the Hebrew letters that corresponded to thirty-six.

Was he one of these men? He had far too many faults, he knew that; his anger flared out too easily, he coveted the post of Chief Rabbi of Prague, he wanted to know and understand more than was perhaps lawful for a mere man. And how could he take on such a vast responsibility? How could he carry the weight of the world on his shoulders?

"Judah?" Pearl said again. "Are you listening to me? I said Izak wants to talk to you after supper."

He forced his attention back to his family. The conversation turned to his audience with Emperor Rudolf, set for two days hence. Another heavy responsibility, Loew thought.

"Why do you suppose the emperor wants to see you?" his daughter Leah asked.

"I don't know," Loew said. "It's said that Rudolf studies Kabbalah. I'm perfectly willing to discuss this with him, if that's what he wants. My worry is that he summoned me to talk about something else."

"What do you mean?"

"You know how precarious our situation here is," Loew said. Leah shook her head, and Loew had to remind himself that his children had lived here in safety all their lives. "It was only forty years ago that King Ferdinand of Bohemia expelled all the Jews from Prague."

"Did he?" one of the grandchildren asked. "But then why are we here?"

"The next emperor, Maximilian, reversed the order."

"So everything worked out well, then," the grandchild said, taking a last bite of chicken.

Loew smiled. "Yes, but you see, our lives depend on the whim of whoever is in power. And Rudolf, they say, is mad. I will have to be very careful."

"Mad?" Leah looked at him with consternation. "What do you mean? Mad how?"

Now he had frightened the children, and some of the grandchildren as well. "Oh, nothing too strange," he said, trying to sound unconcerned. "He collects things—it's said his castle is filled with paintings and statues and scientific instruments. And he has fits of temper, and banishes his counselors when they displease him."

"That doesn't sound so terrible," Leah said.

"No, as you say," Loew said. "I'm certain I'll be fine." But he caught Pearl's eye and saw that she shared his worry. One misstep on his part, and they might all be exiled again.

Someone knocked at the door. "That will be Izak," Pearl said, rising. "Should I tell him you'll see him in your study?"

Loew nodded. He took one of the candles and headed back into the house. It was only as he opened the door to his study that he realized he hadn't asked Pearl which Izak had come to see him: there must be dozens in the quarter.

As he lit a lamp he noticed that the book on his desk was open to page thirty-six. He closed it angrily and sat behind the desk.

A young man came into the study. His face was thin and bony, with a protuberant chin, and he had curly, sandy-colored hair. Now Loew remembered him from the school; he had been a good student, though not a brilliant one. What was his father's name? Izak son of . . . He shook his head at his absentmindedness.

To Loew's surprise a young beautiful woman stepped in after him. "This is Sarah," Izak said. "We want to be married, and we want you to perform the ceremony."

Now Loew remembered what he had forgotten earlier, and a great sadness came over him. "Sit down, please," he told the couple. He looked from one of them to the other. "I'm afraid I cannot marry you."

"Why not?" Izak said.

"Because you're illegitimate," Loew said to him. "I'd give anything not to have to say this, but the law does not allow you to marry."

"What! What do you mean?"

"Just as I say. The law forbids illegitimate children to marry."

"But—but I want to get married. Sarah and I want to get married. She knows I'm illegitimate, and she doesn't mind."

"Unless you can tell me that your mother married your father—"

"Of course she didn't! He's probably that peddler who comes to the Quarter every few weeks—he has a child in every town, or so I've heard."

"Then I'm sorry," Loew said.

Sarah looked stricken. Izak stood and began to pace in a tight circle.

"Well, the hell with you, then!" Izak said. He went to the door and opened it.

"Where are you going?" Loew asked.

"To find someone who will marry us."

"Everyone you talk to will tell you the same thing."

Izak left without saying anything more. Sarah hurried after him. The door closed behind them.

Loew sighed. One more problem, he thought, though not as serious as King Rudolf's summons. Serious to Izak, though. He stood and headed back to his family.

IZAK RAN OUT INTO THE NIGHT AIR, LEAVING SARAH BEHIND. His mind whirled. What would happen to him if he couldn't marry? A long sterile life and an unhappy one, with no wife, no children, no comforts . . .

He was so occupied with his thoughts that he nearly knocked someone down. He smelled a terrible odor, the stench of a person who hadn't washed in years, and he reached out and grabbed what felt like a bundle of rags. The rags shouted; he saw now that he had hold of an old woman. He steadied her and she grinned, showing three or four rotten teeth. He had never seen her in the Quarter before.

"Whoa!" she said. "Where are you going in such a hurry?"

"Nowhere," he said.

"Well, you haven't reached nowhere yet," she said. "You're still somewhere."

"Who are you?" he asked, studying her by the light of a nearby lamp. The colorful layers of clothing she wore hid her shape; she could have been fat or thin or anywhere in-between. Her face was narrow and almost bronze from the sun; she had dark brown eyes and a long pointed nose, almost a beak. Her ears were pointed as well, and several thick wiry hairs grew from them. She seemed to have no lips. "You don't live here."

"Anyone can walk through the streets, can't they? Or run through them, in your case."

She had stopped grinning; she looked almost concerned. "I just found out I can't get married," he found himself saying. Well, why not? He would never see her again in his life. "Apparently bastards can't marry."

"That's too bad."

"I should have lied to him. I should have told him that horrible peddler married my mother. And why didn't he, anyway? Why should I be punished for something he did? I'll kill him if I ever get my hands on him, I swear I will."

"Slow down. Lied to who?"

"Rabbi Loew."

"Ah, Rabbi Loew. He's a great magician, isn't he?"

He stared at her. "Where did you hear that?"

"Everyone knows it. Magicians are flocking to Prague, now that Emperor Rudolf is here. There's another great one coming from England. . . ."

He barely heard her. "Well, he can't help me," he said bitterly.

"Don't give up hope just yet. You asked me who I am—my name's Magdalena. What's yours?"

He had no intention of giving her his name, but to his surprise he said, "Izak. Izak, son of no one."

"Good evening, Izak son of no one. Maybe we'll meet again."

She moved away, melting into the shadows of the twisting streets, leaving him alone with his thoughts.

TWO DAYS LATER LOEW STOOD IN HIS TINY FRONT ROOM, GETting ready for his meeting with Rudolf. Half the men in town seemed to be crowded in with him, all of them offering advice and clothing. He studied a coat from one, a pair of trousers from another; both were brown, though of different shades. Still, they would probably pass muster. They had to; they were the newest things anyone owned.

The town barber forced him into a chair and began to trim his unruly beard. "Whatever you do, don't mention King Ferdinand," someone behind him said.

"Why not?" This was another man, from another part of the room.

"He's the one who expelled the Jews. You don't want to remind him of that, don't want to have him start thinking that's a good idea."

"But they're proud of their families, these kings and emperors."

"That's true. You'll have to flatter him, flatter all of them. Tell him how magnificent he is. Magnificent, that's a good word. And his father and grandfather, and anyone else he's related to, no matter what they've done to us."

"I hear he hates his brother Matthias."

"Yes, that's true. Don't mention Matthias. Everyone else, though—everyone else is magnificent."

"Why does he hate his brother?"

"Who knows? Just don't mention him, that's all."

"Do you say 'Your Highness' or 'Your Majesty'?"

" 'Your Magnificence—' "

The barber had finished and was holding a mirror up to Loew's face. Loew studied himself, noting the graying brown hair and beard, the level brown eyes behind his spectacles. His face would match the clothing, at least, he thought wryly. Was he ready? Was this a face Rudolf would trust?

He was as ready as he ever would be. "Listen, people," he said. "I need to be alone to think. Everyone outside. Now," he added to a few people who seemed inclined to stay behind.

He put on the town's clothes and took one last look in the mirror the barber had left. There were heavy lines on his forehead, cut there like rivers scoured deeply into the earth. He took a deep breath, steadying himself, and set out for the castle.

He returned five hours later, tired, footsore and humiliated. Some of the men of the town had gathered in front of his house, waiting to hear what had happened.

"How did it go?" one of them asked.

"It didn't," Loew said.

"What do you mean?"

"As I said. He didn't see me."

"Why not?"

"I don't know. I waited in a room for hours. There were other people there, all of them waiting for an audience, but no one was called. One of them told me it was the fifth time he had been summoned, but that so far he had never seen the emperor. Another said that if I wanted to see the emperor I should talk to the man who grooms his horses."

"His horses?"

"Apparently that's who he's taking advice from these days. He's dismissed all his counselors again."

"Well, but this is good news, isn't it? It means he's forgotten us. We can go on the way we were."

"That isn't true, unfortunately. I was invited back. After we had all been there for hours a man came into the room and told us all to go. Except me, he said. The emperor wanted to see me again."

"When?"

"A few weeks from now. He'll have probably forgotten by then. Nevertheless, I have to go."

DEE HAD KNOWN MAPMAKERS IN HIS YOUTH, ORTELIUS AND Mercator, the best in the world. The journey from Cracow to

Prague was a short one as the crow flew, but the road on land wound over a good many mountains; it would take a while to reach his destination. And Jane—traveling with the children would take her several weeks, perhaps even a month. Still, she should be in Prague before the child was born.

The coach rocked as it made its way down a steep path. He smiled, thinking of the child. Some might find all this fecundity embarrassing—he was, after all, nearly fifty-seven years old—but he had spent his youth in studying and had come late to the joys of marriage and family.

He closed his eyes, remembering. At Cambridge he had studied eighteen hours a day, stopping only to eat, sleep, and go to church. He had wanted to know everything: What were the stars made of? Why did water boil and wood did not? How were salamanders able to live in the heart of fire? What had God and Adam talked about in the Garden of Eden? Did women have fewer teeth than men, as Aristotle said? (Later he had counted Jane's; she had thirty-two, the same as he.) Was it truly possible to create the Philosopher's Stone and live forever?

He learned a good deal; he knew enough magic to satisfy most men. But it was simple stuff; the answers to his most pressing questions eluded him. Only God knew the answers; everything existed in the mind of God. And so he had started trying to summon angels. When Edward Kelley had knocked on his door and introduced himself a year ago, he thought the man had come in answer to his prayers.

"Will King Rudolf want us to search for the Philosopher's Stone?" Kelley asked.

Dee opened his eyes and looked at Kelley, sitting on the bench across from him. "I don't know," Dee said. "Maybe."

"Good," Kelley said. "I am tired of scrying."

Dee studied the other man. Had he truly been sent by God? Then why was he so recalcitrant? Why was he interested only in money and ways to acquire money? Kelley had told him what he would do with the Philosopher's Stone if he had it: he would touch everything he owned and turn it to gold as Midas had, and then live like a king, surrounded by splendor and wealth.

"Rudolf may want us to scry as well," Dee said.

"Then you scry for him," Kelley said. "I am tired."

"You know I can't."

"Then find someone else."

"I have never been able to."

"God damn it!" Kelley said. "I am tired. I never want to see the glass or those damned angels again. Leave me alone!"

Dee caught his breath at the blasphemy. He tried to speak mildly. "We'll see how you feel when we get there."

"I know how I'll feel. Tired." As if to prove his point he closed his eyes and seemed to sleep.

The coach continued over the mountains. They passed tangled forests, the trees growing wildly in the profligacy of summer. Despite Dee's best efforts his thoughts turned sometimes to the spirit's messages. How much of what it said was true? Was his precious library destroyed, and if so had the spirit done it?

How could God permit such a spirit to run loose in the world? Or, conversely, if there were such a spirit, did that mean that God did not exist, or that He was powerless to stop evil? Was everything random, did everything happen at the whim of powers he did not understand? And the feeling of dread would come over him again, the terror of standing naked before such things without even God to protect him.

When this happened he would strain to see beyond the trees to the next bend in the road, hoping to find an inn and firelight and people. But inns were rare in this part of the world, and in the few they did find no one spoke any language they understood. They were forced to convey their needs by gestures.

Once they found a man who knew German, though he

spoke brokenly and with a good many mistakes. But the man was no comfort; he told them a tale about people who could turn into wolves, and another about a Hungarian noble-woman who bathed in the blood of virgins to stay young for-ever. Unbelievable stories, Dee told himself, tales meant to frighten children. His mood did not lighten.

After a while the language they heard in the inns changed from Polish to Czech, and Dee guessed that they had crossed into Bohemia. Czech was a barbarous language with few vow-els; every second word seemed to run aground against the shoals of the teeth and become swallowed.

Finally the land flattened out and they began to see acres of farmland and a scattering of houses. Other travelers joined them on the road, everything from elegant coaches with coats-of-arms on the doors to the mule-drawn carts of farmers bring-ing their produce to market. The traffic raised a fine dust from the road; it sifted in around the closed windows of the coach and covered them in a gritty film.

Smaller roads began to converge with theirs, tributaries to their vast river. Then they were through the walls and in the city. Dee knew only one person in Prague, a scientist and counselor to the king named Thadeus Hageck, and he gave the driver his address on Bethlem Street.

At Doctor Hageck's house they received the first bit of good news in a long time—the first, it seemed, since they had started on this mad journey. The doctor and his family gave them a warm welcome and invited them to stay as long as they wanted, setting aside a portion of their large house for him and Kelley and the others who were coming later. Dee accepted gratefully.

DEE SENT A NOTE UP TO THE CASTLE ASKING FOR AN AUDI-ence. Days passed, but there was no answer.

In the meantime he decided to explore the city. Kelley refused to come with him; he had set out his retorts and alembics and filled Hageck's study with disgusting-smelling potions and philters, leaving only to buy more of the ingredients he needed. The study was very congenial to him; it had been used by alchemists even before Hageck lived there. Mysterious hieroglyphs were carved on the walls, along with birds and fish and flowers and fruit. An earlier alchemist, Simon, had written his name in several places in letters of gold and silver.

On Dee's first day out he discovered a river spanned by a long, handsome bridge. Coaches drove noisily back and forth, their drivers swearing and lashing their whips, but there was space for those on foot as well. Curious, he went across.

On the other side he saw an arch flanked by two towers. As soon as he passed under the arch all the bells in all the spires rang out at once. All over the city something was taking wing, ascending. . . . Were they angels? His heart began to beat loudly. Then they settled back, wings flapping, and he realized that they were just birds, pigeons and seagulls for the most part.

Whatever happened later, this was his first impression, and an enduring one—that Prague was haunted with angels.

This side of the river was grander than the one he lived in. He saw a forest of statues and cupolas and cathedrals, spires and dark towers, a blur of copper domes and red roofs. People thronged the streets, priests and beggars and scholars and tradesmen. Huge houses with carved facades stood by the side of the road, dwarfing the people. Carts and coaches squealed on the cobblestones. And over all of it loomed a castle on a hill, King Rudolf's domain.

He soon discovered that everything had two names in this city, which confused him until he realized that one was German and one Czech. The river dividing Prague, for example—

it had been called the Moldau on his maps, but the Czechs called it the Vltava. He heard a babel of other languages as well, Latin and Dutch and Italian and others he could not recognize. London was as big as Prague, perhaps even bigger, but London was isolated, a backwater compared to this, and the only language one ever heard there was English.

Well, of course Prague would be greater than London, Dee thought. It was the capital of the Holy Roman Empire, a German confederacy that stretched from the Italian states all the way to Russia. And farther still, if you counted all the marriages and alliances the Habsburgs had made. King Rudolf's uncle, for example, was King Philip of Spain, Elizabeth's old enemy.

He felt very small, and sorry for his country and sovereign. They should be greater, an empire, Britannia. After all, he had once drawn up a genealogy proving that Elizabeth was descended from King Arthur.

He began to walk and came almost immediately to a church. It was small and unassuming, nothing like the grand cathedrals the Catholics built. He remembered that there was something called the Czech Brethren, that a man named Jan Hus had once challenged the Roman church.

And yet now he saw that there was a cathedral on this street as well. Did Rudolf allow the two faiths to exist side by side? How could that work, how were they kept from violence? Or did violence flare out anyway?

He should know more about this strange place where he had come to rest, washed ashore like so much sea-wrack. But they had left in such a hurry. . . . He wished he had had more time.

The next day he kept to his side of the bridge. The streets across the river had been clean, far cleaner than those in London, paved with cobblestones and swept often. The streets in his neighborhood, however, seemed to belong to a different city; they were poorly-drained, littered with refuse, so muddy that carts sank up to their axles. There were mice here, too, and other vermin; once he saw a cat study a rat, its haunches twitching, until it finally sprang in a blur of speed.

His wanderings brought him to a walled city within the city. He looked in through an open gate; the people inside went about their business like everyone else, sweeping and building, shopping and gossiping. But why did none of them go out? And why did no one come in? He took a step toward the gate, but several people on both sides frowned at him and he backed away.

On both sides of the river he saw alchemists and conjurers selling herbs and elixirs, powders and gemstones from their booths by the side of the road. A few even claimed to have the Philosopher's Stone. They beckoned and called out to him as he passed but he ignored them.

But there were others in the city, powerful-looking men who walked the streets purposefully, going about on their own mysterious errands. Several times he saw a man wrapped in a black cloak with two giant black mastiffs by his side: one of the dogs had only one eye and the other three legs. And once he saw a tall man who held himself like an aristocrat but wore the clothing of a lower class; he carried a vial and spoke as if to a companion next to him, but as Dee came closer he saw that there was no one there. He longed to talk to these people, to trade knowledge with them, maybe even ask them for help, but something—their mystery, their haughty bearing—stopped him.

On August twenty-fourth a strange thing happened— Hageck's son informed him that, in spite of what the angels had told him, his friend Henry Sidney was not dead. The angels could not lie, Dee knew that. The message about Sidney must have come from the demon, then, and so had the horrible prophecy about Dee's wife. Dee gave thanks that they had left

Poland when they did, that his wife would be fine, that they had, perhaps, escaped the demon's notice.

Three days later an angry and bewildered letter came from Prince Laski. Why had Dee left Poland in such a hurry? Why hadn't he told Laski about his plans? "I am sending a messenger to Prague," Laski said, "and if my man does not get satisfactory answers from you then my patronage will come to an end."

Dee hid the letter away. Now, truly, all his hopes were pinned on the emperor.

He continued to send messages to Rudolf. Once he climbed up to the palace itself, wondering how far he would get before he was turned back. There was an unguarded moat in front of him and he crossed it. A lion roared from somewhere and he looked around in alarm. He saw nothing, no animals, no courtiers, not even any servants.

A man stepped out from behind a hedge. His clothing was good, Dee saw, and he had a well-trimmed beard and full cheeks and lips. Was he from Rudolf's court? Dee headed toward him, formulating a polite German phrase as he went.

The man brandished a rake and yelled something in Czech. Dee stepped back. Was he a gardener? Did even the gardeners dress well in this country? Perhaps he was a courtier who enjoyed working with plants, Dee thought, someone who would report to Rudolf that he had been trespassing. He quickly spoke a few words to change his appearance, shifting his shape so that he seemed smaller and fatter. The gardener returned to his plants and Dee headed back toward the moat, walking slowly so the other man would not realize he had been alarmed.

Jane arrived the next day. She had left Rowland, who was not yet two, in Poland with a nurse, and brought Arthur and Katherine with her. She was not near term but Dee scoured the city for a midwife, wanting to be prepared when the time came. He found only a dirty foul-mouthed crone who smelled of sweat and animals and excrement and other, perhaps worse, things. In his desperation he nearly hired her, but then, fortunately, Hageck found him a stout woman from the country. The woman spoke no German and Dee no Czech, but somehow Dee managed to convey to her that he would have need of her in a few months' time.

Jane and the children settled in. Jane complained about the smell from Kelley's experiments but for the most part she was too busy learning her way around the city to argue as forcefully as she once did. Arthur and Katherine played out in the streets and came home speaking what sounded like whole sentences in Czech or German.

Laski's man arrived, and to Dee's horror Kelley immediately got into a drunken fight with him. Dee wrote of the incident, "God suffered E. K. to be tempted and almost overcome by Satan: to my great grief, discomfort, and most great discredit, if it should come to the emperor's understanding."

But the emperor had not heard, or had taken no notice, because the next day, September third, a man wearing Rudolf's livery knocked at their door. Dee's request for an audience had been granted.

D EE LOOKED AROUND AT THE STRANGE ROOM he found himself in. Shelves and cabinets lined the walls, holding precious items and junk all jumbled together: swords, globes, clocks, and jewelry as well as rusty nails, old spectacles, turtle shells, and gaming dice. An ivory skull, probably human, stared down at them from atop a bookshelf.

Kelley had said nothing since they had been ushered into the room, though he had clutched the velvet bag containing the scrying glass closer to his chest. There was another man in the room as well, and Dee tried to study him without being obvious.

The man seemed all one color—his trousers, shirt, jacket, his eyes and graying hair and beard, all were brown. And yet everything was a slightly different shade, slightly off, as though an entire village had gotten together and loaned him all their best clothes.

Probably, Dee thought, that was what had happened. It wasn't every day a man was summoned by the king; his village would see to it that he looked his best. Was he from the outlying towns then, a farmer? But he was too old to work a farm, older than Dee himself, and his spectacles gave him a scholarly air.

Looking closer he saw that the man wore a yellow circle sewn to his jacket. Dee wondered what that signified. A rank? A craft guild?

The man turned, saw him, and smiled. Dee smiled back, caught off guard. He greeted him in Latin, the universal language of scholars throughout Europe.

The man shrugged; he had not understood. Not a scholar then. He said something in Czech; now it was Dee's turn to shrug.

Dee tried German. The man nodded, apparently pleased that they had happened on a common language. "My name is Rabbi Judah Loew," he said. "May I have the pleasure of knowing your name?"

Rabbi? This man was a Jew! Dee moved back slightly in his chair. Then he felt foolish; the man was an unbeliever, of course, but harmless for all that. They really did not poison wells or kill children.

"Dee," he said. "Doctor John Dee. From England. This is my associate, Edward Kelley."

"Good day, Doctor Dee. I assume you are here to see King Rudolf as well."

"Yes. Can I ask—how long have you been waiting?"

Loew smiled. "Two hours. This time."

"This time?"

Loew looked around carefully, as if to make certain that no one was listening. "His Majesty is in the habit of summoning people he has no intention of meeting. He is a very private person. I have been in this room twice before, and was sent home without an audience both times. And yet other people tell me he has been eager to see them." He shrugged. "I wouldn't know."

A woman came in and began to dust the shelves. "Why does he summon you then?" Dee asked.

Loew shrugged again. "They say he is interested in the Kabbalah."

"Kabbalah! Are you a Kabbalist? Tell me, I have long been curious about something Pico della Mirandola says—"

"I don't know Pico della Mirandola."

"No, of course not. He's a Christian—I should have realized. But listen, can you explain—"

Dee leaned forward, his earlier uneasiness forgotten. A moment later he was deep in a discussion of the transmutation of numbers and the attributes of God. Dust flew from the shelves as the servant continued to polish the collection.

"You have some knowledge of numbers," Loew said. "What do you know about the number thirty-six?"

"Thirty-six?" Dee said. He felt pleased that this man, clearly an adept, would solicit his advice. "It's divisible by a good many numbers: two, three, four, six, and nine, to mention only those under ten. And twelve, of course. Twelve is a powerful number: twelve tribes, twelve apostles, twelve houses of the zodiac. Is this any use to you?"

"I don't know," Loew said. "Perhaps."

The servant stopped her dusting and nodded to Dee.

"Come with me," she said. "His Majesty is ready for you now." Then to Loew, "And you after him."

"What?" Dee said.

"Go," Loew said. "King Rudolf uses his courtiers as servants, and his servants as courtiers. One never knows quite where one stands with him. But go now, quickly, before he changes his mind."

Dee hurried after her and then slowed, trying to compose himself for an audience with the king. Kelley followed.

They walked through vaulted rooms and galleries. Shelves and cabinets and tables displayed more of the king's strange collection: stuffed ostriches, rhinoceros horns, globes and measuring instruments and glassware. Paintings lined the walls, most of them of naked voluptuous women in allegorical poses. A man sat in a small room off the main hallway, twining filigrees of gold around a cup made of jasper. They heard the sounds of saws and hammers, and several times they saw construction going on in different parts of the castle.

Dee looked up to see a man coming toward them. Who would this be? Courtier, servant, artist? "I'm the Lord Chamberlain, Octavius Spinòla," the man said. "I've come to escort you to the emperor." The servant turned away as though indifferent to their fate.

Spinòla bowed them into a long, richly-furnished room and then left them. The walls here were covered in red leather stamped with a coat of arms. Colorful eastern rugs decorated the tables and benches. Then Dee saw the man sitting on an elevated chair at the end of the room, and all his surroundings faded into the background. The man looked familiar—the full lips, the pouches under the eyes, the pendulous cheeks—

"You're the gardener," Dee said, shocked into English. "The man I saw when I crossed the moat. You had a rake—"

"Speak German, please," Rudolf said, showing no sign he had noticed Dee's confusion, or that he had recognized him. He was dressed less showily than Queen Elizabeth, Dee saw; his clothes were a drab black, almost Spanish in their austerity. But his collar, folded in the Spanish manner called *gorguera*, was made of the finest linen, and his chain of office was the purest gold, and his hat was adorned with buttons of ruby and gold. Two men in uniform stood behind him.

"Yes. Yes, Your Majesty. I thought I saw you—" Stop, Dee thought. Rudolf is playing his own game here. Or he has a double, or he is possessed—No. Don't think about that. Especially now.

The king had a copy of Dee's book *Monas Hieroglyphica* on a chest to one side of him. Dee had dedicated that book to Rudolf's father, the Emperor Maximilian II. He was pleased to see it, pleased that Rudolf had taken the time to retrieve it from his library. They spoke politely for a while about the book and its philosophy, though Rudolf admitted it had been "too hard for his capacity" to understand.

"You are the man who can speak to angels, are you not?" Rudolf asked.

"My associate, Edward Kelley, is the one who speaks to them. I merely ask the questions."

"Good. I would ask the angels some questions now."

"Of course. May we use this chest, Your Majesty?"

Rudolf nodded.

There was a landscape on top of the chest, made of inlays of jasper and onyx and chalcedony. Dee moved his book out of the way, then lifted a heavy bronze statue of a horse off the top and looked around for a place to put it. Finally he placed it on the floor, glancing at Rudolf for permission. Rudolf said nothing.

Dee motioned Kelley forward. Kelley opened the gray bag,

took out the cloth and the wax tablets and the scrying glass, and set them in their proper places.

"We must pray first," Dee said.

Rudolf nodded absently.

Dee bent his head. This would be the first time he had used the glass since Poland. If the demon had followed them—but he had no choice. He had promised Rudolf he could show him wonders. A long time ago, this was, when he had written to the king saying that he might some day come to Prague. And—he hated to think it—he was running out of money. Rudolf's patronage would be very welcome.

Please, he prayed to Someone or Something. Please, let the demon be gone.

He looked up. "What are your questions, Your Majesty?"

"Will my Empire remain at peace?" Rudolf asked.

Kelley looked into the glass. Dee's heart was pounding hard.

"The angel Uriel comes to me," Kelley said finally. He looked at Rudolf, then back at the glass. "Yes. The angel tells me that you will usher the Empire into a new age, a golden age filled with peace and prosperity."

Rudolf nodded. Dee began to relax. Uriel was one of the most powerful angels. If they were under his protection then all would go well.

"And what of my brother?" Rudolf asked. "Will he continue to trouble me?"

"I don't—I don't see—"

"My brother Matthias," Rudolf said impatiently. "Matthias, who thwarts me at every turn. Who spends his days and nights scheming to take my throne."

"Matthias, yes. Uriel tells me that you will triumph over Matthias."

Rudolf's lips quirked upward. Perhaps, Dee thought, he was smiling. "When will—"

"But you must take care," Kelley said, interrupting him. "You will defeat your brother only if you mend your sinful ways."

"What?" Rudolf said.

"Mend your sinful ways!" Kelley said. He was shouting now, like a preacher. "If you will hear me, and believe me, you shall triumph."

"What insolence is this?"

"No insolence. I repeat only what the angels say."

"And in what ways do I sin? Tell me." Rudolf's voice had gone dangerously soft.

"No." Kelley stared boldly at the king. "Those sins should not be spoken of here."

"You don't know, in other words. And why not? Because there are no sins. You are nothing but a fraud, a charlatan after my gold. You must be mad if you think I reward displays like this."

"I did not come to you because of your riches," Kelley said implacably. "I was sent to you by God."

"Leave me," Rudolf said.

"The angel Uriel—"

"Leave me! Now! Or I will have both of you arrested." He motioned to his men-at-arms.

"Come, Master Kelley," Dee said, stuffing his things back in the velvet bag. His mind was whirling. Had they truly been visited by the angel Uriel? Did Kelley think that he could say such things to a king? Or had the demon come to wreak havoc on their lives once again? Kelley's voice had changed a little, there at the end. They were no longer welcome at Prague Castle, that much was certain.

Kelley continued to look at the king. Dee clutched him by the sleeve and pulled him out the door.

Rabbi Loew was still waiting patiently. "How is the emperor?" Loew asked. "What is his mood?"

"Choleric. I'm afraid we angered him."

"Oh, dear," Loew said. He stood and headed toward his audience with Rudolf.

GONE WRONG, ALL, ALL WRONG, DEE THOUGHT. HE HAD dragged his family across Europe to this place, he had insulted one of the most powerful monarchs on earth, he had come to the notice of a potent and malign entity. . . .

A terrible longing rose within him to return to England. Jane too, he knew, wanted to go home, wanted to stop their endless voyaging. But he could not afford to uproot his brood and send them traveling again, especially now that Laski had withdrawn his patronage.

And there was another reason, though he shied away from thinking about it as much as he could. The demon had come to them in England; it knew where they lived. It was still possible that it had not yet found them in Prague.

He stopped going out. He sat in his room in Doctor Hageck's house and observed his household—the children's arguments, the stenches coming from Kelley's experiments. He continued to write in his diary but now he left out and changed a good deal. In his version it was the Lord Chamberlain who led them to King Rudolf; the servant did not make an appearance. He did not think about the reason for these changes, though he knew obscurely that they gratified his vanity.

And underneath everything the fear ate at him, gnawing like a rat at his vitals.

He studied his daughter closely. She seemed fine, a happy and carefree three-year-old. He worried about her nonetheless. If the demon possessed her again he would be powerless to stop it, just as he was powerless in most things.

She was too young to question, but he asked Arthur, who was four-and-a-half, if they were unhappy or worried about anything. Arthur looked impatient with the questions, and puzzled as well. "We're fine," Arthur said. He shifted from one foot to the other. "May Katherine and I go play now?"

"If anything is worrying you—"

"I know how to speak Czech," he said. "Listen." He said something quickly: it sounded like gibberish to Dee. "Can you say that?"

"No. Listen—"

"Go on. Say it."

"I can't. Does Katherine—"

"Yes you can. Come on."

"Arthur!" Dee said, his fear erupting into anger. The hurt look on Arthur's face penetrated to his heart, and he repented his outburst immediately. "Go outside and play. I'm busy here." Arthur turned and ran from the room.

A good deal of the time Jane fussed around him, cooking and cleaning and taking care of the children. "Go outside," she told him more than once. "You're underfoot here. I can't get anything done with you around."

Finally he took her advice. He soon found, though, that the city no longer pleased him the way it once did. His steps were uncertain, like a sick man's, and he rarely left his side of the river.

One day he heard the sound of a crowd shouting. He turned a corner and saw that three or four men had backed a boy against a wall. One of the men pummeled him with a club and the others laughed loudly. Another kicked him roughly in the stomach. The boy fell to the ground.

"Here!" Dee called, running forward. "Stop that! I'll call the watch!"

The men looked up. He had no idea how to summon the watch, he realized. And he had spoken in English; they could not possibly have understood him.

The attackers left the boy and advanced toward him. The man in the lead grinned savagely and raised his club.

Dee spoke a few words, hoping to stop them, to take control of the club. Nothing happened; his magic was not strong enough.

Suddenly he heard more shouting; it sounded a long distance away. Three men hurried toward them, their daggers out. The thugs ran. The watch, Dee thought. He had summoned them, and like Kelley's angels they had come.

The man at the head of the watch said something to him in Czech. Dee shook his head. The man shrugged, attempted something in gestures which Dee did not understand, and then led the others away.

"Wait!" Dee said. "What about him? He's hurt!"

The men did not stop. Dee bent over the boy. He was older than Dee had first thought, eighteen or nineteen, with long, unkempt sandy-colored hair. An ugly rash had broken out on his face, and he looked terribly thin, almost malnourished.

"Are you all right?" Dee asked in German.

The boy said nothing. Another Czech speaker, Dee thought. But then the boy picked himself up, gingerly testing every limb as he went. "No, of course I'm not all right," he said in German. Speaking aggravated the cut on his lip, and he winced.

"Where's your home?" Dee asked.

"I don't have a home."

"Where do you live, then?"

The boy said nothing. He headed down the street. Dee hesitated and then followed him.

After a time they came to the walled city Dee had seen earlier. The boy went through the open gates. Should he go on? Who were these people, anyway?

Rabbi Judah Loew came to the gateway to greet the boy. Where had he come from? What was happening here? It was like a dream, people and places from the past all blending together, none of it making any sense.

Loew stopped when he saw Dee. The boy brushed past him rudely. "What are you doing here?" Loew asked.

"I—the boy is hurt."

"What business is it of yours?"

"I thought I'd help," Dee said. He had not remembered the man being so prickly. "And what about you? What are you doing here?"

"I live here." Loew laughed. "Don't look so confused. This is the Jewish Quarter."

"Oh," Dee said stupidly. He understood a good many things now. Why the boy had been attacked, for one thing, and why the watch had not stopped for him. Jews were probably not welcome outside the walls of the Quarter.

His curiosity, never far from the surface, rose within him. "Who is the boy?" Dee asked. "Why is he so angry?"

"His name is Izak," Loew said. "He's none of your concern."

"Very well," Dee said stiffly. It was no wonder the Jews huddled together in their own town, he thought; if they were all as clannish and impolite as this no one would want to associate with them anyway. He turned to go.

"Wait," Loew said. "I—I'm sorry. I shouldn't have been so abrupt. I need your help in something."

"What?" Dee said. His voice sounded more curt than he had meant it to be.

"Please. Come with me."

He hesitated. It was his curiosity that finally made the decision for him; he had never seen a Jewish Quarter before. With a shock he realized that he had never seen a Jew either, until he had met Rabbi Loew. They had all been banished from England by someone, some king, centuries ago.

He took a breath and stepped through the gate.

The houses here were packed in together beyond what Dee thought would be possible, each one jostling up against its neighbor. Great crowds of people thronged the streets. Loew led him through crooked little lanes, past crooked little houses with overhanging eaves. Someone somewhere was singing in a minor key. From somewhere else came a strange smell, a delicious smell. Geese squawked. Everything seemed different, exotic, as though he had arrived not in another city but another continent.

They went through a square, and there Dee saw the most curious thing yet. He stopped.

"What is it?" Loew asked.

"The clock," Dee said. "It's—"

Loew looked at him, clearly puzzled.

"It runs backwards," Dee said.

Loew laughed. "Does it? Perhaps it is your clocks that run backwards. Have you ever seen written Hebrew?"

Of course. Hebrew ran from right to left. Now he saw that the clock bore Hebrew letters instead of numbers. "I studied Hebrew at Cambridge, actually," Dee said. "Along with Greek and Latin. All the classical languages."

Loew said nothing, but for the first time Dee thought he looked impressed.

They left the square and continued along the twisted cobblestoned streets. It was as though the clock had given him a clue, had shown him a way of translating the entire town. Everything here was the same, really, only backwards, as if seen in a mirror. It was not as exotic as he had thought.

Now that he was paying more attention he saw that the people's clothes were shabbier than those he had seen outside, and that everyone wore the same yellow circle as Rabbi Loew. So that was what it meant. And he noticed that on every street someone would stop and stare or point at him. You would think, Dee thought in annoyance, that they had never seen a Christian before.

"Did you get your audience with Emperor Rudolf?" Dee asked.

"Yes. It was not as bad as I feared it would be. He wanted to discuss Kabbalah." Loew looked troubled. "But it's dangerous to come to the attention of kings. Now that he's talked to me he'll probably invite me back."

"Why is that dangerous?"

But Loew was turning in at one of the houses. As they stepped inside a woman came out to greet them. "Judah," she said. "Did you find Izak? Is he hurt?"

"Yes and yes," Loew said. "Unfortunately. And he still wants nothing to do with me, with any of us."

"Poor child," the woman said. She came farther into the room and saw Dee. "Oh," she said. Her eyes showed the same mixture of curiosity and distrust he had seen from the townspeople. She turned quickly away.

"I brought a guest," Loew said. "This is Doctor John Dee, from England. And this is my wife Pearl."

"England," Pearl said, wonderingly, as though it were a place out of legend.

"He's going to help me with my studies," Loew said.

They headed back into the small, cramped house. Loew ushered him into a dark room smelling strongly of leather, then opened the windows. As Dee's eyes adjusted to the light he saw the source of the smell: bookshelves lined three walls, holding thick squat books, their titles etched on the spines in gold. Unfamiliar objects crowded the small room: branching candelabra, parchment covered in Hebrew letters, scroll-coverings made of threadbare dark velvet embroidered in silver and gold.

Loew sat at his desk. "Choose a book," he said.

"What?" Dee asked.

"Choose a book. Any book, any of the ones in my library."

Dee reached out at random and pulled a book down from the shelves. It was the *Sefer Yetsira*, the Book of Creation, with a commentary. He had never seen this book before, though he had heard of it, and he looked at it with real curiosity.

"Open it," Loew said.

Dee opened it.

"What page are you on?" Loew asked.

"Thirty-six," Dee said.

"Ah," Loew said. "You see?"

"See what?"

"Thirty-six. Whatever book I open, whatever I choose to study, that number is always there. I wondered if this held true for other people who use my books. Apparently it does."

"A coincidence, surely?"

"Is it? Open another book."

This time Dee found he had chosen a volume of the Talmud. He opened it near the end.

"What page?" Loew asked.

Dee looked at the number. "Thirty-six," he said with surprise. Of course—Hebrew books were backwards, like the clock. He had actually opened it near the beginning. "Let me try again."

He took down another book and opened it. "Page eighty-five," he said, a note of triumph in his voice.

Loew looked over his shoulder. "A commentary on Exodus. The thirty-sixth chapter, thirty-sixth verse."

Dee read the Hebrew and saw that Loew was right. "Very well, I believe you. But why—"

"If I knew that, I wouldn't have asked you here."

"I'm afraid I have no idea."

"Do you know any reason why this number might be significant?"

"Only what I told you when we met." Dee hesitated. Given this man's clannishness, he thought, it was astonishing that he was asking a Gentile for help. Something must be worrying him a great deal. "Why ask me? Surely someone more familiar with Kabbalah might know."

"I've asked everyone I can think of. I brought you here because—well, because I thought I heard your voice once. It came to me out of nowhere. You were saying something about coming to Prague."

"I was?"

"It appears we are fated to meet for some reason." Loew sighed. "There is a Jewish tradition—but I was hoping it wasn't that, I was hoping there might be another explanation."

"What is the tradition?" Dee asked.

"That the world rests on the shoulders of thirty-six righteous men. And if something happens to any one of these men, if they die before their time or leave the path of righteousness, the world will come to an end. They are called the *la'med vavniks*, from the Hebrew letters that correspond to—"

"Thirty-six. I know."

"Yes, of course. Of course you would."

"But why should this disturb you?"

"Because—because I am afraid I am one of the thirty-six. And I don't think I am up to the task."

Dee looked at him sharply.

"Judah!" Pearl called. "Judah, your students are here."

"I must go," Loew said. "We'll discuss this some other time. I have no pupils Tuesday, the day after tomorrow, you can come then—"

"Listen," Dee said quickly. "I have an associate who can speak to angels. I'll bring him along if you like. We can discover God's will in all this."

"Speaks to angels? There is an angel mentioned in the Talmud, Anael, who is said to answer all questions, who makes God's secrets known to man. Perhaps—"

"Judah!"

"Please come," Loew said. "I'll be waiting."

DEE HAD NOT GONE FIVE STEPS BEFORE HE FOUND HIMSELF lost in the maze of the Jewish Quarter. Every street, every house looked like one he had just seen. Several times he passed synagogues, an amazing number of them for such a small space. It showed great piety, he thought, or else a great deal of contentiousness among different factions, each one insisting on its own place of worship.

Once he came to a walled cemetery and paused to look inside. Tombstones were crowded in together and pushing up against the walls, new and old, straight or leaning dangerously or rotting on the ground. Bent and shriveled elder trees grew along the paths. The trees were the only greenery he had seen in the Quarter, but if this was a garden it was a malevolent one, each stone a noxious weed straining toward the light. He shivered.

"Do you know the story about this cemetery?"

Dee whirled around quickly. He smelled the woman before he saw her; perhaps her foul odor had given rise to his morbid thoughts. She was anywhere between fifty and ninety, bent over like a crescent moon.

"Who are you?" Dee asked.

"We met before," the woman said.

"I don't remember—" But suddenly he did. This was the midwife he had nearly hired for the birth of his child. She wore layer on layer of ragged clothing in different colors. Her face and what showed of her arms were very dark, burned by the sun.

He turned away; he could not seem to look at her for very long. "What do you want?"

"Do you know the story about this cemetery?"

She was speaking English, Dee realized, but not very well. Unthinking, he had answered in the same language. He switched to German, hoping that was her native language. "No, I don't," he said.

"There was a terrible plague here just a few years ago, in 1582," she said in very good German. "They say that one night during the plague Rabbi Loew walked through the cemetery, and that he met a woman, a tall woman dressed in white, with a white veil covering her face. She was holding out a piece of paper, and Rabbi Loew tore it from her hands and ran with it to the safety of his house. And there he saw that it was a list of names, names of people who were about to die in the plague, and that his own name was among them. But because he had torn the list from the hands of Death they all survived."

"Wait a minute," Dee said. "Are you telling me that no Jews died during the plague?"

"Some did, certainly," the woman said. "He didn't manage to get the whole list, you see."

Dee did not know what to make of this. It couldn't be a true story, surely.

"And now we come to what I want," the woman said. "I have heard of you, Doctor John Dee. Your reputation has preceded you, all the way from England. I would like to be your pupil. I would like to learn what you know of magic."

"What? No. It's impossible."

"Why?"

"Well, because—women can't learn magic. Everyone knows that."

"Do they? What's in a cock that's necessary for the study of magic?"

He remembered now how foul-mouthed she was. "It's not that. Woman's minds are weak, they are flighty and lack stability. They could not take on the responsibility."

"I would say it's just the opposite. We are responsible for everything, for all of life, from the pain and blood of birth to the laying out of the dead. Everything in the world was born between our legs."

Everything in the world was created by God, Dee thought. But he would not argue with this woman. "I'm sorry. No."

"Well," she said. "I hope I can someday change your mind. In the meantime I notice that you are nowhere near the gate you came in."

"Yes, well. I seem to have gotten lost. Do you know the way out?"

"Me? With my flighty and irresponsible mind? How could I possibly know something like that?"

"Don't toy with me," Dee said. "Do you or don't you?"

She laughed, showing three or four brown and broken teeth. "I could say I'd lead you out in exchange for lessons in magic. But I won't. Come with me."

She rucked up layers of her outer garments and tucked them into her skirt, then began to walk. Dee had no choice but to follow.

Loew had not taken him this way, he thought. They went through back alleys, shadowy unpaved streets crowded with warehouses and workshops. She moved swiftly for a woman of her age.

"Tell me something," Dee said. He was breathing faster from the exertion, but she hardly seemed winded. "What are you doing here? You're not a Jew, are you?" Say what you like about the Jews, Dee thought, he hadn't seen anyone in the Quarter as unkempt as this woman.

"No. I followed you here."

"You followed—" The gall of this woman! "That was unwarranted, quite unwarranted. I will not have you following me again."

They passed a butcher shop. The smells of the slaughtered animals coiled out into the street and mingled with the woman's stale odors. Men carrying a side of beef paused to look at them. This time Dee couldn't blame them; the woman looked like one of the city's gargoyles come to life.

"I've been here many times, though," she went on. "Rabbi Loew is a powerful man, a great worker of magic."

"And I suppose you asked him to be your teacher as well," Dee said. He wondered what Loew had made of her.

"I've never spoken to him. But I don't think he'd make a good teacher—he's too—too—" She struggled for the word. "He wants mastery over everything."

"Why do you come here, then?"

"I go all over. I've been everywhere in Prague, and a good many places out of it."

"Isn't that dangerous for you?"

"Who would bother a harmless old woman, Doctor Dee?" she asked, grinning her horrible grin.

They came out to a cobbled street, with the gate ahead of them. "My name's Magdalena," she said. "It's only fair I tell you, since I know yours."

He made his farewells and hurried outside the Quarter.

HE FOUND HIS WAY TO HAGECK'S HOUSE WITH NO TROUBLE, and went straight to the study to tell Kelley about Rabbi Loew. Kelley was busy pouring a bright green liquid from one vial to another, but partway through Dee's tale he stopped and turned to him. "Thirty-six righteous men, you say?" Kelley asked.

"Yes," Dee said, pleased that Kelley was taking an interest. "I asked him if he would like us to speak to the angels about him, and he said he would."

"Did he?" Kelley said absently. His brief spark of interest was gone; he seemed focused only on his work.

"We'll go the day after tomorrow," Dee said.

Next he went to tell Jane about his encounter. He found her in their bedroom, mending one of the children's blankets. "Good," she said when he had finished. "You've been too preoccupied lately—it's good you found someone to talk to. But do you have to take that man Kelley with you? Yes, I know," she said wearily, as Dee made ready to answer her. "He is the one who can see angels."

But the next day, as Dee sat down to breakfast, he noticed that there were no sounds or smells coming from Kelley's study.

"Where is that dreadful man?" Jane asked him, pouring his breakfast beer.

"Which dreadful man?"

"Kelley, of course. He's usually early for breakfast. I went to knock on his door but there was no answer. Perhaps we're finally rid of him."

"I hope not," Dee said. "Tomorrow is the day we visit Rabbi Loew."

After breakfast he looked in Kelley's workshop and his bedroom, then went in search of Doctor Hageck. He found him in his study, sitting behind his desk and going over some accounts.

"Do you know where Master Kelley's gone?" he asked.

"I haven't seen him since yesterday," Hageck said. "He's usually in that room of his, searching for the Philosopher's Stone. Do you know if he's made any progress?"

"I don't, no."

Hageck glanced up from the papers in front of him. "I've heard some disquieting news," he said.

Dee looked up sharply. Had Hageck learned about the demon, was he about to order them out of his house? "What news?" he asked.

"Someone I talked to saw you going to the Jewish Quarter."

"Yes, that's true," Dee said, surprised.

"What is it you do there? Good Christian men in this city do not mingle with those people. Nor do they mingle with us."

"I—I've been talking to an interesting man, Rabbi Judah Loew. Do you know him?"

"I don't know anyone in the Quarter. You shouldn't either, if you're wise."

"Why not?"

"Why not?" Hageck said, puzzled. "You know what the Jews are like."

"No, not really. There are no Jews in England."

"Ah, well, that explains it. They're vicious and cunning and greedy—they'll cheat you out of everything you own. And it's said that they need the blood of Christians to live, that they kidnap baptized children—"

Dee began to laugh.

"What is so amusing?"

"I haven't seen anything like that. I think those are stories, nothing more."

"You don't know. You said yourself you've never met a Jew before. I tell you this for your own good, believe me. Stay out of the Quarter."

Dee nodded without committing himself, but he knew that nothing would keep him from visiting Loew again. His curiosity had been aroused.

Kelley returned that evening. "Where have you been?" Dee asked.

"About," Kelley said. "I've been thinking of renting my own place. I need to spread out if I'm to continue my experiments."

Jane's expression showed her pleasure as clearly as if she had spoken. Fortunately, Kelley was turned away from her and facing Dee. "But how will you afford it?" Dee asked. "You told me you had no money—"

"You needn't concern yourself with that."

Had Kelley found a patron? Or—unlikely as it seemed—had he discovered how to make the Philosopher's Stone? Perhaps he had returned to his old ways, to whatever crimes he had committed before Dee met him. But Kelley's expression permitted no questions. Dee could only hope that whatever Kelley was up to, it would not come to the attention of King Rudolf. And if Jane was happy . . .

"Remember that we're to see Rabbi Loew tomorrow," Dee said.

"Of course," Kelley said.

Dee rose early the next day and was pleased to see that Kelley was already at the table. Jane served them breakfast, and when they were done they packed up the scrying stone and the other implements and headed out to the Jewish Quarter.

As soon as they went through the gate Dee realized that he was unsure how to find Loew's house. He headed down an unfamiliar street lined with shops: a cobbler's, a tailor's, a silversmith's. A few more streets took him to the town square, and he knew the way from there. He strode purposefully on ahead until they came to Loew's house.

Loew opened the door to their knock. "I remember you," he said to Kelley. "You were waiting for King Rudolf with us."

Kelley nodded.

"Well," Dee said. "Shall we get started?"

Loew led the way to his study and opened the windows. His desk had been cleared for them, Dee saw. They brought out their implements, the cloth, the wax tablets, the stone.

Suddenly Loew stepped back, shocked. "What's wrong?" Dee asked.

The other man pointed to an inscription in Hebrew on one of the tablets. "We almost never write the hidden name of God," he said.

"Do you want us to stop?" Dee asked.

"No, no. Go ahead. The damage is already done."

Dee set the showstone on the stand and motioned them to pray. "Good," he said when they had finished. "Ask the angels—we would like to know the significance of the number thirty-six."

"Thirty-six," Kelley said. He looked into the glass. "Madimi says that it is the number after thirty-five."

Loew looked doubtfully at Dee. "Madimi is a child," Dee explained. "She very often says just what comes into her head."

"A child?" Loew said. "Do angels have ages?"

Dee had never thought of that. They must have, though, since that was the way Kelley saw them.

"Now I see the angel Uriel," Kelley said. "He tells me that there are thirty-six righteous men on whom the world depends."

Dee saw Loew tense out of the corner of his eye.

"None of these men know who they are. Each lives in ignorance of his purpose in the world. At the moment of their appointed death, though, they are granted understanding, and they must name an heir to carry on their work. And of course this heir does not know what he has been called upon to do, until it is his turn to die.

"And he says that you—that Rabbi Loew—you are not one of them, as you feared." Kelley's voice grew stronger, deeper, and the cadences he spoke in were different. Dee had never heard him like this; he thought that an angel might actually be speaking through him. "You are the thirty-seventh. You are charged to watch over the others and see that they do not come to harm. If they die before their appointed time they cannot name their heir, and the world will end. There is one here in Prague, especially, who must be guarded, whose life may be in danger."

"Here?" Loew asked. "Who is he?"

"It doesn't matter," Kelley said. His voice changed again, becoming low and raspy. It sounded familiar, horribly familiar. "He will die, whatever you do. All is lost, hopeless. Nothing you do can make the slightest difference."

"Who—who are you?" Dee asked.

"Silence!" Kelley said.

And then all the world went blank. Dee could say nothing, see nothing, hear nothing. He struggled to form words, to scream aloud for help, but he could not move.

4 DEE'S MOUTH MOVED WITHOUT HIS VOLITION. "He will die, the world will end, and then we will finally have our triumph," he heard himself say. "The world will be remade in our image."

The thing was inside him now. His muscles bunched and released under the thing's control; it was a sickening feeling. He still could not see.

Loew was saying something, but he could not hear what it was. Where was Kelley?

The thing laughed. "Your children will die," he/it said. "Everything will die, earth, air, fire, water. This world will become our paradise."

Dimly he could hear Loew shouting in Hebrew, reciting some sort of chant or prayer. He struggled to open his eyes.

He felt his hand reach out. His fingers brushed something round. He lifted it; it felt cold and heavy in his grasp. The showstone.

He raised the stone as if to throw it. Kelley screamed. Loew's chanting became louder, and this time, after great struggle, Dee was able to open his eyes. His hand was poised to throw the stone at Kelley.

Do it, the thing whispered within him. *Throw it. Why can he see angels and you cannot? Is that fair?*

Why not? he thought. Why *could* Kelley see angels, after all?

Kelley screamed again, shrilly. The sound brought Dee back to himself. Good God. Where had that surge of anger come from? What had he been about to do?

He forced his fingers to straighten. The stone dropped and landed with a crack on Loew's desk. He struggled to follow Loew's chanting, the sinuous turns of the melody.

His control continued to return, a little at a time. Thank God, he thought. Thank God. He took a step and stumbled, then fell into a chair and dropped his head into his hands. He was shivering uncontrollably.

He looked up to see Loew regarding both of them uncertainly. "You have not been entirely honest with me, I think," Loew said. "What was that?"

"I don't know," Dee said. He shuddered again; he could not seem to stop. His voice felt raw, as if he had been screaming for a long time.

"You don't *know*?" Loew asked.

"It is—it is a demon of some sort. A fallen angel. We first conjured it in London—we called it somehow through the stone. It possessed my daughter Katherine then. That's why we came here. The demon seemed to say that we could outrun it."

"And you believed it?"

Dee looked at him. "I did, yes. I was terrified for Katherine. I never thought that it might be lying."

"And so you brought it here," Loew said flatly.

"You don't know what it was like! It attacked my *child*! I was alone, all alone—no one knew enough to help me. No one could possibly help me. Everything I touched had gone wrong."

"But why did you call it up in the first place?"

Dee hesitated. He couldn't accuse Kelley, not with the man standing right there. "I didn't intend to," he said.

"I have heard of these demons," Loew said. "They are souls that were created by God just before the Sabbath. When the Sabbath came he had to stop work and so he could not make bodies for them. Now these spirits fly through the upper air, looking for bodies to inhabit."

"No," Dee said. "It's a fallen angel, one of those that rebelled with Lucifer against God."

"We don't believe that. We believe—"

"It doesn't matter," Dee said. He was in no mood to discuss theology with an unbeliever. "What was it you were reciting?"

"The ninety-first psalm. The song against demons, it is called."

"Which one is that?"

In answer Loew began to recite. " 'Thou shalt not be afraid of the terror by night, nor of the arrow that flies by day. . . . No evil shall befall thee, neither shall any plague come nigh thy dwelling. . . . He shall give his angels charge over thee, to keep thee in all thy ways.' "

"A good psalm to remember," Dee said. He had heard it, of course, but had not known that it could be used to banish demons.

"And a window must be open while you recite," Loew said. "There must be somewhere for the demon to go."

"Is it gone for good, then? Did you get rid of it?"

"No, unfortunately."

"But can you—"

Loew shook his head. "No, I'm afraid not. I don't know nearly enough. But it must be exorcized, and soon. If it becomes strong enough it can inhabit a man completely, taking over his mind and body forever, extinguishing his immortal soul. You were very fortunate here."

"I don't feel fortunate." He tried to laugh, but it sounded hollow.

"There is, of course, a temporary solution, and that is to stop using the showstone."

Dee picked up the stone gingerly and turned it over in his long fingers. Loew moved to stop him but then sat back and let him continue, as if satisfied he would not do anything rash.

The stone was miraculously unbroken. Could he bring himself to stop using it? He had so many questions left to ask the angels. But he would have to—he couldn't risk possession by the demon again.

"And I will have to find this righteous man the angel spoke of, the one who lives here in Prague," Loew said. "In fact our tasks may be related. The demon said that if this man is killed the world will end, and then the demons can remake it the way they want. Perhaps if we find this man, and protect him so that the demon cannot harm him—perhaps then it will go away."

"Find him how?"

Loew shrugged. "I don't know."

"There's too much we don't know."

"Yes. We need to learn more. I will ask rabbis and scholars in other towns for help. And you should talk to people you know, all those alchemists and sorcerers I see in the streets. There seem to be more and more of them every day, ever since Rudolf came to Prague."

"I don't really know them, though. I just arrived here myself."

"Well, then," Loew said. "You should try to make their acquaintance, shouldn't you?"

NEITHER DEE NOR KELLEY SAID A WORD ON THE LONG WALK back. It was noon when they got to the house, but Dee went straight to bed and tried to sleep. It was no use. Almost as soon as he closed his eyes he began to relive the scene in Loew's study, feeling the demon crawl inside him like a worm and then take him over completely. He felt dirty, violated.

After a while he stood and looked through the few books he had brought with him. They were no help, though; none of them dealt with anything like this.

He must have slept; he woke in his bed, the sun shining in his eyes. He felt unrefreshed, as if he had spent the night struggling against an irresistible force, and his sheets were bunched in knots. His mouth was dry as a stone.

He went to the kitchen. Jane was already there, setting out

bread and butter for the children. "What happened to you yesterday?" she asked.

He couldn't say that they were no longer safe here, that their brief feeling of safety had been a fool's dream. That they had not escaped after all. Instead, he told her about what he had discovered at Loew's house, the legend of the thirty-six men.

"And that explains why you slept for twenty hours straight," Jane said sourly.

"I wasn't feeling well," he said.

He could tell she didn't believe him. "Your friend's gone again," she said. "That odious man Kelley."

"Did he say where he was going?"

"He didn't say anything. He was gone before I got up."

Dee went out into the city after breakfast, intending to search for the alchemists as Loew had suggested. Kelley had once mentioned a street called Golden Lane, but Dee had no idea where that was. Somewhere across the river, he thought. But the fear that had dogged him since London kept him on his own side; the other side, he remembered, was haunted with angels.

He ended up in a town square. There was a clock here too, a huge thing of blue and gold, with mechanisms for telling the hour and the month and the signs of the zodiac. What a city this is for timepieces, he thought.

As he watched, the figure of Death came out and inverted an hourglass. Then the apostles paraded in front of him; the clock chimed the hour; various allegorical figures followed, Greed and Vanity and Lust. Greed was represented by a Jewish moneylender; he thought of Rabbi Loew, then remembered Hageck's wild claims and shook his head.

"They put his eyes out, you know," someone near him said.

It was the old woman again, Magdalena; Dee could tell that without even looking, though oddly he could not call up her face. "Whose eyes?" he asked, not turning around.

"The clockmaker's. They didn't want him building anything like this again. About a hundred years ago, this was."

He faced her. "Were you following me again?"

"Yes."

"This is intolerable. I'll set the watch on you. I'm not without influence here, you know. King Rudolf himself—"

"You seemed lost. Is there anything you're looking for? Maybe I can help."

Could she? For the first time he wondered what had brought her to such a pass. How had she come to wander the streets of Prague, as old and infirm as she was? Did she have no family? Or had they thrown her out for working magic?

He found himself, to his own surprise, feeling pity for her. Jane had once told him that he had a good heart, that he could never turn away strays in need of help, not even a criminal like Kelley. "Maybe you can," he said. "I'm looking for alchemists or astrologers. The men who came here because of King Rudolf's reputation."

"Of course—I know them all. Come with me."

He had no choice but to follow her. "Do you know where Golden Lane is?" he asked as they set off.

She laughed. "Oh, you'll find no alchemists there," she said. "The street got its name from the goldsmiths who work for King Rudolf. Or from the rivers of piss that flow through it—there's nowhere to dump the waste."

"Where are we going then?"

"Patience," she said.

Despite this last command they stopped soon afterwards. Magdalena motioned Dee into a tavern. He shrugged and went inside; he had already discovered that Bohemian beer was very good, as tasty as English ale.

The place smelled of cabbages and sausage. His eyes strained to see in the dim light. At first he thought the tavern was empty, but then Magdalena led him toward a trestle table in the corner, occupied by several men. Yellow candles burnt to fat stubs ranged across the table, lighting the men's faces from below.

Now he could see well enough to recognize some of the people he had already noticed in the city: the man in the black cloak, his two black mastiffs lying on the floor near him; the tall man with the aristocratic bearing who had spoken to thin air. Magdalena sat at one of the benches and began talking to someone hidden in the shadows.

The man who spoke to air noticed him and nodded. "Sit," he said. "My name is Michael Sendivogius."

He took a place at one of the benches. The table was made of rough wood and covered with mystical signs scored into the surface, stars and numbers and alphabets, crescents and circles and triangles.

"I am Doctor John Dee."

"Indeed?" Sendivogius said. "I've heard of you. You wrote a number of books, didn't you? *Monas . . .*"

"*Monas Hieroglyphica.*"

But Sendivogius was already introducing the others, too quickly for Dee to remember them all. There was someone from Greece—this was the man with the dogs—and a pair of men from Hungary with nearly identical faces: thin and sharp-planed, with long brown hair. One of the men had jewels plaited in his beard. Then Sendivogius introduced a Scotsman, Alexander Seton. "A countryman of yours," Sendivogius said.

Dee was opening his mouth to explain the difference between England and Scotland when Sendivogius indicated the last person at the table. His hair and eyes and beard were blacker than any Dee had ever seen. He wore a richly embroidered brocade coat, frayed and raveled at the edges.

Dee realized with shock that the man was a Saracen, an infidel. Yet even as Dee thought of bloody religious wars and vowed to have nothing to do with him, he remembered that the word "alchemy" came from "al Khemia," or "from Egypt," and he felt a powerful desire to know more. He noticed, surprised, that the Saracen and Magdalena were deep in conversation.

When the courtesies were done the men continued their conversations among themselves, speaking in a babel of languages. The two Hungarians conducted a heated conversation in a language Dee did not recognize, all sibilants and misplaced accents; it sounded like cats fighting. If this was Hungarian, he thought, it was even more barbaric than Czech.

The Greek man shifted toward Dee. He was somewhere in his forties, with a round face, a black unruly beard, and dirty black hair that hung to his shoulders. His eyes popped from their sockets, the whites mottled and unhealthy, almost yellow.

"Are you looking for something?" he asked. His dogs turned toward Dee as well.

Could this man help him? But before Dee could ask the man spoke again.

"Tincture of mercury, perhaps? Cassia pulp? Vitriol of Mars?"

A fraud, Dee thought, disappointed. He had met men like this often enough, accompanying Kelley to various alchemists and astrologers in England. Almost all of them had proved to be braggarts and mountebanks, people who would claim anything to embellish their reputations.

"I'm afraid I don't remember your name," Dee said to gain time.

"Mamugna. I have a mandrake root, gathered under a gallows at midnight. . . ."

"I—no, thank you. I'm looking for knowledge."

"Yes, of course. You've come to the right place. You have only to ask—those of us who are embarked on the Great Work hide nothing from each other."

This had not been Dee's experience. But he had caught a word farther down the table, something that sounded promising. He held up his hand to indicate to Mamugna that he wanted to listen.

"King Rudolf himself came to Prague only two years ago," Sendivogius was saying. His accent was similar to Prince Laski's, and now Dee realized that despite the man's splendid Latin-sounding name he had to be Polish. "And why? The Holy Roman Emperors traditionally make their capital in Vienna. But Rudolf knows a thing or two about magic. He knows that something is about to happen here. Anyone with even the slightest magical ability feels it."

"Nonsense," Alexander Seton said. "Magic is available everywhere, and to everyone. King Rudolf is a great patron, I agree, but he himself knows nothing."

"But look at him," Sendivogius said. "He rarely leaves his castle, he has fits of melancholy, he throws things. . . . It's clear what has happened to him. He has meddled in things too great for his understanding, and is slowly going mad."

"His entire family is subject to these fits," Seton said. "He is descended on both sides from Joanna the Mad, after all. As I said, it has nothing to do with magic."

"Then what about other rulers near Prague?" Sendivogius asked. "In Russia they call the czar who just died Ivan the Terrible."

"And also there is Báthory Erzsébet," one of the Hungarians said. His accent was very strong.

"Elizabeth Báthory," the other said. "Here it is the family name last."

"Elizabeth Báthory, yes," the first one said. "A princess in my country. The people say that she bathes in the blood of virgins so that she stays always young."

"Rulers have always been mad," Seton said. "This means nothing. It—"

"Prague in the Czech language is Praha," Mamugna said, joining the conversation.

Dee turned to him. What did this have to do with magic? But Mamugna was continuing.

"Praha means threshold," the Greek said. "We stand on the threshold here. Not just between east and west, and between northern and southern Europe, though that is certainly part of it, the fact that we are at the center of the great trade routes of Europe. But we are also between the living and the dead, the spirit world and our own. One step across, and we are somewhere else. And that step can be anywhere in the city."

"Do you mean," Dee said slowly, "that it is easier for spirits to come here than anywhere else? That the—the doorway between their world and ours lies in Prague?"

"Yes, of course," Mamugna said. "And as the door opens wider there will be more and more of them, filling the city."

But my spirit appeared to me in England, Dee thought. "What about possession?" he asked. "Have any of you known a demon to inhabit living bodies?"

"Of course," Sendivogius said. "Such things are common enough."

"What can be done, though?" Dee asked. "How do you force the demon to leave the body?"

"Done?" Sendivogius said. "I don't know that anything can be done. As my colleague here said, in Prague the spirits travel where they like. But are you talking about a specific case?"

"A friend of mine," Dee said. "He called up a demon and now cannot send it back."

"How did he do it?" Seton asked. His eyes glowed like sword-points in the candlelight.

"He used a showstone," Dee said. "He can see angels in the glass."

"Ah," Seton said. "How does he prepare the glass?"

Dee felt despair, and a tendril of the fear that was never far from him now. These men knew very little. They were more interested in learning from him than they were in answering his questions.

"It's best to clean the glass with holy water," Mamugna said. "I have some water that has been blessed by none other than a bishop—"

"Nonsense," Sendivogius said. "All that is needed is ordinary water and vinegar."

"Is it?" Mamugna said. "You see here what happens without careful protection—"

"I had this from the Befaninis, who are cooks for the great house of—"

"Befaninis! But that means little witches in Italian!"

"Just so," Sendivogius said.

Dee rose to go. These men had some knowledge, but it would take weeks to sort out anything useful, and he felt too weary to even begin to attempt it. As he stood he saw Magdalena and the Saracen, talking to each other as though no one else in the room existed. Magdalena threw back her head and laughed, her long beak of a nose pointing toward the ceiling. Dee sat back down, next to Magdalena this time, and tried to hear what they were saying.

They had become serious. "Have you given any more thought to my suggestions?" the man said to Magdalena. To Dee's surprise he had only the slightest trace of an accent.

"Yes, of course," Magdalena said. "But I can find no one to help me. I wish you would stay and be my teacher."

"Unfortunately I cannot. And it is best to have only one teacher, one master. It would be irresponsible of me to start you on a course of study and then leave you."

"I understand."

"I'm afraid I have some business to attend to now," the man said, standing up. Now Dee could see his loose-fitting trousers, as worn as the coat, and supple leather boots. "You'll be joining me for supper at the usual time, I hope?"

"Of course."

"Take care," the man said.

She turned to watch him as he went, and saw Dee. "Would you introduce me to your friend?" Dee asked quickly, before the man could take his leave.

"This is Master Al Salah," she said. Her features were blurred in the candlelight. "And this is Doctor Dee, from England."

The man inclined his head in a bow. "It is a pleasure to make your acquaintance, Doctor Dee," he said.

"The pleasure is mine," Dee said. But before he could say anything else Al Salah bowed again and left the tavern.

Magdalena laughed. "You're wondering what the likes of him has to do with the likes of me," she said.

His expression must have given him away, though he had tried to hide his astonishment. "I am, yes," he said. She would not believe him now if he lied to spare her feelings. "And did you say you're meeting him for supper?"

"He's kind enough to feed me," she said. "Otherwise I would probably starve."

"That's good of him," Dee said absently. His mind was whirling with everything he had heard. It was time to go home and try to make some sense of it. "Goodbye."

"Goodbye," Magdalena said. "I'll see you soon."

Dee left the tavern and headed toward Doctor Hageck's house. Why was this man helping her? Did he see something in her that Dee had missed? Or was he simply being charitable, feeding her to keep her from starving?

That last was probably it, Dee thought. His thoughts turned to what he had learned at Rabbi Loew's, that there was a righteous man, one of thirty-six, here in Prague. Could it be Al Salah? What did that mean, to be righteous? Was it enough just to do good, as Al Salah seemed to be doing?

Or was the man they searched for another of the alchemists?

It seemed unlikely. Poor Magdalena, trying to learn something useful from that mixed collection of rogues and seekers. She at least seemed sincere. Perhaps she was—No. But maybe . . . Had the angel said the thirty-sixth had to be a man? He couldn't remember.

No, it was ridiculous. No one so foul-mouthed could possibly be counted righteous.

His stomach growled, reminding him that he had had nothing to eat since breakfast. The conversation at the tavern had been intriguing enough that he had not thought to order a meal for himself. He forced his thoughts away from the alchemists and hurried home, hoping that Jane would have something set out for the midday meal. Poor Jane, he thought, putting up with his comings and goings at odd hours. If anyone was good, and kind, and righteous . . .

His hunger returned, sharper this time. He thought of the supper Al Salah had promised Magdalena, and he could not help but wish that he had been invited.

THE NEXT DAY KELLEY KNOCKED ON THE DOOR AS DEE AND his family were eating breakfast. "I thought I'd show you my new house," he said.

"Certainly," Dee said. He finished eating and followed Kelley. As he went he saw Jane beam with pleasure, thinking, no doubt, that Kelley would now be gone forever.

They went south a long ways. Dee had learned that the section he lived in was called the Old Town and that to the south lay the New Town, new because it had only been built two centuries ago. He had never visited it, though, and now, as he followed Kelley, he saw that the streets were cleaner and broader and that more care had been taken in laying out the squares and boulevards.

He looked longingly at one of the squares, a pleasant green

spot with benches and fountains and paths marked out with rose borders. He would have liked to pause, to rest a while, but Kelley hurried on.

They passed a number of shops: a glassblower's, a tanner's, a tavern. Each had a door of a different color: butter yellow, grass green, crow black. Suddenly Kelley stopped and peered in a window. "One minute," he said. He opened a brick red door and went inside, and Dee followed.

He found himself in a dim dusty room; what little light there was came through small leaded glass windows and a few squat candles. As his eyes adjusted to the light he saw that the room was very long and narrow, no more than six feet wide but extending back an unseen distance into the gloom.

Now he could make out clumps of herbs and roots hanging from the ceiling, and shelves along the wall holding bottles of different sizes and colors. A stuffed alligator stood on a pedestal. The room smelled of mold and chemicals, and of the leather hides from the tanner's down the street.

"Good day, Master Kelley," someone said.

A man walked toward them from the back of the shop. "Ah, Doctor Dee," the man said. As he came into the light of one of the candles Dee saw with surprise that it was Mamugna.

"Do you know each other?" he asked Kelley. "Why didn't you tell me when Rabbi Loew suggested I look for alchemists?"

Kelley said nothing. "I have that sulphur you wanted," Mamugna said. He took a small red jar from one of the shelves and brought it over; Dee smelled its sharp foul odor. "Did you want anything else? What about you, Doctor Dee? Have you decided you need something after all?"

"No," Dee said, trying to sort out his confusion. How long had the two men been acquainted? Why had Kelley mentioned Golden Lane; had that been an attempt to confuse Dee as to the whereabouts of the alchemists?

Kelley opened his purse and reached inside; Dee heard the heavy clink of coins. He paid Mamugna for the sulphur and they left the shop, Dee blinking in the sun.

A few minutes later they came to an enormous house, almost a palace. It had three good-sized stories with gabled windows, and on top of that a cupola almost tall enough to comprise a fourth. A giant arched door stood in the center. As they came closer Dee saw that it was made of oak and bound in iron; it looked too heavy for mere humans to open.

"This is—this is your house?" Dee said.

"Yes."

Now Dee could see a smaller door set into the left-hand side of the larger one. Kelley took out an iron key and opened it, then led him through a marble foyer. They walked through chilly cavernous rooms, all unfurnished. Their steps rang against the floor and echoed back from the walls. Reliefs of gods and angels floated against the ceilings, gazing down on them indifferently.

"Are you cold?" Kelley asked.

Dee realized he was shivering. But he seemed to be shivering all the time now, trying to stay one step ahead of his fears. "No," he said. "I'm fine."

They climbed a marble staircase and headed down a long hallway. Finally they came to a room in which Kelley had set up his alchemical equipment. All his retorts and alembics and athenors barely filled one of the corners; they seemed to huddle together against the empty space around them. Two alabaster women stood on either side of a cavernous fireplace, their heads holding up the mantelpiece.

"But how can you afford something like this?" Dee asked.

"Do you know what the best thing about this house is?" Kelley said, placing his new purchase in with a clutter of other bottles. "There is a legend that says it once belonged to Doctor

Faust. They say he was carried away by devils through a hole in the ceiling."

Dee had heard the stories about Doctor Faust, of course; everyone had. Faust had made a pact with the devil in exchange for knowledge, and so had condemned himself to eternal damnation. "The best thing?" Dee said uneasily. "You would not consort with demons the way Faust did, would you?"

"I would not?"

"Master Kelley. Promise me you will not profane your gift, the gift God gave you. You can see angels, man. Promise me you will not use such a talent to speak to demons."

"But what is the difference, exactly? How can I tell which ones are the good angels and which are evil?"

"Come, you know the answer to that. The ones we called up together were good angels—"

"Were they? Not at the end."

"Yes, but you did not intend to summon that—that thing. It came uninvited."

"Not true. It came when it was called, you know that."

"What are you telling me? That you summoned it intentionally?"

"*We* summoned it. Remember? You were eager for knowledge, and I called up a spirit that could help us. The knowledge is what is important. It doesn't matter how we get there, or which angels show us the way."

The fear inside him uncoiled. The evil spirit felt very near, waiting. So far it had only come when Kelley had looked into the showstone, but what if the passage between worlds had grown easier, as the men in the tavern claimed? What if it could be called simply by Kelley's blasphemy?

"I had nothing to do with it," Dee said sharply. "It's your fault that we had to run, your fault it stalks us now."

"Is it?"

"I won't listen to this," Dee said. "Good day."

Kelley's laughter echoed behind him as he walked from the room. He left the vast empty building and headed back slowly to the Old Town, deep in thought.

Kelley had gone over to the evil angels. Dee was reluctant to think such a thing about his associate, but he could find no other way to account for the other man's wild talk, his strange accusations. And how else had Kelley been able to afford such a palace?

He felt a deep melancholy at the thought. The two of them had worked side by side for so long, had made such thrilling discoveries together. . . . But Kelley was lost now, seduced away.

The day grew warmer as the sun climbed toward noon, and Dee sweated from his exertions. But he thought of Kelley alone in his large chilly house, and he shivered.

AND THEN IT WAS TUESDAY AGAIN, THE DAY RABBI LOEW HAD no pupils. Dee made his way through the Jewish Quarter easily; he was coming to know the streets and alleyways and shops and houses.

Loew led him back to his study and motioned him to a chair. "You did not bring your friend this time," he said, sitting behind his desk. He steepled his hands in front of him, as if he were praying, and gazed levelly at Dee.

"No."

"Who is he? What is he to you?"

"He was—he was my assistant."

"More than an assistant, surely." Loew hesitated. "I do not wish to offend, but—but I think this man studies dark things. Unlawful things."

"Yes, I've come to the same conclusion myself."

"Good. I'm curious. How did you meet him?"

"A friend of mine introduced us. He showed me—Master

Kelley showed me an ancient manuscript and two phials of powder, one red and one white. Well, red and white are the colors of the opposites of alchemy, are they not? Sun and moon, sulphur and mercury. I thought then that Kelley was a learned man, someone who could teach me a great deal."

"Where did he get these things?"

"He dug them up in Glastonbury," Dee said. Loew looked puzzled. "Where King Arthur is buried."

Loew's expression did not change. Dee heard for himself how extravagant this claim sounded when spoken so matter-of-factly. Somehow in Kelley's presence these things were eas-ier to believe; the scryer surrounded himself with an aura of mystery that was difficult to challenge. And then Dee remem-bered something else Kelley had told him: that he had once dug up a newly-buried corpse and made it speak prophecies. At the time Dee had thought that Kelley had renounced such necromantic practices, but apparently he had been wrong.

"Well," Loew said. "Did you learn anything from the alchemists?"

Before he could answer Loew's wife Pearl came into the room, carrying a tray with two cups. She set the cups in front of them; they were in the Bohemian style, with flowers etched on the glass. Dee had seen nothing like them before he had come to Prague.

He studied the liquid through the glass suspiciously. It was a dark brown; it looked like something Kelley would use for one of his experiments. "Drink," Loew said. Pearl left, taking the tray with her.

He sipped cautiously. It was hot and strong and very bit-ter. "What is it?" he asked.

"Coffee."

"What on earth's that?"

Loew smiled. "The Turks drink it," he said. "We get it from them."

"They've never brought it to England," Dee said. He was starting to feel more alert, as though he had moved into another, clearer realm. He took another sip.

"The Jews import it, mostly," Loew said.

"Ah, that explains it, then. We have no Jews in England. One of our kings expelled them, I don't remember which—"

"Edward the First. In 1290. But it is not true that there are no Jews, you know. There is a small community of Portuguese exiles who fled during the Inquisition, and there are some Italian court musicians. And Queen Elizabeth's physician, Roderigo Lopez, is a Jew."

Dee looked at him, surprised; he would not have thought Loew would take such interest in so distant a country.

"We need to know which countries are safe for us and which are not," Loew said. "We have been forced to leave our homes with only a moment's notice. With such a small population it appears that England is not safe, at least for now." He took a sip of his coffee. "So," he said. "What do you have to tell me?"

"I talked to some of the alchemists," Dee said. "I'm afraid I did not learn much from them. They have only bits and scraps of knowledge—none of them truly understands alchemy or sorcery or can tell us anything about what is happening here." He summarized the little he had learned at the tavern.

"I wrote to a friend in Moravia," Loew said when he had finished. "I was the chief rabbi there, you know, before I moved to Prague to marry Pearl. He too sees signs of something about to happen. He mentioned a door between worlds, just as these men did. And he too thinks that the door is widening."

"Judah!" Loew's wife called. "Izak is here!"

"I'm sorry," Loew said. "It's important that I talk to him. Do you mind waiting?"

"No," Dee said. "Not at all."

Loew left the study. Something like five minutes passed, and then ten. Bells rang out in the city, calling out the hour. Dee became impatient; he stood and began to pace, studying the rows of books as he passed. He was pleased to see that he had not forgotten his Hebrew.

Suddenly he realized that he could hear voices from outside the room; they had been growing louder without his noticing. "And you're glad, I suppose," someone said; Dee thought it was Izak. "Glad I couldn't find anyone else willing to marry us."

"Not glad, no," Loew said. "I would truly have liked to perform the ceremony. But God's will—"

"God's will," the other voice said mockingly. "It is God's will that I be prevented from marrying because of something that is not my fault, something I had nothing to do with. If anyone should be punished it should be my mother—her and that horrible peddler who's probably my father. I heard he has a child in every town he visits."

"We must try to find out what God intends for you. Since he does not intend for you to get married—"

"Then to hell with him."

"What?"

"To hell with him. I shit on him. He's not my God—no God of mine would be so cruel."

"I understand how you must feel—"

"Do you? Do you really? How can you possibly? How many children do you have, seven? Imagine having none, imagine living out your days alone, with nothing and no one to comfort you. Imagine your name dying with you. Imagine dying alone. And all for a mistake your mother made years ago."

"I hope you'll come to see—"

"I don't know. I don't know what I'll do. Maybe I'll convert."

"Convert?" Loew said. Dee thought he sounded genuinely shocked. "I beg you—please don't do anything without speaking to me first."

"I wonder what the Christians say about bastards marrying. Or the Moslems. You can have more than one wife if you're a Moslem, I think. Maybe I'll go to Constantinople."

"Stay here. Please. It's not as if you're banned from the synagogue, or cannot be buried in the cemetery—"

"Why would I want to go to the synagogue? Or to the cemetery, for that matter? No, I'm leaving. Nothing you say can change my mind."

"At least keep to the faith of your fathers—"

"My fathers!" Izak said scornfully. "What do I owe my fathers?"

"You'll come to understand—"

"I doubt it," Izak said. Dee heard the sound of a door slamming, and then Loew's footsteps coming toward him.

"I'm sorry I kept you here for so long," Loew said, taking a seat. "Where were we? Yes, my friend in Moravia—"

"Why is he so angry?" Dee asked.

"It's none of your affair."

"Perhaps I can help."

"The only one who can help Izak is Izak himself. There's nothing you can do."

"How do you know that? At least tell me what's wrong so I can judge for myself."

"Very well." Loew paused a moment and then said, "He wishes to marry."

"Is the woman unsuitable in some way?"

"No. No, unfortunately she is not, or he might give up this dream of his. He cannot marry her because he is illegitimate."

"He cannot—I don't understand. Does she object to his parentage?"

"As far as I can judge these things she loves him very much. Fortunately, she has since been married off to another man, and she may forget him in time. He cannot have her because it is the law. Because the Torah tells us that bastards cannot marry."

"But—do you mean to tell me he cannot marry anyone? That his life is ruined because of something his parents did, something that's not his fault? It's true that bastards are coarser than other people, not as civilized, but if the woman here is willing—"

"I knew you wouldn't understand. We are sworn to God to keep his commandments—"

"I can't believe you could be so cruel. My God, if I was that boy I would leave too. And to tell him to keep to the faith of his fathers! His father deserves nothing from him."

"So. You were eavesdropping on our conversation. Are you a spy then, as well as an expert on our laws?"

"I couldn't help but overhear. Your voices were raised."

"That does not give you the right to lecture me about my religion. Especially in my own home."

"I wouldn't dream of telling you what to do."

"That is exactly what you are telling me." Loew pushed away the remains of his coffee; it was cold now, and looked like mud. "It's clear that we cannot work together. I feared it would end this way. We should each of us stick to our own people."

Dee had nothing to say to that. He remembered Doctor Hageck's advice; it had been nearly identical, and now he wondered if the other man had been right after all.

"Farewell, then," Dee said, and left Loew's house.

Halfway to the gate he saw the old woman, Magdalena, unmistakable even from a distance because of the layers of clothing she wore. And there was someone with her, someone who looked like . . . Izak?

It *was* Izak, he saw. How did they know each other? What in God's name had the two of them found to talk about?

He took a different way, not wanting to talk to either of them. When he got to the gate he turned to look back on the close-packed city, the small leaning houses and tangled streets. I will never see Rabbi Loew again, he thought. A pity, in a way—he was obviously a man of great learning. Strange, though. A very odd people, the Jews.

5 DEE WAS GROWING SICK OF PRAGUE. HE HAD not succeeded in winning Rudolf's patronage; Kelley had taken a dangerous, unlawful path; Loew had proved to be stubborn and irrational; and despite all his efforts the demon still stalked him. Although it was December he decided to go back to Poland to fetch his son Rowland and the nurse.

When he returned he continued to keep busy, as if work were a form of exorcism, holding the spirits at bay. His family had grown too large to impose on Doctor Hageck any longer, and with Jane due in a month or so it would become even larger. And Hageck, his face hard, had mentioned that someone had seen Dee go to the Jewish Quarter once again, and Dee, heartsick at all his failures, had not bothered to tell the other man he had visited the place for the last time.

Taking his cue from Kelley he rented a house for them, though it was by no means as grand. His money was dwindling rapidly; if he did not find a patron soon he did not know what would happen. He could not return to England; it was clear he could only learn more about the demon in Prague.

Jane's time came in the middle of February and he sent for the midwife he had hired. After a few nerve-wracking hours of waiting he was ushered into Jane's room to find he was the father of a baby boy. They named him Michael, as he had planned.

He thought carefully about Michael's baptism. Some of the sects of the Czech Brethren were close to his own faith, but Dee, remembering the Catholic church they had visited on Christmas day, chose the church of St. Vitus instead. He did not think too closely about his reasons for this; he knew only that he was coming to understand why some men needed a priest standing between themselves and God. Or between themselves and God's enemies, as in his case. The Catholics, unlike the Anglicans, still had the rite of exorcism.

On March eighteenth he led his brood to the cathedral. It was every bit as splendid as the churches he remembered from King Henry's day, before Henry had ordered them all destroyed. He stood admiring the huge vaulted nave, the frescos and stained glass windows in muted red and gold, the mosaics of precious gemstones. Only when Michael was safely baptized did he allow himself to think about the demon, and about what he had feared might happen to his youngest child. For a brief moment he felt secure, sure that no demon could break through those barriers of sanctity.

The next day, Doctor Hageck's son came to call on them. One of Rudolf's messengers had left a note for Dee at his old lodgings, the boy said. Dee opened the note and pursed his lips in surprise, then called out for Jane. King Rudolf had summoned him to the castle again.

THIS TIME THE LORD CHAMBERLAIN LED HIM THROUGH ROOM after room, each one larger and more impressive than the last. All the rooms displayed bits and pieces of Rudolf's collections, what Dee now knew was called the Cabinet of Curiosities. They passed armillary spheres and unicorn's horns, maps and books and clocks and chalices. Several times Dee saw something he would have liked to study more closely but the chamberlain urged him on, moving so quickly that all the wonders passed in a blur.

Finally they came to a vast antechamber. Murals of gods and goddesses covered the walls and ceiling, the women plump and naked or nearly so. Dee thought he could tell what kind of woman Rudolf preferred just from the pictures he displayed. A fire blazed in one of two great fireplaces, though it was nearly spring and the other rooms had felt warm enough without one. Spendthrift, Dee thought disapprovingly, remembering how he and his family had portioned out their wood to last them through the winter.

Now he noticed that there was another man there, sitting in one of the chairs scattered around the room. As he came closer he saw to his displeasure that it was Rabbi Loew.

Loew nodded to him and he nodded back. Apparently they were going to say nothing to each other. Good, he thought. That was the way he wanted it as well.

A few minutes later the chamberlain ushered them both through a maze of hallways and into another room. It was the same room Dee had seen before, though the chamberlain had led them to it by a different route. There was Rudolf on his elevated chair, and there were his guards behind him. This time, though, another man stood to the king's right. Kelley.

Dee nearly stepped backwards in shock. How had Kelley gained Rudolf's favor, especially after the disastrous prophecies he had made the last time? And why hadn't he said anything about Rudolf's patronage the last time they had talked?

"Master Kelley here has been telling me a great many interesting things," Rudolf said without preamble. "The sort of things I need to know from my loyal subjects." He frowned and looked at Loew, and Dee saw a look of fear pass over Loew's face before he was able to control himself. The king could probably make things very difficult for the Jews in his realm.

"Apparently the world depends on the lives of thirty-six righteous men, is that correct?" Rudolf went on. Loew nodded. "And you have discovered, using the showstone of Doctor Dee here"—this time it was Dee's turn to nod—"that one of these men is here in the city, in Prague. Why wasn't I told this from either of you?"

"We didn't know you thought it important, Your Majesty," Dee said.

"You didn't know!" Rudolf said. "Something like this, happening in my own city, and you didn't think I'd be interested? Fortunately I have men like Kelley to keep me informed of such matters."

Dee looked at Kelley, but the other man would not meet his gaze. "Let me see if I understand this rightly," Rudolf said. "If this man dies before his allotted time then the world will end. Or, more properly, start over. Someone could seize control at the moment of this man's death and refashion the world to his desires."

"Yes, Your Majesty," Loew said. "That is why his life is so important, why we must discover who he is and protect him. We cannot let him die now—if he does, as you say, our world may end."

"That is not what I said," Rudolf said. "They say you are a man of learning, and yet in this matter you are as slow-witted as you are disloyal. I would like this man found, and then I would like him killed."

"What!" Dee said.

"Are you questioning me?" Rudolf asked. "I will have him killed. Oh, don't look so horrified—I don't expect either of you to do it. I have men I can call on for this kind of work. No, I need you for other things. You must find this man for me."

Dee could keep silent no longer. He had to know, even if Rudolf took his life for asking. "Why, Your Majesty?"

"It should be obvious," Rudolf said. "I will be the one to mold the world into its new shape. Master Kelley and I are already studying what will be necessary."

"What shape will that be?" Dee asked cautiously.

But the emperor seemed pleased to talk about his plans. "First we will get rid of my brother Matthias. I can't have him killed—he has too many friends, and they would be quick to start a civil war if he dies. But I can make it so that he doesn't exist, that he never existed. That he was never born to torment me with all his plots and plans, his machinations behind the scenes. He thinks I don't know his designs against me, but I do.

"Then I will make it so there is no death," Rudolf continued. "Others will continue to die, of course, but not me and not those in my favor. I will live forever—then I will not have to meet God at my death. Or perhaps—perhaps I will make it so there is no God. No God but me. No sins but what I say is sinful."

Rudolf paused as if to gather his thoughts. For the first time Dee understood that the emperor was not just eccentric, as he had thought, but quite mad.

"You will find this man for me, do you understand?" Rudolf said.

Loew nodded. "Yes, of course," Dee said, starting to feel relief. Was that all the king wanted, a simple promise? He could hurry home, move Jane and the children to Poland or somewhere safe, quit this haunted city of demons and angels. . . .

Suddenly he saw a velvet bag lying on one of the marble tables. His scrying glass. He had thought he'd hidden it away after that last disastrous time they'd used it, but apparently Kelley had stolen it.

Rudolf followed his gaze. "Your showstone, yes," he said. "Such a thing should have been given to me in the first place. You will look into the glass, both of you, and find me this man."

"But I can't see anything," Dee said. "I have never been able to—"

"Silence!" Rudolf said. "You will do as I tell you." He motioned to his men-at-arms. "Take them to the Daliborka. We'll start our experiments tomorrow."

THE GUARDS LED THEM OUT OF THE CASTLE AND DOWN A LANE past Rudolf's outbuildings, chapels and foundries and stables and a gunpowder magazine. They stopped at a squat round tower. Loew, beside him, sucked in his breath.

One of the guards took out a rusted key and unlocked the door. The door groaned as it opened, the old iron protesting. "Inside," said the guard.

They found themselves in a tower of uneven stone. A dank chill rose from the floor. Water had run down the walls leaving dark stains: rust red, blood red, black.

The guard closed the door; they heard the key snick in the lock. Light came from a small window far overhead. Now Dee could see a raised circle banded with iron in the center of the small tower; he wondered what it was for.

Dee sat against the wall and put his head on his knees. What would Jane think when he didn't return home? Could he write to her, send her a note somehow? Surely they wouldn't deny him that much.

He looked at Loew, who was pacing restlessly in the small room. Undoubtedly Loew was worried about Pearl as well. A wave of fellow-feeling rose up in him, and for the moment it did not seem that important that they had quarreled the last time they met.

"What are we doing here?" he asked, breaking the silence. The stone walls swallowed his words almost as soon as they were out. "Was King Rudolf serious?"

Loew said nothing for a long moment. Finally he sat gingerly next to Dee and nodded. "He's as mad as your alchemist friends said. It's probably true that Matthias wants the throne, but Rudolf suspects plots and counterplots everywhere. Whether it's the influence of Prague, of the spirits that are leaving their realm and coming here—" Loew shrugged. "How did Rudolf get the stone?"

"Kelley gave it to him." Dee shook his head. "He must have stolen it from me. I'm sorry. This is all my fault."

"Your fault? Why?"

"I brought Kelley to you—that's where he learned about the thirty-six. I should have known from the beginning that he'd prove false. Jane warned me. . . ."

"How could you have known, though? Your friend is very plausible—even I can see that."

Dee stirred as he thought of something else. "Kelley can't see anything in the stone. If he could he would have already helped Rudolf. It was all lies, two years of lies and pretty stories. I should have realized. He told me once that a friend of mine died, but then later I learned that the friend is still alive."

"Some of it must be true, though. The part about the thirty-six men—we have no reason to believe that's false. The number thirty-six appeared in other places. And then there's your demon—it seems to come when Kelley uses the stone."

Dee shuddered at the mention of his demon. He had worn a thin cloak suitable for spring for his visit to the castle, and now he pulled it closely around him. "I can't look in the stone for Rudolf," he said. "You saw what happens."

He roused himself for the first time since they had been imprisoned. He spoke a few harsh words. The iron door rattled in its frame. Loew looked up, startled, then nodded as he saw what Dee was doing.

Dee spoke louder. The door shook more fiercely, and something—a hinge, a nail—broke with a sharp crack. The door strained against the lock, the iron squealing.

The lock held firm. Dee continued to speak incantations for a few more minutes, forcing the door back and forth in his frustration, but nothing gave. Finally he sank back, exhausted.

For a long time he sat despondent, thinking about how Kelley had played him false. Once Kelley had made the world come alive for him; an angel lived in every object, in every word, so that even conversation became a miraculous act, an act of prayer. Now the world was empty; it had all been lies.

EVENING CAME. THE HIGH WINDOW IN THE TOWER TURNED slowly dark; the flagstones they sat on grew colder. Just when Dee thought the emperor had forgotten all about them he heard the sound of the key in the lock and the door opening. Two guards came inside carrying a tray of food and a chamber pot.

"Can we have pens and paper?" Dee asked one of them.

The guard ignored him and set the plates down on the raised area in the center, one for Dee and one for Loew. "The king says you can eat this," he said to Loew. "He says he doesn't want you to starve, after all." He and his fellow left, closing the door behind them.

Dee's plate held bread and chicken and sausage. He glanced at Loew, who was looking doubtfully at his meal. "What did he mean?" Dee asked. "Why wouldn't you be able to eat that?"

"We have our own dietary laws," Loew said.

What dietary laws? Dee wanted to talk further, to ask more questions, but he remembered the last time he and Loew had discussed Loew's God. Finally the rabbi shrugged and murmured a prayer. They both knelt awkwardly before the raised circle and began to eat.

After supper he stood and began to pace. "I have to write Jane," he said. "She's a sensible woman but she does worry. And Michael is barely a month old." A terrible thought came into his mind. "Rudolf won't do anything to my family, will he?"

"Probably not," Loew said. "But then I wouldn't have thought he'd imprison us either."

"Wait—he doesn't know we've moved. His message was delivered to our old lodgings. I'll have to keep him ignorant—I'll write to Jane care of Hageck. He'll know to send it on."

Loew smiled grimly. "What about me?" he asked. "I've lived in the same house for years."

"I don't know. God, I don't know. If we don't give Rudolf what he wants he'll keep us here forever, or kill us. And if we do—if we do the consequences don't bear thinking about."

Night had fallen outside. He was suddenly too tired to worry about Jane, about Kelley. He lay down on the flagstones and then, curling himself up to conserve warmth, he prepared to sleep.

The stones were hard and uncomfortable and very cold. He could not remember a time since he had come to Prague that he had not been chilled to the bone. He would not be able to sleep here. He had lost the knack of it, had forgotten how one went about falling asleep. He would never sleep again.

But when he next opened his eyes he saw pale light suffusing the high window, though none of it was strong enough to reach the floor where he lay. His bones ached, and for a moment he thought he would not be able to turn his head. Then, moving slowly and painfully, he levered himself up to a sitting position.

Loew was finishing his breakfast. "The guards have been and gone already," he said.

"Did they bring us paper?" Dee asked.

"I'm afraid not."

Dee ate his breakfast, then sat back against the wall. A short time later the door opened and two guards stepped inside, different ones this time. "Come," one of them said. "The emperor wishes to see you now."

The guards led them back past the outbuildings and through the castle to Rudolf's throne room. Someone had prepared the wax tablets and set up the showstone on one of the tables. He looked around for Kelley and found him standing behind the emperor.

"When did you steal the stone from me?" he asked, unable to contain his anger at Kelley's betrayal. "And why don't you use it yourself, have a few words with your angels?"

Kelley said nothing.

"Look into the stone," Rudolf ordered.

Dee prayed for a moment, then stared down into the stone's glassy depths. "I see nothing," Dee said. He looked up at Rudolf. "I have never been able—"

"Silence!" Rudolf said. He turned to Loew. "Now you."

But Loew failed to see anything as well. The showstone was a piece of glass, prettier than most, perhaps, but glass nonetheless.

Rudolf waved his hand. "Take them back," he said to the guards. "We'll try again tomorrow."

"But we can't see anything," Dee said despairingly. "You might as well let us go home, you can see we're no use to you—"

"I might just as well keep you here," Rudolf said. "You might see something someday, after all."

They were left alone for the evening and most of the next day, long enough so that Dee began to hope the emperor had given up on them. Then, as the weak light was fading from the high window, the guards returned.

They were marched to the throne room again, and Dee was made to look into the glass. Once again he could see nothing there, nothing but the mute glitter of the candles.

He thought of the demon Kelley had summoned. It was very close; he could feel it hovering in the far shadows of the room. They stood a heartbeat away from that other realm, a single step across the doorway. Why not, after all? Especially if the alternative was returning to their grim tower.

He reached out. He seemed to have always known how to do this. The demon—his demon—leapt at him. He tried to deflect it, to turn it toward Kelley or Rudolf, but it engulfed him. He screamed in terror, and then, abruptly, his scream was cut off and he felt the demon take control of his voice.

"So all the fools are here," the demon said. Its voice was whispery and rasping; it sounded like stones on the shore grating together as a wave rolled out to sea. The two guards ran from the room. "King Rudolf, my compliments. You have surrounded yourself with the greatest group of rogues and lack-wits in the history of the world. Not one of them is capable of making his own breakfast, let alone the Philosopher's Stone.

"And Master Kelley." Dee felt himself nod to the other man. "It's good to see you again—I have a fondness for Judases. Tell me, how much did the emperor offer you to betray your friend? How much is that chilly house of yours worth?"

Where is Loew? Dee thought desperately. Why doesn't he recite the psalm? He felt himself drowning under the demon's weight. He would lose consciousness, lose his soul, be unable to step back across the threshold into life and light and sound.

"We are looking for the thirty-sixth righteous man," Rudolf said. He seemed undaunted by the demon's presence.

"There are no righteous men," the demon said. "There is no goodness in all the world. You are on a fool's quest."

"It won't tell us," Kelley said. "It wants the same thing we do—to find the man and kill him and remake the world according to its wishes."

"Ah, Master Kelley, what a clever man you are," the demon said. "Though, unfortunately, just not clever enough. You've tied your fate to the wrong man—Rudolf's brother Matthias will triumph and take the throne. And then where will you be? Selling elixirs from a stall in the road, I don't doubt. And that's if you're lucky."

"No!" Rudolf said. "No, that's not true. I won't let it happen!"

"Such pride," the demon said. "But Matthias knows all about your sins. I warned you when I spoke to you last, remember? All your mistresses, your illegitimate children . . . Matthias will have you declared unfit for the crown."

"It won't happen!" Rudolf said. His calm had deserted him; he was enraged, lunatic. "It won't!"

Suddenly Dee felt the demon loose its hold. The strength left his muscles and he collapsed to the floor.

"Hello again," Rudolf said with the demon's voice. "I knew if I maddened him enough I could find a way in."

"Do something!" Kelley said. "Get rid of it!"

"Yes, of course, get rid of it," the demon said. "You didn't mind when I possessed your friend Dee, or Dee's daughter."

"Last time—you spoke some sort of chant, some spell—" Kelley said to Loew. He looked on the verge of rushing from the room; only his expectations from the emperor seemed to be keeping him there.

Dee stood up carefully. "Let's go," he said hoarsely. "We can escape—the guards are gone—"

"You can't go," Kelley said frantically. "You can't leave it here, loose like this—you have to send it back."

"Unfortunately your friend is right," the demon said.

"Your former friend, I should say. You can't leave me here. Who knows what I might do, especially now that I control one of the most powerful men in the world? It's a hard choice, isn't it? Run and leave me here, or stay and return to prison."

Suddenly Dee understood why Loew had not exorcized the demon earlier. He needed an open window, somewhere for it to go. Dee spoke a few words. Glass shattered in a distant room.

Loew seemed to understand immediately; he began the minor-key melody Dee had heard once before. Rudolf opened his mouth, closed it. Expressions ran like water over his face. Dee watched, sickened, as Rudolf fought with the demon for control.

Loew's voice grew louder. Rudolf said something but it was drowned by Loew's chanting. "Help," Rudolf said weakly. "Help me."

Dee relaxed; the demon was leaving. Or was this one of its tricks?

"Get it out!" Rudolf said. "Ah, God, get it out of me!"

Loew sang one final phrase. Rudolf slumped in his throne. "I want that thing out of my kingdom," he said. His voice was thin but as assured as ever. "You brought it here, Master Kelley, now you send it back wherever it came from."

"I had nothing to do with it," Kelley said. "It was Doctor Dee—"

Dee did not stay to hear more. He ran from the room, hoping Loew would have the wit to do the same. "Guards!" Rudolf called. "Guards, bring my prisoners back!" But the guards had fled when they first heard the voice. Dee had a moment in which to get free.

He glanced behind him as he ran and saw that Loew was following. They rushed headlong through the rooms of the castle, passing the emperor's wonders on either side of them with every step. Candles shone from the walls, their flames reflected in sheets of gold and silver behind them, though the rooms were empty of people.

Finally Dee stopped, panting, unable to run any farther. Loew had slowed as well. It's hopeless, Dee thought. Look at us, two winded doddering old men. How can we hope to outrun an emperor?

Still, they had lost the guards, at least for the present. He strained to hear beyond the rasp of his breathing. They began to move again, walking this time, going as silently as they could.

"Thank you," Loew said, whispering.

"For what?"

"For breaking that window. That's a useful trick."

"I'll teach it to you. And thank you for reciting that psalm."

A short while later they came to a long hallway with doors on both sides. "Which way?" Loew whispered.

"I don't know. Wait."

Dee peered into the nearest room. Books lined the walls from floor to ceiling. He saw books made of leather and velvet and satin, books bound in maroon and brown and black and orange, huge books locked with iron clasps, threadbare books with broken spines, books squeezed into shelves or balanced on top of each other. He went inside.

"That's not the way out," Loew said. "We have to get going—"

His voice trailed off as he followed Dee into the room. "Look at this," he said reverently, lifting out a book tooled in gold. "*De Arte Cabalistica*. I've never seen a copy."

"And here's a book on Zoroastrianism," Dee said excitedly. "And an illustrated herbal. And look—Copernicus's book, *On the Revolution of Celestial Spheres*."

"Do you believe him?" Loew asked. "That the earth travels around the sun? It flatly contradicts the Bible."

"But his calculations—"

Footsteps sounded outside in the hallway, recalling them to where they were. "Quickly!" Dee said, guiding Loew to a shadowy corner behind a table.

The footsteps paused at the library. Dee held his breath. Two men looked inside. "I thought I heard something in this room," one of them said.

The men raised their torches; light played over the spines of the books near the door. "There's nothing here," the other man said. They studied the room a minute longer and then walked on.

Dee and Loew looked at each other, shamefaced, two old scholars who would drop everything, who would even risk their lives, for a good disputation. Then they both began to smile. For the first time since his disastrous visit to Loew's house, Dee's feeling of kinship with the other man returned.

They stayed hidden until they could no longer hear the men, then left the library and continued down the hallway. One of the doors led to a vast room and they went through it.

This room opened onto other rooms, and others beyond that. Dee had not realized how enormous Rudolf's palace was. And each room held pieces of the emperor's collection. They passed fossils and coins, skeletons and stuffed animals, mirrors and orreries. Once they were startled by a loud ringing sound; a clock in the room with them had started to chime the hour. As if in answer all the clocks in the collection rang out, a cacophony of bells high and low, near and far. Then there were two bells ringing, then one, and then all the sounds faded into silence.

As Dee entered one room he saw a man sitting at one of the tables at the far end. He jerked back. "What?" Loew whispered, coming up behind him. "What is it?"

Dee put his finger to his lips, then gestured toward the open doorway. Loew looked inside. "My God," he said softly. "It's Rudolf."

The king sat motionless, studying one of the objects on the table in front of him. Dee could barely see it in the dim light; he thought it might be a seashell. They watched for long minutes, neither daring to move, as the king contemplated his treasure. Then they turned and left as quietly as they could.

"All these—these *things*," Dee whispered. "All these priceless things, and he chooses to look at a seashell."

They continued on, through rooms of paintings, of sculpture, of tapestries and glasswork and musical instruments. Their senses became stupefied. Dee opened a door without thinking and something flew at his face. He flung up his hand and cried out.

He stood motionless, watching as the thing fell to the floor. "What is it?" Loew asked.

"Some kind of flying automaton," Dee said, moving closer to study it. "It must have been connected to the door somehow, ready to fly if anyone came into the room." He laughed. "I made something like it once for a play at Cambridge. They called me a witch. Here I would just be another of the emperor's craftsmen."

"Hush," Loew said.

It was too late. Dee heard men speaking to each other around the next corner, probably alerted by his cries. Loew turned to flee. Dee held his sleeve; they could not possibly outrun them.

The men came into view. Guards, Dee saw, wearing Rudolf's uniform. His heart sank.

"What are you doing here?" one of them asked.

Dee smiled, trying to look sheepish. "I'm afraid we're terribly lost," he said. He spread his hands in a gesture of helplessness and held his smile, certain that he looked like the worst sort of fool. "We had an audience with Rudolf and he told us how to get out of the castle, but, well . . ."

"You're nowhere near the audience chamber," the guard said, frowning.

"Yes, that's just the problem, I'm afraid," Dee said. "The more we tried to find our way out the farther away we got. And of course we were dazzled by all the treasures. . . ."

The guard's frown deepened. Mentioning the treasures had been a mistake, Dee saw; he had only made the man more suspicious. "Take off your cloaks," the guard said.

"What?"

"I said take off your cloaks. No one is allowed in this part of the castle except Rudolf. People have stolen things from here before."

"I assure you we are not thieves," Dee said, trying to put a note of outrage in his voice. "We are guests of King Rudolf. Ask him yourself if you don't believe me. And while you're doing that I'll tell him how you've insulted us. I assure you he won't be pleased."

"Tell him whatever you like. He's the one who ordered us to search everyone in this part of the castle—he'll be happy to hear how well we're doing our jobs."

Dee shrugged and dropped his cloak to the floor. Loew stepped forward and did the same, but not before the guard had seen the yellow circle on his breast.

"What are you doing here?" he asked. "I hadn't heard that the king invites Jews for supper." He snickered and motioned to the other guard, who stepped forward and began to search Loew roughly.

"King Rudolf asked me here to discuss Kabbalah," Loew said.

The second guard stepped back, a frightened expression on his face. "Kabbalah?" he said. "What's that—some kind of Jewish sorcery?"

"Yes," Loew said. "The king wishes to learn it from me."

The second guard looked at the first. "It's true—he's always studying some sort of magic or other. We'd better let them go."

"We might as well," the first guard said. "They haven't stolen anything, anyway."

Dee and Loew bent to pick up their cloaks. Dee's hand was trembling, he noticed; he had been calm while facing the guards but now that he was free to go his terror had caught up with him. "How do we get out of the castle?" he asked, his voice shaking slightly.

"Oh, just keep going the way you've been," the first guard said, smiling maliciously.

"But we don't—" Dee said.

Loew put his hand on Dee's sleeve and Dee quieted. They were lucky to leave with their lives, after all. The guards continued down the corridor.

Without discussing it the two men began to run in the opposite direction, rushing heedlessly through room after room. The rooms began to blur around them. Surely they had been here before, they had seen this double-headed monster, that statue of Mercury.

"Look!" Loew said suddenly.

Dee followed his gaze. Several rooms ahead of them he could see a formal garden with a fountain near the entrance. They hurried toward it.

He strained to hear Loew behind him but could make out only the laboring sound of his breath. The garden lay ahead of him like a sight of paradise. He put on one last burst of speed.

But as he drew nearer and began to slow he saw that there was something wrong with the garden. Its flowers were blooming, for one thing, though spring had hardly begun. And there was no splash of water from the fountain. No wind shook the trees. It was a painting, a mural completely covering one wall.

He stopped, gasping for breath. "It's hopeless," he whispered. "It's all a giant maze. We'll never get out."

Loew said nothing. He was breathing hard.

Then Dee noticed something extraordinary. A small summerhouse stood at the right of the painting, near the bottom. Its door was open, and beyond the door Dee could see a single tree, its branches stripped bare by winter. Was this another illusion? It didn't matter; the emperor's guards would be on them at any moment.

He ran. He could hear Loew calling after him, but he could not spare breath to explain. The air began to smell fresher; he had not noticed how stifling the palace was. Then he stepped through the door.

The sky outside was black and filled with bright stars. Loew came through the door after him. "It's night," Dee said stupidly.

"It is," Loew said. His voice was filled with amazement. "We have to hurry. The guards could still be following us."

Despite what Loew said they could only walk; their final sprint had taken all their remaining energy. They made their way slowly through the lanes surrounding Rudolf's palace, the outbuildings looming dark against the night sky.

Dee felt oddly disoriented. Was this the true sky, the true stars? Or were they still trapped in a room of the Cabinet of Curiosities, enchanted by an astonishingly lifelike painting of the sky and the stars?

A lion roared nearby, startling him from his reverie. "The emperor's menagerie," Loew whispered.

Other beasts were sounding now, squawking and gibbering and howling. Something or someone shrieked out, "Help! Help!" Dee shivered violently and turned toward it.

Loew held him back. "They are peacocks," Loew said. "Nothing more."

"They sound human," Dee said. He shivered again.

They walked on, hoping the guards had not been drawn by the noise of the animals. It was too dark to see much: several times they stumbled on the uneven cobblestones or lost themselves in a warren of alleyways. Once they passed the menagerie again, coming at it from a different direction.

Finally Dee noticed that the ground began to slope downward, that they were leaving the precinct of the castle. The usually bustling city below the castle was silent and deserted. Dee's feeling of unreality grew.

"How do we know this isn't just another part of the emperor's collection?" Dee asked. "How do we know that Prague, that the world, is not just one of his illusions, another room in his palace?"

Loew said nothing. Dee stopped and saw that he was lagging behind and breathing hard.

"Do you need help getting home?" Dee asked, concerned. The man was even older than he was, after all.

To his surprise Loew nodded. "I do, yes. Thank you."

They staggered through the city like two drunken revelers. Once they sat on a low wall and gathered their breath. Three prostitutes passed them, tripping over their finery.

"What are you going to do now?" Loew asked.

"God, I hadn't thought," Dee said. "I can't stay here in Prague, that much is obvious. I'll have to go somewhere Rudolf can't reach me. Poland, probably." He laughed without mirth. "I left Poland to escape the demon, but it seems to have followed me here. Well, at least my family can stay where they are—King Rudolf doesn't know how to find them. What about you, what will you do?"

"I have the beginnings of an idea," Loew said. "But I'll need your help. Can you find safe lodgings for the night and come to me tomorrow?"

Dee shook his head. "I can't—the emperor—"

"You can't set out for Poland tonight. You said yourself

Rudolf doesn't know where you live. Go see your wife, sleep at your house tonight, and then come to me sometime tomorrow. Tomorrow evening would be best. I'll meet you at the town hall, at nine o'clock. Under the clock, the one you say runs backwards." He smiled; it had a bitter tinge. "I think my first feeling about you was correct, that we're both in this together. Whatever it is."

L OEW LET HIMSELF INTO HIS HOUSE. PEARL HAD not gone to sleep or had woken early; she was sitting by the hearth, staring into the flames. She gave a startled cry when she saw him. "Oh, thank God," she said. "Are you all right? Thank God you're safe! What happened to you?"

"I was in King Rudolf's jail," Loew said. He sank into a chair, more tired than he had ever been in his life. "I only just managed to escape."

Pearl put her hand to her mouth. "In jail? But why?"

"Rudolf wants some information." Loew hesitated, then told her what they had learned about the thirty-six men. As he spoke he felt a great weariness fall from him. He had wanted to shield her from danger, but now he saw how good it was to share his burden with someone he loved.

"But what can we do?" Pearl asked. She looked around wildly, as if she thought Rudolf's men would break into their house at any moment. "Will he come here?"

"Not tonight, I don't think. We didn't see any of the watch on our way home. And perhaps he'll forget all about us, or go into seclusion and ignore everyone. It's happened before. Besides, the emperors don't like coming here. It's traditional for them to stay away from the Quarter."

"But what if he does? Will we have to leave Prague?"

"It may come to that. But first we must find a way to protect ourselves."

"How?"

"I have an idea." He stood and kissed her, then held her close for a moment. "I'll discuss it with Doctor Dee tomorrow."

"Can you trust him?"

"I think so, yes. He's a Christian, of course, and he has all the peculiar ideas Christians have. But I think he's less hostile to us than others would be, and he's interested in learning." Loew almost smiled, remembering the two of them in the emperor's library, the lure of the books making them forget for the time that they were in danger of their lives.

He yawned widely. "I'll be in my study. Could you bring me some coffee, please?"

"Of course."

He took a candle and lit the way to his study. Then he sat at his desk, his head in his hands. A knock at the door roused him.

It was Pearl with his coffee. He took it from her and drank it quickly. "Will you be all right?" she asked.

"I think so."

He waited until she left, then took a book from his shelf and set it on his desk. It opened to page thirty-six, and he scowled. He paged back and forth, looking for a passage he remembered.

There it was: "On Making a Man of Clay." Next to that was a note he had written, an idea he had had about the proper word to inscribe on the man's forehead. It was as if he had always known he would come to this moment.

But to make a man, a golem as it was called. . . . How could he possibly think himself worthy? Only God could create life.

But the being would not be precisely a man. It would have

the soul of an animal, not a human; it would be missing the light of God.

And he had no other choice. The emperor had forbidden the Jews to take up arms and learn how to defend themselves; it had made them easy targets for the mobs that overran the Quarter from time to time. He could not possibly gather a fighting force in the short time he had, even supposing he could find someone to train them. And the golem, of course, would be useful in protecting the thirty-sixth man, should he ever be found.

He shook his head, trying to drive away his melancholy thoughts. The man would be found, and Rudolf would respect tradition and not enter the Jewish Quarter. Everything would work out for the best.

He sat at his desk and prayed for the rest of the night, hoping to make himself pure for the task ahead of him.

DEE STAYED INSIDE THE NEXT DAY. AS HE HAD FEARED JANE had been terribly worried, and he told her how he and Loew had been imprisoned. He did not mention the demon, though, saying only that they had managed to escape from the castle.

"But the king will still be looking for you," she said.

"Yes, I'm afraid so. I'm sorry, sweetling—I'm going to have to go away again. I'll have to see if Prince Laski will receive me once more." She sighed, and he brushed her cheek with his hand. "I know how difficult this is for you and the children. Loew has an idea, a way to protect himself from the king. I'm going to visit him tonight."

All the while they talked he listened for a knock at the door and the sound of the king's men forcing their way inside. At dusk he said farewell to Jane and set out for the Jewish Quar-

ter, keeping to the shadows, ready to turn back if he saw anyone suspicious. As he went he thought of the psalm Loew had
recited: "Thou shalt not be afraid of the terror by night. . . ."
The night grew darker; he wrapped his cloak around him.

When he reached the square he heard the town hall clock
strike nine, and then the faint echo of all the clocks across the
city ringing out. Someone stood in front of the town hall holding two lit torches.

It was Loew. He saw Dee and smiled. "You made it after
all," he said. "I was afraid you'd gone to Poland."

"My curiosity got the better of me," Dee said. "I could not
resist the riddle you posed last night. What is it you have
planned?"

Loew handed him one of the torches. "Light is said to
drive away demons," he said. "The Talmud says that carrying a
torch at night is as good as having a companion, and moonlight is as good as two men. There will be a full moon tonight."

They began to walk. He led Dee not to his house but along
an unfamiliar cobblestoned street. Houses flickered in the
torchlight. Light shone out from some of the windows, the
golden glow of hearth-fires. He saw people eating supper, talking, laughing, reading, and he wished he could return to his
own home and sit by his own fire with Jane. He had never felt
so much of an outsider.

They traveled for a while without speaking. Suddenly Dee
smelled a familiar odor in front of him, of water and rich thick
mud. A few steps more brought them to the banks of the
Moldau. The moon began to rise, as full as Loew had promised; its silver light pooled out across the water.

The lane ended. They walked the last few yards in mud,
their shoes sinking as they went. Loew set his torch upright in
the sand, and Dee did the same.

"Come," Loew said. "I'll need your help. We are going to
create a man from the mud."

A man? Could Loew truly create a man? Some people, Kelley among them, thought that the Philosopher's Stone could animate a lifeless vessel, but Dee had never heard of anyone who had done it successfully. Did Loew know the secret?

Loew knelt and began to shape the clay. Dee shook off his doubts and bent alongside him.

As they worked the moon rose fully. Its light shone down upon them, illuminating the figure as it slowly took form. Dee shoved his hands into the wet mud and felt it slip between his fingers. It was lifeless, inert. Could it possibly be roused to life?

He molded the curve of a shoulder, the flat plane of a chest, added mud to thicken the muscles of the thigh. To his surprise he saw Loew sculpt a penis and testicles for the thing; he wondered why, since it would never have the opportunity to use them. The only sound as they worked was the quiet slap of the river against the shore. Their torches hissed and went out, but the moon gave enough light to work by.

At one point he saw Loew separate the jaws and put a piece of paper in its mouth. Then he wrote something on its forehead in Hebrew characters. *Emet*, Dee read. Truth.

Dee sat back and wiped his forehead, realizing as he did so that his face had gone as muddy as his hands. He could see now that one of the thing's arms was longer than the other; he had not managed to match the one Loew made. He bent back to work, to correct his mistake, but Loew held up his hand.

Loew stood and tried, futilely, to brush the mud from his trousers. "I need you to recite a psalm," he said. "The one hundred and thirty-ninth. It says—"

"Wait," Dee said. "We're not finished, are we? The arms are wrong. And see—the features are misshapen. Look at its mouth and nose and eyes—they're far coarser than a human's."

"We can't waste any more time," Loew said. "I don't

know how much longer this will take, and we have to finish before the night ends. To some people, what we do here is witchcraft."

Dee nodded reluctantly.

"The psalm," Loew said. "You must say, 'My body was not hid from thee, when I was made in secret, and curiously wrought in the lowest parts of the earth. Thine eyes did see my substance, unperfect, and in thy book all my members were written.' And you must walk in a circle about the body as you recite."

Dee stood. He suddenly realized how tired he was, how unused he was to hard labor and no sleep. "And what will you do?" he asked.

"I will circle the body as well," Loew said. "I will speak the *shem*, the name of God. I will combine the letters into all the permutations there are."

Dee nodded. He had written the hidden name of God on one of his wax tablets; he remembered now that Loew had been alarmed when he had first seen it. It consisted of the letters Yod Hay Vav Hay—YHVH—though no one was certain exactly where the vowels should be placed or how it was pronounced. Kabbalists combined the letters into all their possible forms—only twelve words, since two of the letters were the same—in order to work their magic.

They began to walk around the body, their feet leaving tracks in the mud as they went. Dee recited the verses he had been given. He could dimly hear Loew speaking words as well, but he could not make them out. After a while he noticed that they were circling counterclockwise, going backwards like the clock in the town square.

He could never remember afterwards how long they had walked. It felt like hours; his legs ached and began to tremble, and his voice grew hoarse. The words he spoke sounded meaningless. Once Loew stumbled, and he hurried forward to support him.

After a while he felt certain that they had failed, that the body would never come to life. He wondered when Loew would realize this, when he would call a halt to his experiment.

The moon began to set. He could no longer see the river, could barely see the body they walked around. The moon glinted on the thing's face.

The moonlight moved over the coarse features. No—the light was not moving at all. The head was turning slowly to one side.

Dee blinked. The face seemed stationary now. Surely he had not seen what he had thought he had seen. His circling turned him away from the body, and when he was facing it again it looked as lifeless as before.

Then the thing opened its eyes. Dee gasped and stood still. Loew pushed him roughly, indicating that he should continue walking; he did not stop chanting as he motioned.

Dee took a step forward, and then another. He was trembling strongly now, and not from tiredness. The thing sat up and studied its hands, turning them back and forth. Its head was cocked to one side as though it was puzzling something out.

"Good," Loew said. "You may stop now."

Dee sank gratefully to the ground. The thing seemed to study him. Its irises were not much more than depressions in the clay of the eyes, like thumbprints, but the eyes moved and seemed to see. It was all one color, hair and eyes, tongue and teeth, the muddy color of a riverbank.

The clay man got slowly to its feet. Dee had not realized how tall they had made it; if he were standing it would tower over him, and he was not a small man.

"I should tell you how to return it to clay," Loew said. "In case something happens to me. First you must take the piece of paper from its mouth."

"What did you write on the paper?" Dee asked. He could not take his eyes from the thing.

"The name of God, the *shem*," Loew said. "Then you must erase the first letter on its forehead, the *aleph*. When you do this it will simply say *met*, or 'dead.' "

Dee nodded.

"We call this a golem," Loew said. "It has a soul like the souls of animals, but it lacks the light of God." Suddenly, unexpectedly, he grinned. "I wasn't sure I could do it. I have never heard of anyone succeeding."

He sat abruptly near Dee. "I will call him Yossel," he said. "He will ring the synagogue bells." He laughed giddily.

Was he delirious? Dee wondered. Or was he simply elated at his success? Dee thought that he could not blame him for either. They had done something incredible here.

"We must go," Loew said, turning serious. "I will take him home, and he will give us protection from the king's men. And you will go to Poland."

His voice had turned cold; it was as if he regretted his earlier giddiness, as if he felt embarrassed at showing such emotion to a man he thought of as an outsider. Still, Dee had heard the laughter, and he could not help but feel more warmly toward him.

"I wish you luck," Dee said. "Farewell."

"Farewell," Loew said.

The golem moved. "Arrr elll," it said, the words coming from deep within its chest. Its voice sounded like rocks rumbling down a mountain.

Loew turned to it, his face shining in the darkness. "I had hoped you would be able to speak," he said. "You must say 'farewell.' "

Dee took his leave. Behind him he could hear the rough

voice of the golem and then Loew's careful enunciation, sounding like the point and counterpoint of prayer.

He made his way through the darkened city. With the moon down the stars looked brighter, more substantial. For a moment he saw them as an exhibit in the Cabinet of Curiosities, the emperor's astonishments, spread out across the table of the sky.

He shook his head. He was tired, more tired than he had ever been in his life. More tired than when he had spent eighteen hours a day studying at Cambridge. It was only the fear of the king's men that kept him from sleeping in one of the grassy parks, or on one of the benches by the city's many statues and fountains.

He came to his house and climbed up the stairs to the bedroom he shared with Jane. She stirred when she felt him lie next to her but did not wake. He slept nearly a day and a night, dreamlessly, and when he woke it was almost dawn of the next day.

He stood. Jane looked up at him from the bed. "What on earth did you do?" she asked. "You're covered with mud."

He looked down at himself, saw the streaks on his hands and clothes. There was mud on the bed linen as well. "I'll tell you while I get ready," he said.

He went outside, pumped water for himself, and carried the bucket to the bedroom. As he undressed and wiped away the traces of the riverbank he told Jane what he and Loew had done together. She looked at him in astonishment when he described how the clay man had sat up and studied its surroundings.

"Be careful," she said when he had finished.

"I will," he said. "But I think Rabbi Loew is trustworthy, at least—he won't play me false, as Kelley did."

"No," she said. "I think you're right about him."

Her agreement warmed him; he had confidence in her level-headed judgment. For the rest of the morning they packed together for his journey, then he kissed her and said goodbye to the children, and left for Poland.

PEARL WAS WAITING UP FOR LOEW WHEN HE CAME HOME; SHE had warned him that she would not be able to sleep. Her eyes widened when she saw the dark shadow behind him, and she backed away as it followed him into the house.

"What—what is that?" she asked.

"A golem," Loew said. She put her hand to her mouth, her eyes flickering nervously between the two of them, and he added quickly, "It will protect us from the king."

"Is it dangerous?"

"No, not at all. It obeys my every command. Yossel, sit over there." The golem bent itself awkwardly into the chair Loew had indicated. "You see?"

The fear began to leave her eyes. "Yossel?" she said, almost smiling.

"Yes, well, it needed a name."

"Where will it stay?"

"I thought in Bezalel's old room."

"And you're certain it's harmless?"

"Completely."

She studied the golem a while. "What a thing," she said softly. "What a thing to have created. You still amaze me, Judah. Could you make it stand up again? I think it might break that chair."

Loew smiled and told it to stand, and the golem did as he asked.

Over the next few days he spent all his free time with the golem. He hurried through the rest of his duties—teaching, counseling, leading prayers—eager to get back to his son's old room, to learn more about Yossel, and to teach it.

Yossel learned quickly. Loew taught it words by pointing

to things; the golem remembered almost everything and in a very short time they were able to have simple conversations. He found chores for it around the house, and, as he had promised, he had it ring the synagogue bells.

One day Loew took down a book and opened it. "What is in that box?" Yossel asked. Its voice was deep and slurred, but Loew had come to understand most of what it said.

"This? This is not a box."

"What is it, then?"

"It's a book. You read from it." He looked down and noticed with annoyance that he had turned to page thirty-six.

"I read from it?"

"What? Oh, I see. No, not you. I read from it, I and other learned men. See these marks here? They are words—they tell me things."

Yossel moved closer and peered at the upside-down book. "They look like fire," he said.

Loew glanced at the golem, suddenly uneasy. Jewish mystics had compared the sinuous Hebrew letters to fire before; some said that the Torah had been written before the creation of the world, in tongues of black fire on a page of white fire.

"I would like to learn to read," Yossel said. "I would like the fire to tell me things too."

Loew's uneasiness grew. The golem had never asked for anything before; he had thought it would do as it was told, without desires of its own. "No, that's not possible," he said.

"Why not?"

"No more questions," Loew said sharply. "Come outside with me—I need you to chop some wood."

"What is chop?" the golem asked. "What is wood?"

IN POLAND PRINCE LASKI RECEIVED DEE COLDLY. HE COULD not understand why Dee had left with no explanation, he said, and he pointed out acidly that he had still not been made king, that King Stephen Báthory continued to sit firmly on the throne of Poland and Hungary.

Dee did not know what to say. Kelley had been the one to predict the kingship for Laski, and Kelley, Dee now knew, had played him false. But when he admitted that Kelley had made mistakes, that, for example, Sir Henry Sidney had not died when Kelley had said he would, Laski grew colder still.

Laski gave him a small room in his manor house, a room that Dee suspected had once been used for servants. It took five steps to cross its width and six for the length; he knew this because he spent a good deal of his time pacing. The room held a bed and a chest and nothing else, and despite the fact that it was April a cold wind forced its way through the walls.

He asked for a desk and a chair, but Laski put him off with vague promises. While he waited, he studied obscure books in Laski's library. The library was dark and gloomy and smelled of old wood; there were no windows, almost as if Laski had not wanted anyone to visit. If so he had gotten his wish; dust lay like fur on the books and shelves and piled up in the corners. One day the candle he had taken from his room burned down while he was reading, plunging him into darkness. He formed a small glow-light, enough to help him find his way from the room, and then went to beg for candles from the servants.

He spent days in the library, running his candle along the spines of the books, sometimes seeing the flame reflected in the shine of a leather book or an incised gold title. Finally he came upon something that looked interesting, a Latin treatise on astrology. The book was nearly two feet high, and heavy, but he managed to carry it to the table and open it. Almost immediately he found a passage about thresholds and doorways to other worlds.

"In some years," the book said, "the other worlds lie closer to our own, and it is possible to walk from one to another as easily as one might walk through the doorway of one's own house. Yet there is great danger here, for the spirits can venture into our world as well. And there is another danger, for we have evidence that learned men in previous Threshold Years have managed to return the spirits to their own realms, and in doing so have had to shut the door and secure it strongly, with the result that the spirits, both good and ill, were not able to find their way to our world for years, if not centuries. And there is also evidence that the next time the worlds move closer to each other it will be the last, that if the door closes it will close for the last time, that the spirits will come no more to our realm. And the stars say that this will happen in the year 1586."

Dee translated the passage and sent it to Loew. "This says the door might be closed in the next year, in 1586," he wrote, "and yet it was written in 1471, over a hundred years ago. I believe that whoever wrote it knew a great deal about the subject. Unfortunately he does not indicate how to close the door, nor how to secure it, and I think that it is only when the door is closed that I will finally rid myself of the demon. Though I have to say that I, for one, will be sorry to see the spirits come no more."

He wrote other letters, a few to Loew but most of them to Jane, glad that he had taken the time to teach his wife to read. He wondered how his children were doing, especially Michael, who was still so young; and how Jane was coping without him; and whether the golem had learned any more words, and if it had had to protect Loew from the king; and many other things besides. He wished that there was some way to talk to them from a distance; perhaps if two parties had scrying glasses, and angels could be summoned to deliver messages. . . . But no, he had had quite enough of angels for the present.

Loew answered his letter about doors and thresholds a week later. "I, too, would be sorry to live in a world without spirits," he wrote. "We believe that there are angels for everything: angels to heal and to slay, for memory and for forgetfulness, an angel to preside at each of the four seasons of the year, angels for every month and star and hour.

"The king has not yet moved against me. We have men who watch him closely, and these people say that he has gone into seclusion, that he speaks to no one, that the affairs of government are being taken care of by his counselors and, for all I know, his scrubbing women and horse grooms. I think it would be safe for you to return, to see how the land lies, at least to visit your family. And you can see how my creation is doing; it has learned a great deal since you left us. You could always go back to Poland if you feel you are in danger here."

Dee read the letter with growing pleasure. It would be good to return to Prague, to see his family and Loew, if only for a little while.

He arrived in Prague a few days later and spent the day with Jane and the children. Late the next afternoon he told Jane he would be visiting Rabbi Loew and set out for the Jewish Quarter. Loew's wife Pearl answered the door.

"He isn't here," Pearl said. "He's talking to the chief rabbi and a few others."

"I thought he was the chief rabbi," Dee said, surprised.

"Oh, no. They have not seen fit to appoint him."

She spoke with some bitterness; Dee thought that this must be a sore point with her. But to his annoyance she would not meet his eyes. He remembered now something Loew had told him when they were imprisoned together, that men were not allowed to look at any woman other than their wives, and that the same was true of women and their husbands.

"How long will it be before he comes home?" Dee asked.

"Not very long," Pearl said.

He began to walk aimlessly through the Quarter. He ended up once again at the cemetery and stood a moment studying the jumble of headstones. A picture came to his mind, unbidden, of layers and layers of skeletons, all of them tumbling together promiscuously beneath the earth.

He continued walking. He was not as familiar with the Quarter as he had thought, or he had forgotten a good deal of what he knew, because in a few moments he found himself completely lost. The sun began to set behind the little crooked houses; shadows stretched out before him on the street. It would soon be too late for visiting. He quickened his steps.

Nothing looked familiar. The houses seemed to close in on him. One or two candles burned within, shining against the darkness.

Ahead of him he saw three schoolboys carrying satchels, talking and laughing as they came up the street. "Excuse me," Dee said.

The boys stared at him. Two ran off, laughing, but one stood his ground.

"I wonder if you can show me the way to Rabbi Loew's house," Dee said.

"Certainly," the boy said. "This way."

He headed down one of the streets and Dee followed. The boy fidgeted; Dee guessed that he preferred conversation to silence, and he was soon proved right.

"Do you see that man?" the boy said, pointing to two people in close conversation. "That's Mordechai Zemah. He's a printer. When King Ferdinand wanted to expel the Jews twenty years ago, Zemah traveled all the way to Rome and got an audience with the pope. And somehow he convinced the pope, and the pope convinced the emperor, and we stayed here. And the man talking to him—he's an astronomer named David Gans. He corresponds with Tycho Brahe at the Uraniborg Astronomical Institute."

Dee looked at the two, amazed. He had heard of Brahe, of

course; every educated person in Europe had. More went on in this little quarter than he had ever imagined; listening to this boy he could almost believe he stood in a town filled with legends, a place where heroes walked. And then of course there was Rabbi Loew, whose creation of the golem would probably become another of the town's myths.

"That man over there," the boy said. He indicated a peddler holding a staff as tall as he was and carrying a heavy pack on his back. He wore a long shapeless dark blue cloak with a hood and many pockets, embroidered on the cuffs and hem with colorful peasant designs. The man knocked at the door to one of the houses. "His name is Mordechai, too, like the printer. He comes here every month or so, sells us candles and knives and things."

A woman answered the door. The peddler set his staff against the wall and pulled a ribbon out of his bag. The woman laughed. The ribbon lengthened and changed color.

The boy lowered his voice. "Do you know Izak? People say that man is his father."

Dee did not know how to answer this. "Here he is," the boy said, and Dee looked up the street to see Rabbi Loew heading toward them. The boy wished the rabbi a good evening and then ran for home.

"Good day," Loew said to Dee. "You've taken my advice and decided to risk a visit, I see."

"I'm glad you're safe," Dee said. "You are safe, aren't you? Has there been any sign of the king's men?"

"None, I'm glad to say. But let's not talk about such things. I'm afraid I can't spend as much time with you as I'd like. The Sabbath is coming and I have to prepare. Walk with me—I'll show you how Yossel is coming along."

Dee eagerly went with him down one of the cobblestoned lanes. "The Sabbath? But it's only Friday."

"Friday, yes. We celebrate the Sabbath on Saturday, you

know, and we start our days on the evening before, at dusk. What nonsense was that child telling you?"

"Oh, all sorts of things." Dee repeated the conversation but left out the part about Izak's father; he did not want to argue with Loew today.

They reached the house and went inside. Loew led Dee not to his study but toward another room. "This was my son's bedroom," Loew said. "I suppose there are some advantages to seeing your children grow up and leave the house."

"I didn't know you have children," Dee said.

"One son and six daughters, all grown now. My son Bezalel is also a rabbi. What about you—how many children do you have?"

"Three sons and one daughter. All of them still children—the youngest, Michael, was born a few months ago."

"Then you have some wonderful experiences ahead of you," Loew said. "My family is the best part of me."

Dee's eyes had grown accustomed to the dim light and he saw the genuine pleasure on Loew's face. Another thing we have in common, Dee thought. No matter how hard he tried to distance himself from the other man, he was constantly reminded of their similarities.

Something moved in the gloom. He turned, startled, and saw the golem sitting on the bed, its head nearly touching the ceiling. Someone had lengthened its clothes, Pearl probably, but they were still too small for its enormous frame.

"Good day, Yossel," Loew said.

"Good day," the golem said. Its pronunciation was a little better, but Dee wondered if he would have understood the words if he hadn't known what it was saying.

"This is Doctor Dee," Loew said. "He was present at your birth."

The golem turned to Dee and nodded, looking out of its strange flat eyes.

"Well," Loew said. "I said there has been no sign of the king, but since I wrote to you the chief rabbi has heard certain rumors—"

"I told Pearl that I thought you were the chief rabbi," Dee said.

Loew shook his head. "I'm afraid I don't have that honor. I had hoped, of course. . . . But he's a good man, a very good man." Loew paused. "A good man. I wonder . . ."

"Could he be the thirty-sixth?" Dee said, completing Loew's thought.

Loew shrugged. "Lately I can't hear anyone called a good man without wondering about him."

"Why does the rabbi think the king will move against you?"

If he made a reply Dee never heard it. Someone shouted from the street. "Rabbi Loew!" someone called. "Rabbi Loew, they're coming!"

Loew hurried back down the hallway to the front window. Dee, following him, was in time to see about a dozen uniformed soldiers marching slowly along the narrow cobblestoned street. A child scampered out in front and threw a stone at them. One of the soldiers drew his sword but another motioned to him to ignore the child, and they continued until they stopped at Loew's house.

"Now we see," Loew said. "Now we see whether I created well or ill. Yossel!"

The golem came down the hallway. It had to duck to avoid hitting the ceiling, and this gave its walk a strange, shambling motion. As Dee scurried out of its way he could not help but notice once again that its arms were of different lengths.

The golem thrust open the door so fiercely that it slammed against the wall. It walked out into the street, unfolding to its great height. Groups of onlookers came out into the street to watch: women in aprons, interrupted while cooking the Sabbath meals; men in the midst of dressing for services. Several of them gasped and began to back away. Someone screamed.

The golem moved without hesitation toward the soldiers. The man in front launched his sword at it; the sword sank deep into the golem's chest but it continued on. It lifted the man who had thrown the sword and hurled him to the ground.

A few of the soldiers broke and ran, but most stayed in formation. One thrust his sword into the golem's thigh. The golem swatted him away. The man fell backwards, into the arms of one of his fellows, and they both went down.

All the soldiers were running now. One stayed long enough to throw his sword and then joined his fellows; the sword dangled from the golem's upper arm. Others were picking themselves up from the ground and hobbling away, some wincing in pain.

A few children followed the soldiers, taunting and jeering, but Loew called them back. Then he turned his attention to the golem. "Yossel!" he said.

The golem glanced at him and began to walk away from the rabbi's house. It plucked out swords as it went— from its chest, arm and leg—and threw them to the ground. "Yossel!" Loew called. "Come back!"

The golem seemed not to hear. It hit out blindly, its fist ripping through the fragile wall of a house. Someone inside screamed. Loew and Dee ran after the golem, both of them calling out for it to stop.

The golem was moving faster now. It tore the thatch from the roof of one of the houses, pulled down a balcony from another, grunting as it worked. People ran from their houses and then stood silent, horrified at the destruction. "Make it stop!" someone yelled to Loew. "Make it stop!"

"What is happening?" Dee said, panting as he tried to follow the golem. "Why isn't it stopping?"

"Its power grows during the week," Loew said. "It's the strongest on the Sabbath. I usually take the *shem* from its mouth before the Sabbath starts, but now I fear I won't have time. I've never let it stay conscious during the Sabbath before—I don't know what may happen."

The speech had winded him. He stopped and looked into the sky. "Almost dusk," he said. "The Sabbath is almost here. I have to do something."

Abruptly he turned and began to run down another street. "Wait!" Dee called. "Where are you going?"

"To the synagogue," Loew said. "I have to tell the congregation to recite the service as slowly as possible. They have to see to it that the Sabbath does not come."

Dee stood uncertainly, wondering which way to go. Then he hurried after Loew.

Loew came to one of the synagogues Dee had seen before and ran through an entrance decorated with grapes and vine leaves. Inside it was very dim; the only light came from candles in hanging bronze lamps. He heard singing in a minor key, and only then was he able to make out the congregation, sitting in wooden benches gone dark with age.

Loew shouted something. The man at the front of the room, standing before an embroidered curtain, glanced at him, annoyed, and the two began to argue in loud voices. Finally the man—the chief rabbi, Dee guessed—shrugged and motioned Loew forward.

Loew began to sing very slowly, and the congregation followed his lead. Slower and slower went the songs and chants, dragged out as long as possible, until it seemed that each note was held for minutes at a time.

Dee went back to the door and looked outside. Darkness was filling the streets. He heard the sound of glass shattering, of someone shouting for help. Heavy footsteps headed toward the synagogue.

The golem loomed out of the darkness. It stopped at the sound of singing, its head cocked to one side, then said something in its gravelly voice.

"What?" Dee asked.

"Where?" the golem said slowly.

"Where? Where is Rabbi Loew?"

The golem nodded. "My creator," it said.

"He's inside the synagogue," Dee said.

The golem moved toward the doorway. Dee blocked him, his heart beating hard. "You can't disturb them now," Dee said. "The services have begun."

"Services," the golem said. Then, speaking even slower, as though it was formulating the ideas for the first time, it said, "I want to pray too. I want friends and family, want respect, want love. I want what he has, my creator."

The golem sat; its speech, its new thoughts, seemed to have tired it. Dee moved forward warily. Behind him he could hear the slow singing of the congregation.

"Who would you pray to?" he asked. He wanted to keep the golem talking, but at the same time he was genuinely curious. "To God or to Rabbi Loew? It was Rabbi Loew who created you, after all."

"I would—" The golem stopped, its mouth comically open. "I would pray—"

Dee summoned his courage and reached into the golem's mouth. It was strangely dry. He felt for the piece of paper under the tongue, grasped it and pulled it out.

The golem closed its eyes. Its head sagged. Dee exhaled softly with relief.

He went back inside the synagogue and held up the paper. Loew nodded. He sang for a few moments longer, finishing a prayer, Dee thought, and then gave up his place to the chief rabbi.

Loew walked back to where Dee stood and took the paper

from him. "Thank you," he said quietly. "Please, stay until the service ends. They are almost finished—we very nearly didn't make it in time."

Dee nodded. Loew took a seat in one of the benches but Dee continued to stand at the rear, feeling out of place. He studied the curtain at the front; it was embroidered with silver and gold thread and with pearls, and shimmered in the dim light. At one point in the service the rabbi opened it and Dee made out the scroll of the Torah behind it.

As his eyes grew accustomed to the light he saw a dark irregular stain on the eastern wall. He wondered what it was, whether it had some sort of religious meaning.

When the service came to an end he asked Loew about it. "That?" Loew said. "That is blood."

"What?" Dee asked. All the rumors he had heard about Jews, about how they stole baptized babies and drank their blood, came back to him. Had he been too trusting? "Why is it there?"

"The Quarter was attacked once, about two hundred years ago. They killed three thousand of us. We keep the blood there in their memory."

Dee could say nothing. Suddenly he thought he understood everything: why these people kept to themselves, why they hedged their lives about with laws and proscriptions, why Loew had grown so angry with him. Three thousand people. He could not imagine so large a number killed.

His expression must have mirrored his thoughts, because Loew smiled suddenly. "But come, my friend," he said. "Let's not talk of such unhappy things on the Sabbath. Show me what you've done with Yossel."

It was the first time Loew had called him "friend." They went outside and saw that a crowd had formed around the golem.

As Loew came closer the people backed away, murmuring

among themselves. Several of them glanced at Loew but no one met his eyes. Loew was becoming a legend, as Dee had thought he might, but his accomplishments were well on the way to making him feared rather than loved.

The golem sat, still inert, its head fallen against its chest. The crowd dispersed, the darkness closing around them as they went. Loew and Dee were left alone with their creation; it was barely visible in the light from the synagogue. "I must tell you," Dee said, "that it spoke to me. That it said it wanted friends, a family. That it wanted to pray."

"Did it?" Loew said. "It's said several worrisome things to me as well. Perhaps I did wrong to create it."

"If you hadn't you'd be in the king's jail right now."

"Yes, of course, you're right," Loew said. "We can't move it—it will have to stay here until the Sabbath ends. I'd hoped to let as few people as possible know, but now of course the whole town is in on the secret.

"It couldn't be helped."

"No, that's true," Loew said. He hesitated. "Would you like to have Sabbath dinner with us? I'm certain Pearl has made enough for one more—she never knows when I might bring home some traveling scholar."

"Yes, I'd like that," said Dee.

7

IT WAS VERY LATE BY THE TIME HE FINALLY LEFT the Quarter and made his way home. He walked slowly, thinking of Loew's family around the dinner table, their faces shining in the candlelight.

Two of Loew's daughters had come, along with their husbands and children.

He had drunk another odd beverage, this one called "tea."

He had watched as Pearl had lit the Sabbath candles, as the family prayed and sang and ate. "The Sabbath must be welcomed like a bride," Loew said. "She restores our souls for the week ahead."

At one point Pearl set out a loaf of bread and a cup of wine on another table. Dee looked at Loew, a question in his eyes, and Loew said, "Even the dead are allowed to celebrate the Sabbath, even the most wicked among them, and they must be made welcome. When the Sabbath ends they must go back to their torments. Then we light candles and burn spices to protect ourselves from the stench of the fires of Hell."

The next day Dee stayed at home with Jane and the children, telling Jane about his adventures, trying to summon the energy to leave once again. Rudolf had not forgotten about them, as he had hoped. But where would he go? Prince Laski would not welcome him, he knew that much.

Arthur and Katherine played around him, running and screaming, until he thought he would go mad from all the noise and his own inactivity.

"Listen to this," Arthur said. "*Strč prst skrz krk*. It's a sentence with no vowels. Can you say it? It means 'Put your finger down your throat.' "

"No," Dee said.

"Why not? Say it."

A knock sounded at the door and Jane went to answer it. She came back with an odd look on her face. "One of your strays," she said.

He was almost relieved to find Magdalena standing at the door. "The alchemists would like to talk to you," she said. "Something happened last night, and we want to know what it was."

"Nothing happened," Dee said.

"Nonsense. We all felt it."

Dee shrugged. "Very well," he said. He had no intention of giving up Loew's secret, but it would be good to leave the house for a while. He said goodbye to Jane and walked with Magdalena to the alchemists' tavern, once again marveling at how spry she was for such an old woman.

Everyone nodded to him when he came in, and as he took a seat at the scarred table they all clustered around him.

"So," the Scotsman, Seton, said. "What was it that happened last night? I sensed something coming from the Jewish Quarter, and of course we all know that you have become close to Rabbi Loew."

"How do you know that?" Dee asked. Then he remembered Kelley's meeting with Mamugna, and he looked at the Greek man reproachfully.

Mamugna met his gaze openly. "There are no secrets among us," he said.

"Tell us about Rabbi Loew," Sendivogius said. "We have heard that he is a great magician."

"He probably is," Dee said. "I know very little about him."

"What did you two do last night?" one of the Hungarians asked. Dee had learned that their names were Zoltán and László, though he still had trouble telling them apart.

"Nothing," Dee said. "We did nothing."

"I cannot believe that," Seton said.

The door opened and another man came inside. At first Dee could only see shadows, but as the man headed into the light Dee realized it was Kelley. His heart began to pound.

Everyone greeted Kelley, and he nodded back. "Why have you come here?" Dee asked. "Are you going to report our doings to the emperor?"

"The emperor?" Sendivogius said. "Do you work for Rudolf now?"

Kelley smiled around the table. Dee remembered that smile, how it had nearly always followed one of Kelley's fits of anger. The smile had not lost its charm, apparently, because the alchemists quieted to hear Kelley speak.

"Yes, I'm ashamed to say I did once work for Rudolf. I succumbed to his wiles, his flattery."

"His wealth," Dee said.

"Yes, if you like," Kelley said. "He offered me a great deal. But it was for an evil cause, and I have quit his service. I repent all that I have done."

For a brief moment Dee believed him. Then he remembered all the lies, all the pretty stories about angels. "Nonsense," he said. "Rudolf rewards you too well. I can't believe you would give up that huge house of yours, let alone all the money he must be paying you."

"I have, though," Kelley said. "I grew afraid of the flames of hell. What the emperor asked me to do is wrong, evil."

"What did he want from you?" Seton asked.

"Do you know the story of the thirty-six?" Kelley asked.

All around the table people shook their heads.

"It was a Jewish legend originally," Kelley said. "Rabbi Loew could tell you more about it. Or my friend Doctor Dee here, if he cared to."

A few of the men looked at Dee. It was amazing, Dee thought, how Kelley had managed to turn the alchemists against him, all the while presenting himself in the best light possible. He felt a vast frustration; he knew, to his sorrow, how far Kelley had allied himself with evil forces, and knew too that no one around the table would believe him if he told them. They had all fallen under his enchantment.

Everyone grew quiet as Kelley spoke of the thirty-six righteous men who upheld the world. "So what do you think?" Sendivogius asked when he had finished. "That the thirty-sixth is one of us?"

"Me!" Mamugna said, laughing. "It's me."

"No, me!" said one of the Hungarians.

"Seriously, though," Al Salah said. "What do you want from us?"

Dee had not heard Al Salah speak all evening. Kelley turned toward him, seemingly unable to resist the man's natural authority.

"I wondered if any of you know who the man is," Kelley said. "Or if you have any guesses."

"I wouldn't tell you if I did know," Dee said. He looked out at the others. "Can't you see? He's lying. He'll report whatever we say to Rudolf. He's lied to me before, many times. He told me he could see angels in my scrying glass, but he saw nothing, nothing at all."

"Nothing?" Kelley said. "I called up a demon, according to you."

The others studied Kelley with new respect. "So this was the friend you spoke of," Mamugna said.

"He summoned a demon, yes. That's the sort of man he is. He pursues knowledge but doesn't care how he gets it. Demons, angels, it's all the same to him."

"All of us wish to acquire knowledge, though," Mamugna said, his face impassive.

"And why do you want the name of the thirty-sixth man?" Dee asked. "Tell us that."

"I would think that much is obvious," Kelley said. "We must protect him from the emperor, of course. If Rudolf finds this man before we do he will kill him."

"Why would he do that?" Sendivogius asked.

"The world becomes malleable if the man does not die at the appointed time. If Rudolf kills him he can make the world over the way he wants it."

"Imagine what a world created by Rudolf would be like," Seton said.

"Yes, imagine," Dee said. "Don't tell him anything. He's working with Rudolf, not against him."

"There's no real evidence of that—" Sendivogius said.

"Evidence! I saw him in Rudolf's throne room! He stole my scrying glass!"

"Yes, but as he says, he's repented." Sendivogius turned toward Kelley. "I'd like to help you, but I have no idea who this man could be."

"Nor I," Seton said.

The others—Zoltán and László and Mamugna—shook their heads. Kelley shrugged. "Well," he said. "Please let me know if you discover anything." He grinned; Dee saw a flash of the old Kelley, the man filled with plots and mischief. "I live in Doctor Faust's old house."

Several of the others looked at him with a mixture of fear and admiration: here was someone unafraid to sleep in a house where a man had been snatched by demons. And yet even that fact failed to dissuade them, Dee thought. They all wanted what Kelley had, his air of wealth and power; they didn't care how he had gotten it.

Kelley left, and the rest of them followed soon after. Dee found himself walking next to the Scotsman, Seton.

"Are you certain he's not to be trusted?" Seton asked. He was speaking English, but his accent was so distorted that at first Dee had a hard time understanding him.

"Yes," Dee said.

"I think I can discover who the thirty-sixth man is," Seton said. "But I don't know if I should pass this information on to Kelley."

"You must not tell him anything." Dee's curiosity got the better of him and he asked, "How would you do it?"

"Come visit me tomorrow and I'll show you."

Dee hesitated. He should be packing, should be deciding where to go and what to do next. But Loew had told him to find out all he could from the alchemists, and he had to make certain that Seton would not pass on any discoveries to Kelley.

"Very well," Dee said. Seton gave him directions, and the two men separated for the night.

"Who was that odd woman?" Jane asked when he came home.

"Odd woman?" Dee said. "Oh, Magdalena. One of my strays, as you said."

"Where does she live?"

"I don't know. On the streets, I think."

"On the streets! And you never invited her here for supper? Men!" She looked at him fondly and shook her head.

He had never thought of it. He marveled at how good she was, and wondered, not for the first time, whether she might be the thirty-sixth.

The next day he made his way to Seton's house. The house was small, with peeling paint and cracked shutters. The steps up to the front door listed to the right, and creaked ominously as he climbed them. Five or six orange cats lay on the porch.

None of the other houses in the neighborhood looked much better. Dee felt surprisingly reassured by this; these people were probably not in Rudolf's service, then. Not for them the echoing, glacially cold mansions of the very wealthy.

Dee knocked on the door. He was looking forward to this meeting; it had been a long time since he had had someone to share his work with. And it would be good to speak English with someone besides Jane and the children. He had been feeling marginal, unimportant, like a note scrawled in the borders of text in a book. Even a heathen like Al Salah was more at home here.

The door opened. "Come in, come in," Seton said. He led Dee through several very tiny rooms and into what looked like a small study.

A scrying glass stood on one of the bookshelves. Dee stepped back in alarm, and Seton looked at him, puzzled. "I—

I have sworn off scrying glasses," Dee said, trying to make a joke of it.

"Yes, I remember," Seton said. "Master Kelley used yours to call up his demon, is that right? Don't worry—we will do nothing like that here."

He sat at a desk, picked up a pen and dipped it into an inkwell. Then he closed his eyes, spoke a few words under his breath, and put the pen to a piece of paper.

Nothing happened. Dee watched him for a moment and then looked away, thinking it impolite to study a man who could not see him. His eyes rested on a skeleton of some animal on the shelf in front of him. It looked like a cat; he thought of the cats he had seen on the porch and stirred uneasily.

He glanced back at Seton. The other man still sat as he had, though now drops of sweat were beaded on his face. Suddenly his pen moved in a strange jerking motion, as if someone, or something else controlled it.

The pen jerked again, then swung back and forth across the paper. It described one arc, then two, then three. Then it moved to the top of the page and began to scribble rapidly. Seton muttered as he wrote—a long stream of unintelligible sounds.

Dee looked at the paper. Seton was scrawling words over other words, words over meaningless designs; Dee could make out nothing he understood. Seton became more agitated; he spoke faster and faster, his breathing grew harsher, his pen flew across the page. Sweat dripped to the paper, mixing with the ink.

Finally he stopped and opened his eyes. The page was covered with names now; even some of the desk had been scribbled over. Seton studied his handiwork. "Good God," he said.

Dee turned the page to face him. "I can't read this," he said.

"No, but I can. Here, I'll write out a list for you."

Seton bent over a fresh piece of paper and set to work. "Jan the tavern-keeper near the town hall," Dee read, upside-down. "Wolfgang, counselor to the king. Beggar, Town Square."

Seton continued until he had written six names and descriptions. "How are we going to find all these people?" Dee asked. "And even if we do, how will we know who is the right one?"

"I don't know," Seton said. He sanded the paper dry and handed it to Dee. "Perhaps we should show this to Master Kelley. He might have resources we don't."

"I told you—he'll just give it to Rudolf. Why doesn't anyone believe me about him?"

"Well, because we have no evidence that he would do such a thing. You're the only one who thinks so poorly of him."

And even if I proved Kelley's treachery beyond a doubt, Dee thought, would you still give him your list? Are you the same as him, do you just want power and Rudolf's patronage?

He shook his head. He had never been so suspicious of everyone before. It was because he missed Kelley, because he felt Kelley's betrayal like an absence in his heart.

"I'll see you at the tavern tonight, then," Seton said. "We'll compare notes."

Dee nodded and took his leave.

He spent the rest of the day going over the list. Several of the names were far too general to be useful—"Traveler, Jewish Quarter," for example. Loew might be able to help with that one, and perhaps some of the others. He took out pen and ink and paper, and began a letter telling Loew what he had seen at Seton's house.

"These are the people Seton listed for me," he wrote. "Petr, servant to Count Vilém of Rosenberg; traveler, Jewish Quarter; beggar, Town Square; Jan the tavern-keeper near the town hall; Wolfgang, counselor to the king; and Anna, wife of

Václav the cobbler. I realize that some of these descriptions are very vague, but perhaps you can search some of them out, especially the ones who live in or near the Jewish Quarter."

When dusk fell he folded the list and placed it in his purse, then made his way to the tavern. Most of the alchemists had arrived by the time he got there, their familiar faces shining in the row of candles, but he did not see Kelley anywhere.

Mamugna was talking quietly to one of the Hungarians. Every so often he would glance around to make sure he was not being overheard, though Dee had no doubt he was trying to sell the man useless potions or equipment. Al Salah and Magdalena were deep in conversation. Seton nodded at Dee.

The door opened. The candles guttered in the wind. Kelley came inside, followed by another man. The second man hung back and sat on a bench outside the ring of candlelight.

Kelley took a seat near Dee. "Good evening," he said to the other alchemists. "Has anyone learned anything about that matter we discussed the other day?"

"The thirty-sixth man, you mean?" Seton said.

Kelley winced, as if he did not like to hear his affairs talked about so openly.

A noise came from the other end of the table. Dee and some of the others turned to look. Both of Mamugna's dogs were growling at the newcomer, their hackles raised.

"Who is that man?" Dee asked.

"Just a servant," Kelley said. "But getting back to what we were discussing—"

"I've discovered a few things," Seton said. He moved to sit next to Kelley. "I have a list of possibilities."

"Are you giving him the list, then?" Dee asked angrily. "Are you ignoring everything I've said to you, all my warnings? He'll just hand it over to Rudolf, you know that."

One of the dogs whimpered softly. Both of them were

backing away from Kelley's companion now, their tails tucked between their legs.

"Who is that?" Al Salah asked.

"I told you," Kelley said impatiently. "He's my servant."

Dee strained to make out the man in the dim light. He had drawn his cloak tightly around him and wore his hood low on his face; it was as if a piece of the darkness had shaped itself into a man. And there was something odd about the way he held his cloak, but Dee could not puzzle out what it was.

When he turned back he saw that Seton had given Kelley the piece of paper. He was too late. But what did he think he could do, anyway? If he snatched it away Seton would simply copy it over.

"This is interesting," Kelley said. "Yes, very interesting. Do you think we can get to these people before Rudolf does?"

"I don't know," Seton said. "I have no idea who some of them might be. 'Beggar, Town Square,' for example—that could be any number of people."

" 'Traveler, Jewish Quarter,' " Kelley read. He turned to Dee. "Rabbi Loew might know who this is."

"Do you think I'd tell you if he did?" Dee said. "Haven't you heard anything I've said?"

"Come, come. I told you I—"

Dee was no longer listening. The shadowy man moved into the light, and suddenly Dee realized what had been puzzling him. He lunged across the table and grabbed the man's cloak, ripping it apart. All around him men were shouting and pointing. "Look!" Dee said, struggling to make himself heard in the din. "His hands!"

The man's hands were backwards, the thumbs on the outside. Someone screamed. Someone else shouted something in Latin. Several men jumped up with their hands at their swords; the bench clattered behind them to the floor.

Dee began to recite the psalm against demons. The man ran for the door, drawing the tatters of his cloak around him. Kelley tried to follow, but Al Salah held him fast, his sword at Kelley's throat.

"Next time you visit us come without your demon," Al Salah said. "And tell the emperor we know nothing about the thirty-sixth man."

Kelley pulled away and hurried outside.

The alchemists looked around them, scarcely breathing. "Did you know what that man was all along?" Dee asked Al Salah.

"I suspected," Al Salah said. "Dogs can usually tell when something is amiss. And look at these—" He reached down to scratch the three-legged dog. "See the brown spot above their eyes? That means they can see into the spirit worlds."

Mamugna looked surprised; Dee thought that he hadn't known what his dogs were capable of.

The alchemists began to leave, glancing nervously about them. No one, it seemed, wanted to stay in a room where a demon had been present. Dee followed Al Salah and Magdalena out the door.

"Seton and Kelley are working together, of course," Al Salah said.

"What?" Dee said. "No—they can't be."

"They already had that list. They were hoping to draw you out, to get you and Rabbi Loew to add names to it."

"But I was there when Seton wrote it. He went into some sort of trance—"

"You were duped, I'm afraid. Seton put on a show for your benefit. They probably used a scrying glass to get the names originally."

"But it's much too dangerous to use a glass now. Our world and the demons' world are far too close." Dee shivered.

"Oh, my God. So that was where this—this thing came from. Kelley's companion."

"Yes. It must have stepped across the threshold into our world when they used the glass. You mentioned something once about calling up a demon. Is this the same one that visited you before?"

"No. No, the other one—my demon—cannot assume human form. I think it's jealous of us—of our joys, our loves, even of the fact that we live and breathe. It's waiting for a body to inhabit." Dee shivered again. "For my body, I think. Why on earth would Kelley and Seton use the glass again? Kelley's seen how dangerous it is."

"You know why. They will do anything for riches, for the emperor's favor. They are desperate to find out what you know."

"But I don't know anything!" Dee said in frustration. "I have no idea who this thirty-sixth man is. My best guess so far is that it's you."

Al Salah laughed. "No, I'm afraid not."

"How do you know?"

He laughed again. "It's true—I wouldn't know it if I were. Isn't that what the legend says? But I think I would have guessed. I, too, have heard this legend, and have wondered who the man might be."

"Have you learned anything? Do you know who he is?"

"No, though I have a list of possibilities myself."

Al Salah handed Dee a sheet of paper. "How did you get this?" Dee asked.

"Don't worry—it wasn't by supernatural means. I asked questions, talked to people, kept my eyes open."

Dee took his own list from his purse and compared it to Al Salah's. Al Salah, like Seton, had written six names, but two of them were different. In his confused state Dee thought that the numbers must be significant—six times six, after all, made thirty-six.

"Listen," Al Salah said gravely. He studied Dee in the dim light. "There are a great many dangers surrounding you. Not just your demon, and this man Kelley. . . . The king, it seems, is interested in you as well."

Dee laughed harshly. "You could say that," he said. "I spent a few nights in his jail."

"He must be trying subtler methods now. I'm certain he told Kelley to gain your trust, to say that he had repented." Al Salah was silent a moment. "You must leave Prague immediately."

"I know. But where should I go?"

"Not Poland this time, I think."

"How—how did you know where I was?"

Al Salah ignored Dee's question. "King Rudolf knows that you have met Prince Laski, and that Laski would give you a place to stay. What about Hungary? Do you have friends there?"

Dee shook his head. "I wrote a letter to King Stephen once, asking for patronage. He seemed interested, but then, well, we got caught up in all this. . . ."

"Good. Perfect. Go to Hungary."

Another journey, Dee thought. Well, it could not be helped. "Could you send your list to Rabbi Loew?" he asked Al Salah. "Judah Loew, in the Jewish Quarter. I've sent him mine as well. Maybe he can find out who this man is."

"Of course. I'll be leaving Prague next week—there's some business I have to attend to at home—but I'll send the letter before I go."

What had he heard recently about Hungary, about King Stephen? The Báthorys, that was it. Elizabeth Báthory, who was said to bathe in the blood of virgins to keep herself young. Was she Stephen's sister? His cousin? Every ruler within a hundred miles seemed to be going mad. He thanked God that Queen Elizabeth of England was far away enough to escape the contagion, that she at least was still sane. When would he see her again?

BEFORE THEY PARTED FOR THE NIGHT AL SALAH told Dee a little about Hungary. It had been divided into three parts: one part under Turkish rule; one under King Rudolf and the Habsburg empire; and one ruled by King Stephen, though Stephen had to swear fealty to the Turks and pay them tribute. Stephen had married into the royal Polish family and had become king of Poland as well.

Dee tried to enter the house and go up the stairs quietly, but Jane must have heard him, because she was sitting up in bed as he came into the bedroom. He climbed into bed and drew her down next to him, holding her. "I'm afraid I'm going to have to leave you again," he said.

She stirred and sighed; her breath was warm against his neck. "You're always leaving us," she said. "Where are you going?"

"Hungary."

She sighed again. "I wish you didn't have to go."

"I'm in danger here—"

"I know. It's that man Kelley, isn't it? Didn't I warn you about him?"

"Kelley, yes, and Rudolf too. Remember when I told you about the thirty-sixth man? Rudolf thinks I know who he is."

"Let's go back to England," Jane said suddenly. "Let's get away from Rudolf, away from this crazy country."

"I wish we could, sweetling. I can't afford to take all of us to England. I have to find patronage from someone. Maybe King Stephen—"

"Maybe. It's just—I miss you when you're gone. I feel lost here—I don't know the language, the customs. I want to go back to England."

"I'll get us all back," Dee said. "I promise."

The next day he booked passage on a coach to Stephen's province, which was called Transylvania. The coach drove south and east, passing Vienna, and Dee wondered if it was true that Rudolf had moved the capital from that city to Prague in order to be closer to the spirits.

They left the city behind them and entered a wood. As they continued the trees crowded closer and closer around them, blocking out the sun, turning everything gray and vague. The road they followed grew narrower, nearly disappearing in places in all the vegetation. Squirrels leapt to the top of the coach and ran along the roof, their steps loud in the silence. Other animals cried or chittered within the dense forest.

One evening he heard a pack of wolves howl in the distance. "Here we are—we are here. Here we are—we are here," they seemed to sing in their thin weird voices; their howls ascending and descending like a scale. The hair on his forearms stood up; it seemed to him that they were declaring their mastery of the forest, reminding them that humans had only managed to carve out a pitiably small realm of order and light.

At the taverns where they stopped for the night he began to hear more Hungarian, and another language spoken by dark bearded men that he assumed was Turkish. He had not realized that these infidels pushed so far westward, so close to the capital cities of Prague and Vienna, and it made him apprehensive about the fate of Christendom. Then he remembered Al Salah; he had almost forgotten that the man was a heathen.

Someone who spoke German told him about the Turkish sultan, Murad III. "They say that he has forty concubines, and that he spends all his time with them and neglects his duties to his country. They say he has a hundred and thirty sons. Nothing at all like his grandfather, Suleiman the Magnificent, the man who conquered Hungary. They called Murad's father 'the sot,' and it looks as if Murad is no better."

Another mad ruler, Dee thought, but he said nothing of his suspicions to the other man.

They traveled on. The forest gave way to flat green fields. They passed flocks of hundreds of sheep, and twice Dee caught a glimpse of a huge white fleecy dog, something like an enormous sheep itself, driving the herds.

At twilight the coachman announced that they had reached Stephen's capital, the town that had become the seat of government after the Turks occupied Budapest. Gyulafehérvár, the town was called, and Dee's heart sank when he heard the coachman speak the name; he would never get used to these long unpronounceable Hungarian words.

Exhausted, he made his way to an inn Al Salah had recommended. He climbed the stairs to his room, dropped his bags to the floor, and slept until morning.

The next day he sent a request for an audience to the king, then studied his two lists and began a letter to Rabbi Loew. "A man at the alchemists' tavern named Al Salah has given me a list of people, one of whom might be the man we seek. He claims he did not acquire this list by supernatural means, and I believe him. I asked him to send it on to you, but in case you do not receive it I will tell you that it is similar to ours, though it does not have Wolfgang the counselor or the beggar in the town square, and does include two others: Jaroslav, a stable-owner near Cattle Market, and Samuel son of Abraham, in the Jewish Quarter. If you look for these people please be careful—Al Salah suspects that Seton is working with Kelley, and I have to say I agree with him."

As he had done in Prague, he explored the city while wait-

ing for Stephen's answer, but the town proved to be a drab
backwater, nothing like Rudolf's glittering capital. There were
few parks and statues, no magnificent houses or great carriages
or elaborately costumed courtiers. The only languages he
heard were Hungarian and Turkish. And he felt none of the
excitement of Prague, the sense he had had there of being at
the center of things. No one stopped to speak to him, or even
met his eye; they seemed sullen, filled with frustrated anger.
Well, he thought, they lived in what was practically a conquered country after all, forced to pay tribute to the Turks.

Several times he heard an eerie, insinuating melody float
out over the town: the Moslem call to prayer. He watched, fas-
cinated, as turbaned men from all over stopped what they were
doing and made their way to a mosque.

At last a letter came from Stephen's chamberlain granting
him an audience. Like King Rudolf, Stephen had built his castle on top of a hill for defense, but as Dee climbed upward he
saw that the resemblance ended there. In front of him was
what looked like a pile of gray stone; grim turrets stood out
along the walls and a great iron gate guarded the entrance.

He presented his letter to one of the guards, who opened a
small rusty door in the gate and motioned him inside.

Stephen's castle was so dimly lit he could barely see the
guard in front of him. He followed the man through a series of
vast, drafty rooms made of gray and blood red stone. Tarnished swords and shields hung on the walls. There were no
rushes or tapestries to soften the chill, and no chimneys for
ventilation; several times he smelled a thin, acrid smoke that
made his eyes water. Furry gray-green moss grew underfoot.

They climbed a stone staircase that seemed to have been
built for giants, then headed down a wide corridor. Portraits
lined the walls, the first paintings Dee had seen in the castle.
Stern, judgmental-looking people in dark colors stared down
at him as he hurried past.

Finally the guard stopped. Ahead of them was a knot of people, a group of men talking to a group of women. A man in a coat made of a patchwork of fur bent his head over the hand of one of the women. The woman nodded back to him coldly.

Dee noticed, surprised, that his guard had backed away, a look almost of terror on his face. The man in fur took no notice. "I assume you are Doctor Dee," the man said in passable German. He had dark, nearly black hair, and unexpected green eyes under black eyebrows. His features were almost delicate, his cheekbones high and sharp, like Zoltán and László's. "Welcome, welcome. I am István, king of Hungary and Poland. I hope you have had a safe and pleasant journey."

István? thought Dee. Probably Stephen in Hungarian. He nodded politely.

The king turned to the woman whose hand he had kissed. "This is my royal cousin, the Countess Erzsébet," he said. She had the same startling coloring as her cousin, dark hair and green eyes, but her face was rounder and her mouth was fuller and redder. She looked very young, around twenty or so. "She is visiting me for the present. But come, let us find somewhere to talk."

He led the party through one of the doors off the corridor. The room they came to was startlingly cold; it was no wonder, Dee thought, that King István dressed in furs. He wished he had some furs of his own. And yet it was May twenty-third, nearly summer. He wondered if summer ever came to this place.

"You wrote in your letter to us that you speak to angels," István said. He took a chair and motioned Dee to a rough wooden stool opposite him. He wore silver and iron rings on every finger, each with a different colored jewel.

"I wrote that letter a long time ago," Dee said cautiously. "Since then I have learned how dangerous it is to summon spirits, especially now. I have had to abandon my experiments."

István looked puzzled. "Then I do not understand why you are here, Doctor Dee," he said.

"I have—I have made other experiments as well," Dee said quickly. "Alchemy, for example. I believe I am close to learning the secret of the Philosopher's Stone."

"Indeed?"

"Yes." Dee swallowed, feeling wretched. He had no interest in riches and knew very little about the Philosopher's Stone; Kelley had been the one who had pursued experiments with lead and gold and mercury and sulphur. And yet here he was, claiming mastery of the subject. How was he different from Kelley and all the other mountebanks at the tavern? But he had to live, had to find a safe haven away from Rudolf.

Almost as if he had read his mind, István said, "And why didn't you give this knowledge to Emperor Rudolf?"

"Rudolf and I have had our differences."

István sat back, a pleased expression on his face. "Good," he said. "Rudolf occupies a third of Hungary, land he has no right to whatsoever. And here we are, caught between the Turks and the Holy Roman Empire, doing our best to see that the infidels do not overrun western Europe, and where is our thanks for it? What has Rudolf ever done for us? Or the pope, for that matter, or anyone? But as long as I wear the iron crown of Hungary I will see to it that this land, at least, stays free of foreign influence. We can use all the gold you can make for us."

He motioned to one of his men, his rings a dull glimmer in the gloom. "See that Doctor Dee is settled comfortably in the castle. Make sure he has everything he asks for. What sort of equipment do you need, Doctor?"

What did he need? He tried to remember what Kelley had ordered back in England, things Dee had had to pay for. Absurdly, the only thing that came to mind was Mamugna saying, "A mandrake root, gathered under a gallows at midnight . . ." He tried to concentrate.

"An athenor," he said. "Various containers, mercury, sulphur, other things. . . . I'll write you a list."

"Good, good. Let me show you to your rooms, then."

"I have to go back to my lodgings and get my bags—"

István waved his hand. "I'll send someone for them. Follow me."

They retraced their steps down the corridor, passing the room he had seen Countess Erzsébet and her retinue going into. Two women were heading toward Erzsébet's door; neither of them, Dee noticed, was the countess herself. István nodded. "Good day, Anna, Marie," he said.

"Good day, King István," the women said, bowing slightly. They smiled and continued on.

István ushered him into rooms on the other side of the corridor. The guard, who had followed them, looked fearfully over his shoulder at Erzsébet's rooms as though he expected a hideous monster to emerge at any second.

Dee's rooms were as large as the others he had seen, and fashioned of the same cold stone. There was no fireplace. "I'll need a furnace," Dee said.

"Of course, of course. A furnace for Doctor Dee," István said to one of his men. "And paper, a pen, an inkwell. And a servant or two. And now I'm afraid I'll have to say farewell. Affairs of state."

The king and his men left. Dee took one of the rough wooden chairs and sat, feeling cold and alone and miserably homesick. He wished he had his bags, so that he could pile on layers and layers of clothing. He wished he had a companion, someone to talk with, Jane or Loew or Al Salah. He wished that Kelley . . . But it didn't do to think of that.

He walked to the door and looked out cautiously. The two

women, Marie and Anna, were leaving Erzsébet's rooms again. They nodded to him; this time he thought their smiles seemed almost mocking, as though they knew an embarrassing secret about him. He inclined his head toward them and they continued down the corridor, laughing softly.

Finally a servant arrived with paper and a pen, and another came a few moments later with his bags, and he was able to set to work.

He spent the next few days in his rooms, setting up an alchemical workshop. For most of that time he saw no one except the servant assigned to clean his rooms and bring him food, a young woman named Judit. She spoke only Hungarian, but he found himself looking forward to her visits, the way she would put her head around the door and say cheerfully, "*Jó napot kívánok*," which meant something like "good day."

King István gave him a generous allowance. He kept enough to live on and sent the rest back to Jane. The first thing he would buy, he decided, was warmer clothing, so when he finished with his workshop he set out from the castle.

He found a market in a square; it was something like the Cattle Market in Prague but much smaller. Vendors displayed the usual Czech glassware and German Bibles, but there was also merchandise from the east that Dee had never seen before, turquoise and ivory and silk and coffeepots. Men argued the merits of cattle and horseflesh; fishwives shouted into the din. Someone was scolding a man trying to sell a cookpot.

He found a woman displaying coats, picked out one made of fur, and indicated he wanted to buy it. The woman spoke rapidly and loudly in Hungarian, none of which he understood, and at the end of it he found himself the owner of the coat. He had no idea if the price he had paid for it was fair or not.

On his way out he passed a jeweler and saw a silver brooch in the shape of a sleeping dog. The dog was stretched out full length, its head resting between its paws. He and

Jane had had a dog like that once, back in England, before they had started all this traveling. . . . Without stopping to think he bought the brooch for her, paying the first price asked for it.

A week later he received a letter from Rabbi Loew. "I thank you for the letters you sent," Loew wrote. "As you indicated in the first one, though, the lists are frustratingly vague. The man described as 'Traveler—Jewish Quarter' could be any one of a number of people. Travelers come here from all over the world, from Egypt, Turkey and Spain. Caravans come through, too, from Trebizond and Samarkand, and our friends stop to visit us then. I will see what I can discover, however."

He wrote back to Loew, working until late in the afternoon. The light through the windows began to fail and he stood to get some candles. He felt lightheaded and sat down quickly, and it was only then that he realized he had had nothing to eat that day, that Judit had not come to bring him breakfast and clean out his rooms.

He straightened carefully and went out to the hallway. Erzsébet and her women were returning to their rooms. "Excuse me," he said.

The countess turned to him. Her mouth looked unnaturally red. He thought of baths of blood, then told himself sternly not to let his imagination run wild.

"*Szervusz*," Erzsébet said. He had heard the word before; it seemed to be corrupted Latin and to mean "at your service."

"My servant is missing," Dee said. "I don't wish to bother your cousin over something so trifling, but I was wondering if you might know where I could find his chamberlain. . . ."

He trailed off. There was no expression at all on her face, and he wondered if she had understood anything he had said. Then she said in perfect German, "Judit, yes. She is my servant now."

"Your—"

She seemed to enjoy his discomfiture. "Yes, I had my cousin István assign her to me."

"But what do I do? Where do I find a new servant?"

She shrugged and opened her door. One of the women—Anna? Marie?—turned and looked back at him, smiling her cold malignant smile.

He shrugged and headed down the stairs, looking for István or his chamberlain. He kept close track of the rooms he had gone through, but after a while he found himself thoroughly lost, as confused as he had been in King Rudolf's castle. He remembered the feeling he had had then, that the world and everything in it was just a extension of Rudolf's Cabinet of Curiosities, and once again he wondered if he had ever truly left the emperor's castle, or if he had merely found himself in some neglected corner of it.

People passed him in the corridors, chattering in Hungarian, but no one stopped when he tried to speak to them; no one seemed to understand German or Latin or, when he tried it in desperation, English. A group of servants brushed by him carrying dishes of what smelled like mutton, and his stomach clenched in hunger.

He stared after them, wondering where the kitchen was, and if he could find some food there. Someone behind him spoke his name.

He whirled around. He could see no one he recognized. He had probably imagined hearing anything; hunger had confused him, along with the strangeness of the castle. Then someone came toward him out of the gloom.

"Hello, Doctor Dee," Magdalena said. Her features were blurred in the dim light of the corridor, but there was no mistaking her bent outline, or her odor.

"What—what are you doing here?" he asked. "I say that a lot to you, don't I? But this—how did you get here? Surely you didn't follow me into Hungary."

He was babbling, relieved to find someone, even Magdalena, that he knew. "I didn't have to follow you," she said. "Al Salah told me where you were going."

"But what on earth are you doing here?"

"Following you." She grinned, showing her few teeth. "Al Salah suggested it, actually. He was worried about you. Hungary is a dangerous place, just as dangerous as Prague, though in different ways."

"And he thought you could protect me?"

"Why not?" She grinned again. "He knows a great deal, does Al Salah. And he thought you might be a good teacher for me."

"I told you before—I will not be your teacher. I hardly know anything myself." Though he could, he thought, teach her a simple shape-changing spell. Perhaps if she didn't look so monstrous she would have an easier time of it. But no—it was dangerous to teach women magic; nothing good could come of it.

"People who are still learning make the best teachers, Al Salah says. They have not become set in their ways—they do not think that what they believe is the only true way."

"He seems to have said a good many things. Does he have any idea what I should do next?"

"He's gone back home, to Constantinople. But I have an idea. I could pose as your servant—that way I could stay in the castle and keep an eye on you. And I could tell you everything I overhear, all the rumors and gossip."

"I just lost my servant, actually. I was going in search of another one."

"There you are, then. No one will notice another servant in the castle."

"Do you speak Hungarian?"

"A little."

"And a little English, and probably Czech—"

"A little."

"Where did you learn all this? What happened to your husband—is he dead? Why aren't you sitting by some fireside, with all your grandchildren taking care of you?"

"It's a long story, Doctor Dee. I'll tell you someday, if you truly want to hear it. Right now, though, I should get you some food. You look as if you're about to die of hunger."

"I might be, actually. Do you know where the kitchen is?"

Magdalena nodded. He realized he had come full circle to the castle's main entrance, and that he could find his way back to his rooms from here. He gave Magdalena directions, told her to watch out for Countess Erzsébet, and went back upstairs.

She appeared half an hour later, with some of the mutton he had coveted earlier, some stuffed cabbage, and, amazingly, a mug of good Czech beer. "I've discovered a few things," she said.

He nodded, too busy eating to answer her.

"They're all terrified of Erzsébet in the kitchen," Magdalena said. "While I was there two of her women came down for her supper, and everyone served them as quickly as possible to get rid of them. Then when the women left they all started talking."

"What did they say? Why are they so afraid of her?"

"You heard the stories at the alchemists' tavern. They think she kills virgin girls and bathes in their blood to keep herself young."

"And does she?"

"No one's disappeared from the castle since she got here, if that's what you mean. Some of the servants thought she might have taken someone from the town below, but no one's been reported missing."

"Did the kitchen staff say anything else?"

"Everyone was complaining about her serving women.

They think that they're too good for us, they never mix with any of the other servants. One of them, Anna, is Hungarian—she comes from Sarvar, Erzsébet's estate. The other one is French."

"Marie?"

"Yes. She's a Protestant, apparently, a Huguenot. She fled here to escape persecution by the Catholics. King István believes in religious freedom, did you know that? He's Catholic himself, but he allows Protestants to worship here, and even Jews."

Dee wondered if Rabbi Loew knew that. Probably he did. But Magdalena was saying something.

"The countess and her retinue will only be here for another month," she said. "They're all looking forward to the day she leaves."

"Good. Maybe I'll be able to get my old servant back. Did you see her? Judit?"

"No."

Dee frowned. Magdalena raised her eyes to meet his. Suddenly Dee felt certain they were both thinking the same thing. Where had Judit gone?

MAGDALENA TOOK HIS DIRTY DISHES TO THE SCULLERY AND did not return that night. He wondered where she was bedding down, if she had found the servants' quarters. For the first time he marveled at her resourcefulness, her ability to find a place for herself in any situation.

Another week passed. One day he heard voices outside his door and opened it to see Magdalena talking to one of Erzsébet's women. "This is Marie," Magdalena said. "I was just asking her if she had seen Judit lately."

"Yes, please," Dee said. "How is she?"

"No good," Marie said. Her German was overlaid with a

thick French accent. Her face was wide and very pale, her hair and eyes light brown. She had compressed her mouth into a thin line and Dee realized that she was smiling, that she had learned to imitate Anna's expression, or that Anna had imitated her. Both her hands held a fragrant-smelling covered bowl. "Sick. Sick, yes?"

"What's wrong with her?" Dee asked.

Marie shrugged; either she didn't understand the question or didn't know. She lifted the bowl. "I take. Take for Judit."

Now Dee saw that underneath the bowl Marie carried a worn black book. "What are you reading?" he asked, not expecting her to understand.

She drew her lips into a line again. "Bible," she said.

"Do you read the Bible a lot, then?" Dee asked.

"Must to go," she said. "*Szervusz*."

She turned and headed toward Erzsébet's suite. To Dee's surprise Magdalena hurried forward and opened the door for her.

"The Bible, my ass," Magdalena said, coming back to Dee.

"Hush," Dee said.

Magdalena pulled him inside his rooms and closed the door. "I'll wager it's a book of poisons, complete with pictures," she said.

"Is that why you opened the door for her? To get a closer look?"

Magdalena grinned and nodded. "I couldn't see anything, though. She kept it under that bowl she was carrying. Suspicious, don't you think?"

"Not really. How else would you carry it?"

"And what about the way she hurried away from us? Obviously she didn't want us to ask any more questions."

"She had to get to Judit. The woman is sick, after all."

"She has that look, you know. The same as that other one, Anna. As if she knows all about you, all your secrets and everything. As if she's disgusted by you, and she's certain everyone else would be too, if only they knew what she does. I feel like dirt every time I see either one of them."

"She can't help how she looks," Dee said, though he too had felt discomfited by her smile.

Magdalena didn't seem to hear him. "I'm thinking of going into their rooms and looking around. Checking on that book, for one thing."

"You can't do that—it's far too dangerous."

"Oh, no. No one ever notices a servant. They'll just think I'm changing the bed linen or something."

"Please don't do it. You've been very helpful so far, very brave. I don't want anything to happen to you."

Magdalena brightened at his praise. She had been eating more at the castle and had filled out, and suddenly Dee realized that she might be younger than he had first thought, perhaps fifty or even forty. Then she looked down and her wiry gray hair fell in front of her face, shadowing her features.

"Don't worry," she said. "I'll be careful."

THE NEXT DAY, DEE LEFT HIS ROOM AND HEADED TOWARD THE stairs, intending to walk to the marketplace for supplies. The countess Erzsébet came toward him in the gloom.

He nodded toward her. "Doctor Dee," she said. "My cousin tells me you're an alchemist."

"Yes, that's true," he said cautiously.

"I thought we might have a talk some day. I myself dabble in certain—disciplines."

"It would be my pleasure," Dee said, his curiosity, as always, getting the better of him. "What disciplines are those?"

"Have you noticed how easy some spells have become? How simple it is to work magic these days? Why is that, do you suppose?"

"There is a door to other realms, and it is opening wider every day. Various powers are coming through, are seeking our world. But be careful—not all of these things work for good."

"Is there any way to open the door still wider?"

He shook his head. "That would not be wise. You can't predict what these powers will do if they are let loose on our world. The wise man will seek ways of closing the door."

"Ah, but I am not a man, Doctor Dee." She bit down hard on a fingernail; he noticed now that all her nails had been chewed to the skin, leaving raw-looking scabs.

"No," he said. "All the more reason not to attempt to open the door wider. Women's magic is weak and uncertain, it lacks guidance—"

She laughed. "Nonsense," she said. "I see you are no wiser than the rest of the fools my cousin patronizes. Good day, Doctor Dee." She gathered her skirts in her hands and continued on down the corridor.

"Wait," he said. "Be careful!"

She opened the door to her rooms and closed it behind her, giving no indication she had heard him.

He stood a moment in the corridor, gazing after her, thinking about their conversation. Her comments had been strange, off the point; she had not answered him but had gone her own way, following her own thoughts. He shook his head uneasily and went downstairs.

LOEW LEFT THE JEWISH QUARTER AND SET OUT INTO THE streets of Prague, looking for Jan the tavern-keeper. He had had a rare argument with Pearl that morning and felt glad to be away and enjoying the sunshine. Pearl had told him, not for the first time, that she wanted Yossel out of their house.

"And where would he go?" Loew had asked.

"I don't care. Somewhere else. You saw how dangerous he is."

"No one would take him, you know that."

"Of course they won't. And you know why. Because they're all terrified of being murdered in their beds, that's why. Like we will be, if you keep him here."

"I told you—he's completely harmless—"

"Harmless!"

"Yes. It's true I lost control of him once, but it won't happen again. I'll make him sleep when the Sabbath comes, that's all."

Now he thought about his creation. For a while after Yossel's rampage he had ordered the golem never to leave his room. And to his relief Yossel had obeyed him; whenever Loew passed the room he saw him sitting on the bed, his eyes fixed on nothing. Loew could not help wondering what he thought about. Finally he went inside and spoke to him, but the conversation did nothing to dispel his uneasiness: the golem asked when he would be allowed to study, to pray, to leave the house and take part in the life of the town. "When will I learn to open the box of fire?" Yossel asked, and Loew was puzzled until he realized that that was how the golem referred to reading.

After these talks Loew tried to find him chores: chopping wood, hauling water, moving furniture. He took him to the house whose roof he had wrecked, hoping to make amends by having him do repairs, but the owner had been so terrified he would not let the golem come close.

Suddenly Loew realized that he was thinking and speaking of Yossel as "he" and not "it." When had that happened? He shook his head and went into a nearby cookshop.

No one in the cookshop had heard of Jan the tavernkeeper, and a few of them eyed him warily, wondering, no doubt, what he was doing outside the Quarter.

He left and continued walking. The hours passed quickly.

Morning became afternoon; the shadows stretched out like cats along the cobblestoned streets. He did not wish to be late for evening prayers. In desperation he questioned a few men on the street, but they all shook their heads or brushed past him without speaking.

Finally one man stopped. "Jan's tavern, yes, of course," he said. "Two streets that way, and then turn left."

"But I was there already, and I didn't see —"

"It's behind another cookshop, in an alley. You can't find it by accident—you have to know where it is."

This sounded promising. Loew walked back the two streets, saw the alley he had missed, and turned left. There in front of him was a small tavern. The man had been right: he could never have found it on his own.

It stood in the cookshop's shadow; even on the sunniest of days, Loew thought, it would not get much light. The roof slanted nearly to the ground; candles inside turned the windows to gold. There was no sign anywhere to suggest what the place might be, or who the owner was.

Before today Loew had never visited a tavern owned by Christians. He shrugged, said a small prayer, and opened the door.

He had to duck through the door, and, once inside, saw that the ceiling rose only a few inches above his head. A fat serving man bustled about carrying platters and mugs of beer.

Was this the owner? He looked disappointingly ordinary, short enough so that the low roof did not bother him, with dark brown hair and a face you could pass in the street and never notice.

The tavern was crowded; several people vied for the man's attention. "Jan!" someone called.

Loew's heart beat faster. This was him, then. He no longer noticed the man's ordinary appearance; he thought only that here, in front of him, might be the thirty-sixth, the man on whom the existence of the world depended.

Loew took a seat out of the light of the candles and watched the tavern-keeper. Soon after he sat down, one of the men in the tavern told Jan that he had no money to pay for his meal. Jan shrugged, holding his arms out to the side as if to say, Never mind, there is money here for everyone. A few minutes later he did the same to another man.

The third time this happened a woman walked out from the kitchen and began to berate him, softly at first and then louder and louder. "Are you letting him go without paying again?" she said. "We have no money to feed ourselves—what in God's name do you think you are doing?"

Jan shrugged again. Several of the men grinned and joked among themselves, as if this was a common occurrence. And Loew had to admit it looked a little comical: Jan's wife was thin and even shorter than he was, but her voice boomed out as if it came from a much larger woman.

The woman sighed loudly, a sigh meant to be heard in every corner of the room. Suddenly she noticed Loew and began to head toward him, but stopped when she saw the yellow circle sewn to his jacket.

"And what are you doing here?" she said. "Aren't there taverns in the Jewish Quarter? I suppose you're going to eat and not pay as well—I know you Jews."

"I'd like—I'd like a beer," Loew said.

"Let me see your money first."

Loew began to search through his purse. Just then a man came into the room, and the woman turned away from Loew abruptly. The man's face and hands were a mottled, unhealthy red, as if he had lived out-of-doors for years. He was dressed in rags and had no shoes; his feet were as thick as horn.

"You!" Jan's wife said. "I want you out! Right now!"

"Let him stay, dearest," Jan said. The endearment made the customers snicker again.

"Are you going to give him money again?"

"I suppose so."

"No! No, I forbid it!"

Jan opened his purse. The beggar stood calmly, ignoring the woman, his hand outstretched. "Here you are," Jan said. "Here's thirty pennies, and—wait—here's six more."

Jan's wife seemed to have given up in disgust. She turned back to Loew. "A beer, did you say?"

"Just a minute," Loew said. He looked at Jan. "Why did you give that man thirty-six pennies?"

"Because he's hungry," Jan said.

"What difference does it make?" the wife asked Loew. "Are you here to drink or ask questions?"

"No, I mean, why specifically that number? Why thirty-six?"

Jan looked puzzled. "Because he doesn't care that his wife and children are starving," the wife said.

"I don't know," the tavern-keeper said finally. "It's an important number, I know that much. Every beggar has to get thirty-six pennies. Do you know why?"

Loew shook his head. The wife set down a glass of beer and waited until he paid for it. He drank thoughtfully and then left the tavern.

He hurried home, worried about missing evening prayers. His thoughts swirled like leaves in the wind. Was this a righteous man? He seemed a good man, someone doing the best he could in turbulent times, but was he the one they were looking for?

Perhaps, Loew thought, I don't want to think so. I expected a man filled with wisdom and learning, and he is far too simple. But is it necessary that a righteous man also be a learned one?

A few days later he ventured out to find Jaroslav the stable-owner. Jaroslav proved far easier to locate; the second person he asked gave him directions to the stableyard, and then added, "He's a wonderful man—gives a great deal of money to charity."

Good, Loew thought. He made his way to the stable and went inside. It was a cool dimly-lit place, smelling of animals and leather, hay and sweat and dung. A man came out of the darkness, calling something to someone over his shoulder.

"Are you Jaroslav?" Loew asked.

"Yes," the man said. A small boy ran into the stable and Jaroslav motioned to Loew to wait a moment. The boy was probably his son; with his square face and lantern jaw he looked like a younger copy of the man.

"Did you deliver the horse?" Jaroslav asked.

The boy nodded.

"And it took you—what?—an hour to get there and back?"

The boy nodded, not so certain this time.

"An hour," Jaroslav said. "For a fifteen minute errand. Didn't I tell you to come right back and not dawdle? Didn't I?"

The boy said nothing. Jaroslav grabbed him by the arm and began to cuff him. "I'm sorry," the boy said. "I had to stop and—"

"No excuses!" Jaroslav said, hitting him harder. "When I tell you to come right back, you come right back, do you understand me? Did you get his money, at least?"

The boy nodded. He tried to reach into his purse while his father continued to hit him. "Here it is," the boy said. "Thirty-six pennies to hire the horse, like you said."

"Good," Jaroslav said. "At least you can do one thing right."

He let go of the boy and turned to Loew. But Loew was already leaving the stable, having seen enough.

DEE GOT A LETTER FROM LOEW DESCRIBING HIS SEARCH A few weeks later. After his account of his visit to Jan's tavern

Loew had written: "Even if we never find this man I have already learned something from our quest—I have begun to regard every man with respect, even the most common among them, because any one of them might be the one we seek."

Dee rummaged among the papers on his desk and took out his list, then crossed off Jaroslav the stable-owner and put a question mark by Jan's name. He stretched, went to his door and looked into the corridor. A beautiful woman was coming out of Countess Erzsébet's rooms.

She was not Anna nor Marie nor any of the others he had seen. He watched her idly, wondering what Erzsébet needed with so many serving women and ladies-in-waiting. As she headed for the stairway her shoulders began to round. Her hair grew white from the roots outward, as though an invisible hand was painting it; it struggled loose from its bindings and fell in unruly wires to cover her face. By the time she reached the stairs she was as bent as a crescent moon, and Dee knew who she was. Magdalena.

He left his room and followed her down the hallway. Her gait had become slow, uncertain. He caught up with her easily at the foot of the stairs. "Magdalena," he said.

She turned toward him. "Doctor Dee. I was just going to get your supper."

Her face was guileless. Had he truly seen her as a young beautiful woman? Her hair had been light brown, like polished wood, and her eyes blue as a calm sea. She had stood as straight as a new blade of grass. He strained to see the color of her eyes, but her straggled hair shadowed her face.

"Who are you, really?" he asked.

"What?" She seemed genuinely confused.

"I saw you come out of Erzsébet's rooms just now. You looked far younger, like a maid of twenty."

"I—I did?"

Was she hiding something? An expression passed over her

face—guilt? fear?—so quickly he could not be certain he had really seen it. "I don't know what you're talking about," she said evenly. "That must have been someone else. I have to get your supper now."

He nodded. Then he went back to his room, sat at his desk, and began to shake.

Was nothing as it seemed? Was Magdalena one of Erzsébet's women? Did she bathe in virgins' blood—Judit's blood?—to make herself younger? She had said she wanted to learn magic; what sort of magic was it that she wanted to learn? Kelley's sort, the kind that summoned demons and other evil creatures? Women should not study magic, he thought; they were too weak, prey for evil spirits who used them for their own ends. He had even told her that once.

Was she in league with Kelley, had she followed Dee to Hungary at Kelley's request, to spy on him? Why had she turned up so conveniently in the castle, at precisely the time he needed a servant?

And what about Al Salah? Perhaps they were all working together, perhaps Al Salah had sent him to Hungary for his own purposes. Which one of them had suggested Hungary as his destination? He couldn't remember.

His trembling grew worse. There was no one he could trust. He remembered again how Kelley betrayed him. What about Judah Loew? No, he was being ridiculous.

Someone screamed from across the hall.

Dee hurried outside. The screams were coming from Erzsébet's rooms. He knocked on the door. Anna opened it slightly, not letting him see the room behind her.

"What's happening here?" he asked.

"One of our ladies is ill," Anna said. "We have called a doctor to attend her. I'll have to ask you to leave—we don't want the contagion to spread."

"What's wrong with her?" Dee asked. The scream came again from behind the door.

"I'm sorry—you'll have to go now," Anna said. She began to close the door, and Dee, helpless, had no choice but to back away.

9. LOEW THOUGHT HE KNEW ALL THE PEOPLE IN the Jewish Quarter, but he could not remember anyone called Samuel son of Abraham. But one evening he mentioned the name to a friend, and the friend reminded him that there used to be a Samuel who made furniture, and that his father's name had been Abraham.

"Is he still alive?" Loew asked. "I don't think I've seen him for five years, but I'm certain I would have heard if he died."

"I don't know," the friend said. "You might ask his sister Rachel. I heard something about him, though—that he never leaves his workshop, that he's working on something, I can't remember what. The person who told me this seemed to think that Samuel had gone quite mad."

The next day Loew set out for Rachel's house, remembering what his friend had told him. Could a madman be righteous? Or was it simply that a righteous man would appear mad to other people?

Rachel answered the door, careful not to look directly at Loew. "Yes, Samuel is still alive," she said. "He lives in the workshop behind my house."

"Can I see him?"

Rachel hesitated for a long time. Loew was about to repeat his question when she finally nodded and led him through the house and into the back.

Light poured into the workshop from several windows and lit the single piece of furniture in the room. Loew stopped and stared.

It was a chair, and yet like no chair Loew had ever seen. It was fashioned of cherrywood that had been polished until it nearly glowed. A green stone shone in the center of the back and a shimmering mass of white coruscated out from it; it looked like an emerald surrounded by diamonds, although Samuel couldn't possibly have afforded so many precious stones. Gold and silver filigree twined around other jewels, glittering red and blue and yellow.

Samuel had been polishing the chair as they came in. Suddenly he stepped back, sat on the floor, and began sketching frantically, ignoring his visitors. Rachel said, "Samuel, Rabbi Loew is here to see you."

Samuel looked up, making an effort to come back from wherever he had been. "Good day, Rabbi Loew," Samuel said. "Is he here yet?"

"Who?" Loew asked, taken aback.

"You've come to tell me he's returned, isn't that right? That my task here is almost finished."

"I'm sorry—I don't understand."

"Elijah the prophet. He's coming. This time he will bring the Messiah, and all our suffering will be at an end. And this— this is his chair. The Messiah's chair."

Rachel looked at Loew, an expression of hopelessness on her face. He saw what she had had to endure for the past five years, saw that her brother had quietly gone mad without anyone in the Quarter realizing. Now he noticed that her clothes and Samuel's were very nearly rags, that they both had the gaunt look of someone on the verge of starvation, that their roof—which he could see from the open door of the workshop—needed fixing, and that several of their windows had been covered by wooden boards. But the roof of the workshop was sturdy and all its windows were glass.

"Other people are preparing for him as well," Samuel said, not noticing Loew's horrified expression. "There is a man making his shoes, of the softest leather. And another who is making his cup out of solid emerald."

Loew had never believed that the Messiah would come in his own lifetime. Perhaps he had been wrong, though; after all, why would someone devote his life to such an improbable task if it wasn't true?

The chair blazed in the center of the room, a green and red and blue fire. Loew shook his head. No, the Messiah would not come; none of the signs pointed to it. Samuel was mad, as his friend had said. And it appeared that others in the Quarter had caught his madness as well. They should be found, and helped. Samuel should be helped. And his poor sister . . .

"Who are these other people?" Loew asked.

Samuel went back to his sketching and did not answer. "Can you give me money to continue my work?" he asked, not looking up. "Thirty-six pennies, perhaps?"

DEE SAT IN HIS ROOM AND READ LOEW'S ACCOUNT OF HIS adventure. Spring had turned into summer but he could not get warm; he kept the furnace going at all times and wrapped himself in his fur while he worked.

Countess Erzsébet had not left after the month was up but had stayed on with her retinue. Magdalena said that the rumors about her were growing more and more lurid, and Dee noticed that the household staff tiptoed past her room, casting anxious glances over their shoulders as they went.

"Should we cross Samuel off the list?" Loew had written. "Is he mad? It all depends, I suppose, on whether the Messiah comes or not. For myself, I have gone to the Chief Rabbi to ask if anything could be done for them—so, as you can see, I am not expecting any supernatural aid. The rabbi will make certain that they get alms—though I am afraid Samuel will simply use the money to continue his work.

"I also found Anna, the wife of Václav the cobbler. Rather, I found out what has become of her—she died of a fever last winter. Everyone I talked to could not speak highly enough of her—she was a saint, a kind caring woman who helped everyone she could. Even I, who never knew her, have begun to think we have lost something very precious now that she is gone. But she cannot be the thirty-sixth, then, can she? The thirty-six are the pillars upholding the world, or so I understand it; if one of them topples the world falls, and Rudolf, or anyone, is free to remake it any way he wants.

"There is one more interesting thing about Anna, though—she lived at 36 Karlova Street.

"You ask me how I am. We have not been bothered by Rudolf since that last time. I think he fears my power, fears what I could do if he sends more men against me. Fortunately, he does not know how small my protection is, that it consists of one man.

"I say 'man,' yet of course I know Yossel is not a man, that he lacks a soul, which can only come from God. But we have been talking, Yossel and I, and I have been amazed by his intelligence. Amazed and disturbed, sometimes, because he asks me questions I have not been able to answer. Why can't he pray with the rest of the town? Why can't he study with us?

"But I was telling you about Rudolf. He has always been curious about my knowledge of Kabbalah, and now rumors are reaching him that I have managed to make a man of clay. He is not finished with us here—he will try again, and when he does I do not know what will happen. Sometimes I feel I should return to Poland, and yet I know I must stay here: I have been charged—by God?—to find the thirty-sixth and I must not leave until I do. Your friend, JL."

Dee shook his head. The Messiah would not come, of course. He had already come, and the Jews had not recognized him. It was odd, Dee thought, that he had almost forgotten Loew's false beliefs. Yet if Loew was in England he would be tortured or even burned if he expressed them aloud.

He dipped his pen in the inkwell and crossed off Anna, and Samuel son of Abraham.

A knock came at his door. He opened it to find Magdalena standing there, a tray of food in her hands. She looked, once again, like an old crone, and he wondered if he had imagined seeing her change from a young woman, if Magdalena had been right and he had simply confused her with someone else.

"I must tell you something about Erzsébet," she said, pushing past him into the room. She put the tray on his table and sat down without waiting to be asked. "I was right about that woman, that Marie. She's a poisoner. They all are."

He sat opposite her. His heart was pounding loudly. How did she know so much about Erzsébet? He lifted a piece of bread, then realized he could not possibly eat it and set it back down. He watched her carefully. Would she change shape before his eyes?

She did not seem to notice his discomfort. "I went back into Erzsébet's rooms and started dusting," she said. "Someone isn't cleaning those rooms right—there's an odd smell in there. I don't know what all those women do all day. Anyway, I cleaned Anna's room, and then went into Marie's. She'd left her book, that book she said was a Bible. So I opened it, and the first thing I saw was the words 'pain and poison.'"

"Pain and poison? That's what the book said? Could you read anything else?"

"No, unfortunately. Just as I was looking at it I heard

someone come in. I closed the book and went out quickly, and there were Erzsébet and Anna and Marie. Erzsébet asked me what I was doing there. I said I'd been sent to clean the rooms. Erszébet said that I must be mistaken, that her own servants took care of that. She was smiling. I hate her smile. I curtseyed and said that I must have gotten confused and gone to the wrong rooms. And then I ran down to the kitchen and got your supper, and came back up when I was sure they'd all be back in their rooms."

"Did you see Judit?"

"No."

"Wait a minute. Wait a minute. Marie knows you, doesn't she? We talked to her once, remember? And Erzsébet must have seen you in the hallways. Didn't they think it was strange that you'd gotten confused after you'd been here all this time?"

"I don't think they recognized me."

"How could they not recognize you? You're very memorable. Or did you change shape again? Did you do something in Erzsébet's rooms, take some potion that made you younger?"

"I would never take any potion of theirs. I told you—they poison people."

"You didn't answer my question. Did you change shape again? Is that why they didn't recognize you?"

She said nothing for a long time. She sat up straighter, preparing, Dee thought, to lie again. Then he noticed that her hair was turning darker, that her blurred features were becoming clearer, her skin tauter. The foul odor around her had disappeared; now he could smell only the light sweat of a healthy young woman in the midst of her chores. She stared at him from clear blue eyes.

"Who are you?" he whispered.

"I'm Magdalena," she said. "I'm twenty years old. I've had to disguise myself to be able to live on the streets. Before I learned what simple magic I know, I—well, terrible things happened to me." She shook her head, put her head in her hands. Her hair fell, shining like gold, over her fingers.

She was beautiful, he realized. And yet he was used to speaking to her as if she were sexless, almost as if she were a colleague. To his embarrassment he felt himself growing aroused by her nearness.

She was looking at him, her eyes wide with fear. "Please don't tell anyone. Please keep my secret. I couldn't—I couldn't bear—"

No. He had to banish these dreadful thoughts, had to prove to her that she could trust him even if she trusted no one else. He was old enough that she could have been one of his children. That was how he had to think of her, as a daughter. "Of course I will," he said.

"Thank you. You're—you're very kind—"

"Not so kind. I was cruel to you, several times, wasn't I? So that's why you—" Why you used such foul language, he thought. And why there was always such a terrible smell around you, and why I could never manage to see you clearly. You've learned to keep people at a distance.

"You know what frightens me?" she said. "My magic doesn't work in Erzsébet's rooms. She has some sort of opposing spell, some evil magic. . . . I need your help, Doctor Dee. I need to learn more to stay alive."

He remembered his passing thought, that he could teach her a simple shape-changing spell. "I would imagine you know as much as I do," he said. "But what happened to you? Why are you living on the streets? Where's your family?"

She shrugged. "My mother died, my father put me out. It's a common story."

"How old were you?"

"Eleven."

He drew a breath. His daughter Katherine was nearly four. In seven short years . . . No. It would never happen, he vowed that on everything precious to him. He would care for her from beyond the grave if he had to.

"What are we going to do about Erzsébet and her women?" she asked.

"Nothing. You can't risk going into her rooms again. What she does is her cousin István's business, not ours. And we haven't actually seen her poison anyone."

"István doesn't want to know what she does. Everyone in the kitchens says so."

"Still. There's nothing we can do—we're in danger ourselves. We can only protect ourselves, and trust in God, and hope that everything works out for the best."

She nodded doubtfully and left. But that night he woke from a troubled sleep and thought he heard loud sobs from across the hall. He stood and went to the door, but either the sound had stopped, or it had been part of a malign dream.

SUMMER PASSED INTO FALL. DEE MISSED HIS FAMILY MORE than ever, missed Jane's cheerful common sense and the children's noisy games. At odd times he would remember Arthur saying, "Stick your finger down your throat," and he would smile softly. A letter from Jane would be cherished and read over and over again.

He found himself, almost against his will, becoming interested in the work of alchemy. He had always understood that the goal of the work was not riches or immortality but the creation of a perfect Stone, a mineral forged from the union of opposites. That the Stone, being perfect, could change ordinary metal to gold, or restore a sick man to health, was an added benefit, but not what the true alchemist sought.

King István, he found, had a well-stocked library, and Dee spent a part of every day there, studying the alchemists who had gone before him. They spoke of many different unities: of mercury and sulphur, man and woman, sun and moon, sperm and blood. He began to understand that these were not allegories, or that if they were they pointed to something beyond the creation of a Philosopher's Stone. There was more here than Kelley, with his desire for riches, had realized.

So he puttered around his laboratory, pouring and heating and cooling various substances. Sometimes he ventured out into the town to find the things he needed. And always, as he worked, he felt he was growing closer to something, something that lay just beyond his grasp.

The only thing to break his loneliness was his suppers with Magdalena. She kept the shape of the crone; it took too much effort, she said, to change back and forth. Dee could not help but feel relieved at this; he found it much easier to talk to her when she looked like an old woman.

He asked her, a few times, about her time on the streets, but she would not discuss it except to say that her life had been in danger more than once. So they talked about the letters he had received from Loew, about what made a righteous man or woman, about the town and the people in the castle.

"Do you remember Zoltán and László at the alchemists' tavern?" he asked. "One of them—I could never tell them apart—had jewels braided in his beard. I thought that was a Hungarian fashion, but I don't see anyone doing it here."

"László, yes," she said. "It was a fashion, but hundreds of years ago. They were always very pretentious, those alchemists."

"And yet they had some knowledge, even some wisdom."

"That's true," she said. She studied him a moment. He could still not see her features clearly; he knew now that that was part of her magic. "You've changed since you got here," she said finally. "Once you would have scoffed at the idea that these men had any wisdom at all."

He shrugged. "I've become like Rabbi Loew, I suppose. Anyone might turn out to be the thirty-sixth, anyone at all. Everyone is worth listening to."

"Except Erzsébet," she said, grinning.

"Even Erzsébet. We don't know that she's done anything wrong."

"Oh, come—you can't believe that. I hear things, coming from her rooms. . . ."

He remembered the screams, the sobs. "I do, too," he said uncomfortably.

"There, you see. I have to go back in there, have to find out what she's up to."

"You can't. It's far too dangerous. She's already seen you once. And you'll change shape there, you know that. You can't risk anyone seeing that happen."

"But what if she's torturing people, or poisoning them? What happened to Judit?"

"It's not our business—"

"You've said that. But I think it is. It's my business, anyway. I know what it's like to be terrified, to be at someone's mercy. I'm going in there."

"You can't—"

"Why not? Are you saying you'll stop me?"

"No," he said miserably. "I can't stop you—I know that. I'm just saying that you should think about it, you should be careful."

"I have thought about it, and I will be careful. There's been some talk in the kitchens about Erzsébet and her party going hunting. I'll wait until then, and then slip inside. It'll be perfectly safe."

"When are they going?"

"I don't know yet. I'll find out."

He sighed. "I'll have to go with you, then."

"No you don't."

"Yes I do. I don't like thinking of anything happening to you. You're far too impulsive. I used to wonder why, when I thought you were an old woman. And anyway—" He raised his hand to forestall argument. "—I want a look at that book of Marie's."

LOEW BORROWED A HORSE AND RODE SOUTH TO TREBONA, to the estate of Count Vilém of Rosenberg. The estate spread out before him for miles; he saw breweries, sheep farms, workshops and outbuildings and artificial ponds. He had been able to get away from his teaching duties for two days, but he did not see how he could find Vilém's servant in such a short time. He tied his horse to a tree and set off.

In the first workshop he came to he saw a group of women making soap. He asked if they knew Petr, but they shook their heads and went back to their work.

The second outbuilding contained a huge table holding alembics and pipes and minerals and vials of various-colored liquids. A furnace huffed softly in the corner. So Vilém, like Rudolf, was an alchemist. Somehow this did not surprise him; a great many noblemen had caught the desire to find the Philosopher's Stone from the emperor.

"Hey!" someone said behind him. "What are you doing here?"

Loew turned, startled. The man was tall and well-dressed and carried a clear glass bottle; probably he did experiments for Vilém in the workshop.

"I'm looking for one of Count Vilém's servants. A man named Petr."

For a moment he hoped that this man would be Petr, that the thirty-sixth would turn out to be a scholar after all. "Don't know him," the man said. He studied Loew suspiciously, taking in the unfashionable clothes and the yellow circle. "Did Rudolf send you?"

"What? No, I'm here on my own."

"Because Rudolf wants milord's secrets, I know that much. And he's been known to consort with Jews, to study Kabbalah. Back away from the door, please. Milord doesn't let anyone in here but me."

Loew moved away cautiously. "I'm looking for Petr," he said. "That's all."

"I've already told you I don't know him. If you don't leave now I'll call the guards."

Loew set off again. Fortunately the man entered the workshop and did not see Loew head farther into the estate.

Several hours later he was no wiser. A number of people thought they had heard of Petr, but they could not agree on whether he worked in the main house or the stables or on the sheep farm. He saw another alchemical workshop, this one with nobody in it, and wondered how many alchemists Vilém thought he needed. Once a couple of guard dogs chased him from a building, tails wagging, mad with delight at being called upon to do their job.

Evening came on. He headed back through the estate to where he had left his horse, and rode to his lodgings.

He had no better luck when he returned to the estate the next day, though he did catch a glimpse of Count Vilém and his wife Polyxena riding through their lands. Polyxena was far younger than her husband; one of the people Loew had talked to had said that she was his fourth wife, the daughter of Spanish nobility.

Discouraged, he rode back to Prague. Petr did not seem to work anywhere on the land. He was probably a servant in the manor house, but Loew could not think of a credible reason for presenting himself at the door. Perhaps if he said he was an alchemist. . . .

An alchemist. Yes. When he reached his house he went straight to his study and began to write to Dee, summarizing what he had learned in Trebona. Then he added:

"It occurs to me that you might have better luck. Perhaps you could pose as a scholar of the occult (this would be no pose, really) and spend a few days on the estate. Count Vilém would certainly be interested in meeting someone with your knowledge. I don't know if he would keep your visit secret from Rudolf, but considering his rivalry with the king I think it's possible that he might.

"The names left on the list are: traveler, Jewish Quarter; beggar, Town Square; and Wolfgang, counselor to the king. I have been unable to discover who the first two are, and as for the third, I have been staying out of the king's sight, for reasons you well know. But I will, of course, continue to work on this puzzle."

A FEW DAYS LATER, DEE AND MAGDALENA STOOD BY DEE'S slightly-open door and watched as Countess Erzsébet and her party filed by. When the last woman passed down the stairs they waited a moment and then crossed the hall and let themselves into Erzsébet's rooms.

The rooms were dim; both Dee and Magdalena carried candles. As they entered Magdalena's shape blurred and shifted. Although Dee was waiting for it he still startled at the change. In a moment a young woman stood before him, her posture straight, her eyes blue as the base of the candle flame.

The transformation had absorbed him so strongly that he had not noticed anything else about his surroundings. Now he could smell the bad odor Magdalena had told him about, like something stale and decaying. He scowled, and Magdalena, catching his thought, whispered, "What is it, do you think?"

"Rotting food?" he said, whispering as well. "You're right—they certainly don't do a good job of cleaning here."

"Marie's room is this way," she said, leading him down a corridor and through one of the doors.

As soon as he stepped inside he saw the book, which she had left on a table by her bed. He held his candle over it and saw the word "Bible" printed on the cover. "Look," he said, pointing to it.

"That doesn't mean anything. It's a book of poisons, like I told you. Open it up."

He did. At first he was confused, not able to make sense of the words. Then he realized the book was in French.

"What does it say?" Magdalena asked impatiently.

"Don't you read French?"

"No, of course not."

"Then how did you read the part about the poisons?"

"It's in there, trust me."

Suddenly Dee understood. He laughed.

"What is so amusing?" Magdalena asked, scowling.

"Look." He turned the pages until he came to the Book of Matthew. "It's a Bible, just as it says. Look here, it says 'pain et poissons.'" He laughed again, louder this time.

"Quiet. See, it's a book of poisons. Why are you laughing?"

"It's in French. Marie is from France, remember. This means 'loaves and fishes.' It's the fifteenth chapter of Matthew, where Jesus feeds the multitude with seven loaves of bread and some fishes."

"It means—it's really a Bible?"

"Yes. They're not poisoning anyone, or torturing them. Marie is a genuinely religious person, and all those screams we heard came from someone who was really ill. There's nothing at all suspicious here."

"What happened to the person who was ill, then?"

"She recovered, I suppose. Come—we'd better leave before someone finds us."

They went out into the corridor, Magdalena leading. Just then they heard the sound of a door opening, and voices coming into the rooms. Dee stepped back into the room but it was too late—they had already seen Magdalena.

"Who are you?" someone asked. That was Erzsébet, Dee thought. "What are you doing here?"

"Weren't you in our rooms before?" an unfamiliar voice said, probably Anna. "What are you doing, spying on us?"

"My, she's a young one, isn't she?" Erzsébet said.

Dee stood, irresolute, wondering if he should reveal himself or stay where he was. Nothing bad would happen to Magdalena, though; the countess and her women were innocent, they had proved that much. And he would not like to explain to King István what he was doing in Erzsébet's rooms.

He raised his candle, trying to penetrate the shadows around him. There was an open door in front of him; he went through it as quietly as he could.

"Young and healthy looking," he heard Anna say from the front room.

"I think she'll do fine," Erzsébet said. "What's that light out there? Is someone else here with you? Another young one like yourself?"

They were coming toward him. He lifted the bed covering, blew out his candle and dove underneath. The smell was much stronger here.

He felt something clammy under the bed with him. He turned, reached out to touch it. It was skin, but cold, very cold. He moved his hand, felt long strands of hair.

He nearly screamed. Magdalena did scream, loudly. "Help

me!" she called. "Help!" Her cries became muffled, as though someone had clapped a hand over her mouth.

"Marie, help me get her into the bath," Erzsébet said. "And you, Anna, go see where that light came from. She seems to expect someone to rescue her."

Footsteps came toward the door. Quickly, he clambered out from under the bed. Before Anna's eyes could grow accustomed to the dim light he grabbed the nearest thing to hand — a fireplace poker — and swung it at her head.

The poker glanced off her forehead. She swayed a moment and then came on. He had hit her far too lightly, he realized; he had been horrified at the idea of striking a woman.

She screamed and launched herself at him, punching and scratching. He pushed back. She stumbled. Her head struck the corner of a table and she fell to the floor.

He felt her throat to make certain she was still breathing and then hurried out into the corridor, following the sounds of the screams.

In another room Erzsébet had Magdalena bent over a round iron tub. She held a long knife in her hand. Marie stood next to her, her hands to her mouth.

"Marie!" Erzsébet said. "Stop standing there like a fool and help me."

"What — what you do?" Marie said.

Magdalena screamed again and tried to squirm out of Erzsébet's grasp. Erzsébet hit her hard with the hilt of the knife. "What do you think I'm doing? I'm getting her in the tub so I can cut her open and let her blood run out."

"You — it is true, then?" Marie asked. "The stories — they are true?"

"Don't be such an innocent. You knew what I do here ever since you joined my service. How could you not? You've seen the blood in the tub, heard the screams. You knew all the time."

"No," Marie said, backing away, horrified. She said something rapidly in French; Dee thought it might be a prayer.

"Well, you know now, so help me."

Magdalena twisted and managed to free her head. She bit down hard on Erzsébet's arm. "Ow!" Erzsébet cried. "You little monster!" She brought down the hilt of the knife again.

Dee moved forward. Marie saw him and her eyes widened. He motioned for her to leave the room but she stood there stunned, unable to move.

He slipped in past her, grabbed Erzsébet's wrist and twisted hard. Magdalena bit Erzsébet's other arm, and Erzsébet, distracted by the pain, opened her hand and dropped the knife to the floor. Dee jerked her arm behind her back.

"I've got the knife," he said, though he was having a good deal of trouble picking it up and holding Erzsébet's arm at the same time. "Stay still. You, Marie—go bring me some rope."

Marie stood, uncomprehending.

"Rope," Dee said harshly. "Hurry. Rope, to—to tie—"

Magdalena slid from Erzsébet's grasp, grabbed the knife from Dee, and held it to Erzsébet's throat. Dee pantomimed tying a knot. Marie nodded and ran from the room.

She returned with rope, and the three of them worked to tie her hands and feet. "You truly didn't know," Dee asked Marie.

She shook her head.

"What about the screams?"

She shook her head again. "No—no there."

"What do you mean? You weren't there?" She nodded eagerly. "They waited until you were gone?"

"You knew, you stupid cow," Erzsébet said, struggling against her bindings. "What about all the blood?" Marie said nothing, and she repeated the question in French.

Marie answered her in the same language, speaking for a long time. Dee could make out some of it: that Erzsébet had told her that someone had been ill, that she thought a doctor had come to bleed the patient.

"And you believed me?" Erzsébet asked in French, jeering.

Once again Marie answered in French. Of course she had believed her, she said; she could not conceive that someone would do these things.

"Why did you come back?" Dee asked Marie. "I thought you had gone hunting for the day."

Marie said nothing, but to his surprise Erzsébet answered. "I forgot my favorite hunting knife," she said. "The knife I'll use on you, as soon as I'm free."

"What do we do now?" Magdalena asked.

"Now we go to King István and tell him what his cousin has been up to," Dee said.

"Don't you think he knows?" Erzsébet asked. "He lets me do what I want. He can't afford a family scandal."

"I wonder," Dee said. "We'll tell him anyway, and see what he says. There's a body under one of the beds—maybe he'd like to know about that. Is it Judit?"

"Of course not. Judit was a long time ago—she's dead and buried by now. Though I have to say I miss her—she had such beautiful skin, nothing like that coarse peasant under the bed."

Dee pulled tightly on one of the knots and Erzsébet cried out. "Forgive me," he said. He sounded insincere even to himself.

"Don't be so high and mighty, Doctor Dee," Erzsébet said. "You call on the same magic I do."

"Nonsense," Dee said. He tied the last knot and stood. "Come, let's find King István."

"You do, though," Erzsébet said. "You were the one who told me about the door between the worlds. I summon the powers I use by bloodletting—the blood makes them eager to come through the doorway. And how do you summon them, Doctor Dee?"

"I told you—I'm trying to close the door, not to call upon whatever is behind it."

"I don't believe you. There are things you can learn by opening the door wider and letting these powers come through. You could learn all the secrets of alchemy, you could have riches beyond counting. Even you wouldn't throw away a chance like that."

"Let's go," Dee said roughly. He led Magdalena and Marie out into the corridor and down the stairs. Magdalena had not resumed the crone's shape, he noticed.

They found the king in the audience room, hearing petitions. He nodded to them but continued to listen to the men and women before him. Dee stood against a wall, trying to control his impatience.

Finally István finished and looked up at them. "Yes, what is it?" he asked.

"I—could you come with us, please?" Dee said. "It concerns your cousin Erzsébet."

"Erzsébet? She's not hurt, is she?"

Dee nearly laughed; a combination of horror, tension and relief was hitting him hard. "No, my liege, she's not," he said. "Please. This way."

He allowed István to precede him up the stairs and into Erzsébet's rooms. With a shock he saw that Erzsébet was sitting on a couch in the front room, looking as fresh as if she had just gotten up. He glanced at her wrist and saw the scoring left by the ropes. How had she escaped? Witchcraft?

Suddenly he remembered Anna. At the same moment Anna came out from one of the inner rooms and sat next to Erzsébet, smiling at them triumphantly. "István," Erzsébet said. "To what do I owe the honor of this visit, my dear cousin?"

"I'm not sure," István said. "Doctor Dee? Could you explain yourself?"

"This way, King István," Dee said. He took a candle from the mantelpiece and led the party into the room where he had found the body. The smell had lessened, and suddenly he knew what they would find when they got there. He bent and looked under the bed anyway, but the space was empty.

Dee stood. "I don't understand," István said. "Could you explain what you hoped to find here?"

"I—I saw a body, my liege."

"A body? Do you mean someone was hiding in my cousin's rooms?"

"A dead body."

"What?" With a sudden gesture István took the candle and peered under the bed. "Are you mad, man? Why would there be a dead body here? And how did you come to be in my cousin's rooms, spying under her beds?"

"She had captured my servant, Magdalena," Dee said stolidly. He was fated to play this game out, he saw, though it could only end in one way, with his defeat. Already Erzsébet was grinning at him smugly.

"And why would she do that?" István asked.

"To drain her blood. The blood calls dark forces from other worlds—she admitted as much to me earlier."

"He knows a good deal about dark forces, doesn't he?" Erzsébet said. "Why is that? He looks haunted by something, I think. Ask him what it is—ask him why he had to leave Prague."

"Where is my servant Judit? Ask her that. She killed her and—and—"

"You go too far, my good doctor. I'm afraid I will have to ask you to leave—to leave my house, and leave Transylvania as well. I cannot have you make these wild accusations about my family."

"They're not accusations, my liege," Magdalena said. "She kills people, and bathes in their—"

"Enough!" István said. Was there confusion in his face, just the slightest inkling that Dee and Magdalena might be telling the truth? "You, Marie—what are you doing with these lack-wits?"

"Is—is true, my liege," Marie said.

"Are you all mad?" István said, staring at Marie. "You—I gave you refuge from religious persecution, allowed you to practice your own faith here in freedom, and this is how you repay me? I want you out of here, all of you." He glanced at Magdalena and the confusion came over his face again; he was clearly wondering who this beautiful woman was and why he had never seen her in his household before. "You have one hour to pack up your things and go. And be glad I do not have you prosecuted for treason."

"Yes, my liege," Dee said.

István strode from Erszébet's rooms. Dee and the women followed. As they were leaving Erzsébet moved closer to Dee and put her mouth next to his ear.

"It's so difficult to find burial spots when I travel," she said. "I hardly know the countryside at all."

He whirled to look at her, but her face appeared composed, as if she had never said a word.

DEE PACKED QUICKLY, MAGDALENA HELPing him. It was only when he finished that he realized he had nowhere to go. He was not welcome in Transylvania or Prague, or even Poland, where Prince Laski had been growing more and more angry at not having been made king.

He felt cursed, condemned to wander the earth with no

rest. Like the Wandering Jew, he thought, and reflected how ironic it was that Loew the Jew was snug at home, surrounded by his family.

"What about Trebona?" Magdalena said.

"What?"

"You can go to Trebona, can't you? Loew says that Count Vilém and Rudolf are feuding, so Vilém will never tell him where you are. And Vilém's an alchemist—he'd love to talk to you."

"You read my mind, didn't you?" Dee said, smiling wryly. "Very well, I'll go to Trebona. I might even find Petr, Vilém's servant. But what about you? You can go back home, if you like."

"I'm coming with you. I'll be your servant."

"Oh, God. Look—you can't even stay out of trouble for two minutes at a time—"

"You need someone to protect you—"

"*I* need someone? Who was it who ended up bent over the tub with Erzsébet's knife at her throat?"

"If it wasn't for me you would have starved—you couldn't even find the kitchen by yourself—"

"I'd rather starve than have to worry about you constantly."

"I'm coming with you. If you don't let me I'll just follow you to Trebona."

Dee sighed. "Very well. But for God's sake change back into an old woman. I can just imagine the scandal if I showed up with a young girl as my servant."

Magdalena looked surprised, as though she had forgotten what shape she held. She changed quickly.

"I'm almost getting used to you doing that," Dee said.

They clattered down the steps of the castle. A guard at the entrance opened the iron gate for them. As they went through Dee saw Marie walking toward the town below them, carrying a large leather bag. He ran to catch up with her.

"Marie," he called. "Where are you going?"

She looked back at him, her expression fearful. She relaxed when she saw who it was. "Prague," she said. "I cannot—cannot to stay—"

"Good," he said. "We're headed the same way. I'll see you get there safely."

He took her bag, and the three of them went into the town and caught a coach heading to Bohemia.

WHEN THE COACH STOPPED AT TREBONA, DEE AND MAGDALENA said farewell to Marie and got out. They looked around them; Count Vilém's estate was as large as Loew had said. They passed a sawmill, a soapworks, and other outbuildings whose purposes Dee did not understand before they came to the manor house. Winter had come early this year; a chill rain drizzled down as they made their way to the manor house. He shivered and worried about Magdalena, whose response to the cold was to pile on more and more layers of clothing.

The manor was made of gray stone, darker gray where the rain had washed it. The servant who opened the door looked at them doubtfully. Dee supposed he couldn't blame him; he in his fur coat and Magdalena in her rags must look like beggars or Romanies, the people they had called "minions of the moon" in England. His bags had been scuffed and stained beyond repair by all his traveling.

"I'd like to speak to Count Vilém, please," Dee said.

"What business do you have with milord?" the servant asked.

"I am—I am an alchemist," Dee said, and to his surprise he realized that that was almost true. "I come from England. My name is Doctor John Dee."

"One moment," the servant said, and closed the door.

"Do you suppose he's gone to get the guards?" Dee asked.

"Perhaps his orders are to tell Vilém about any alchemists who show up at the door," Magdalena said.

He wondered how she could be so optimistic, when her entire life had taught her such a vastly different lesson. But just then the door opened. "Count Vilém is expecting you," the servant said.

He led them through a number of rooms, each large and well-furnished but with none of the clutter or excess of Rudolf's castle. Finally the servant pushed open a door, said "Doctor John Dee," and motioned them inside.

Count Vilém of Rosenberg sat in a leather chair and indicated a chair opposite him for Dee. He was a large man, with thick white hair and a bristling white mustache; his face was reddened from working outdoors. No one seemed to notice Magdalena; she took a stool against the wall and settled back into the shadows. The servant bowed himself out.

"Doctor John Dee," Vilém said in German. "You are in Rudolf's service, are you not?"

"No, milord," Dee said.

"No? That is not what I heard."

How much should he tell this man? "King Rudolf imprisoned me, milord. I would not tell him the results of—of some of my investigations."

Vilém smiled. "Good," he said. "Well, you are welcome here, very welcome. I have a workshop you can use, and a room for yourself and another for your—" He glanced briefly at Magdalena. "—your servant."

"Thank you, milord. Thank you very much. I must ask a favor of you, though. It would please me if you do not mention to Rudolf that we are here."

Vilém laughed. "I had not intended to in any case," he said. "Rudolf and I—well, we play an elaborate game. I pretend to be his loyal courtier, and he pretends to be my gracious king, and each of us searches assiduously for the Philosopher's

Stone without telling the other of his progress. To be honest, I fear for the kingdom if Rudolf discovers the Stone before I do. As I said, you are very welcome here."

Count Vilém proved as good as his word. He gave Dee a suite of rooms, a generous allowance, and a fully furnished workshop. Even better, he urged Dee to send for Jane and the children. "There is room here for all of them," he said.

For the first time since he had set out from England Dee felt able to rest, to take stock. It seemed to him that he could finally take deep breaths, could stop looking over his shoulder at something he felt to be gaining on him. In spite of the winter and the settling snow, it was only now that he felt truly warm.

Jane and the family could not travel through the snow, so Dee celebrated Christmas with Vilém and his wife. Vilém was a learned man with a library to equal Rudolf's, and they spent many evenings discussing treatises on alchemy and other branches of magic. Polyxena sometimes joined them and showed herself to be almost as well-read as her husband. She was a small woman, with fine features and dark black hair and eyes; she dressed more sedately than Vilém, in the browns and reds fashionable in Spain. Sometimes Magdalena came down from her room and sat quietly in the shadows as they talked.

"So far," Dee said one evening, "all I've learned is that I don't know anything. I'm beginning to think that all my assumptions are wrong, that the alchemists we're studying aren't writing about turning lead into gold but about something else."

"What, then?" Vilém asked.

"That's what I don't know. Something about—about the union of opposites. The books talk of the marriage of mercury and sulphur, but sometimes I think that's only a code, that they're hiding something important. That they don't mean mercury and sulphur at all."

Other times he talked to Magdalena. She had discovered that Petr worked in the kitchens, and whenever Petr served a dish or cleaned up after a meal Dee studied him surreptitiously, wondering if he was the one they sought.

He asked Magdalena to talk to him as one servant to another, to discover what she could about him. There was little to tell, she reported. He and his wife, a ladies' maid, lived in the servants' quarters on the top floor of the house; Magdalena had a room down the hall from them. He kept mostly to himself, but once or twice, the other servants said, he had stepped in to resolve a quarrel, and had gained a reputation for being a fair and honest man.

"You have not been entirely straightforward with me, Doctor Dee," she said one evening, after she had reported on the latest events in the servants' quarters.

"What do you mean?"

"When I asked you to teach me magic you said you knew very little. And yet when I hear you talking with the count and countess I see that you are very wise indeed."

"You seem to know a good deal already. Where did you learn to change shape like that?"

"A friend taught me," she said. She smiled at some memory. "An Englishman, like you. That is where I first heard of you, and where I learned English. He's gone back to England, though. When I heard you were in Prague I knew I had to seek you out, to continue my education."

Dee thought of the few simple magics he could do—moving things, creating light, changing shape. She already knew how to change shape, of course, but should he teach her the other things? He still believed women should not learn magic; he had only to look at Erzsébet to see where that disastrous path led. On the other hand, one of his tricks might save her life some day.

"Why don't you continue to listen to Count Vilém and me

in the evenings?" he asked, postponing his decision. "You can learn a lot just by hearing us talk."

"But I need to ask questions as well," she said. "And you and the high-and-mighty count and countess ignore me whenever I speak."

"That's not true, surely," he said. "I don't remember you saying anything."

"That's just what I mean. I'm unimportant—no one hears anything I say. I'm a woman—"

"Polyxena is a woman—"

"A servant, then. An old servant. No one is interested in talking to me."

"Well, of course they have to get used to the idea that you know something—"

"You would think they'd be used to it by now," she said angrily.

In the days that followed she did not come down to join their conversations. But Dee soon had other things to occupy him. The snow and ice on the roads melted, and Jane wrote him that she had booked passage for the family to Trebona.

It had been nearly a year since he had last seen her, and when she and the children came into Vilém's house he found himself unable to take his eyes off her. The reddish blond hair was thinner and mixed with gray now, and the lines on her face had grown deeper, but he still thought her the most beautiful woman he had even seen. He held her tightly. "I feel as if I've come home," he said softly.

Michael had grown from an infant to a toddler and was beginning to speak a few words. "He speaks Czech, mostly, and German," Jane said. "So do the other children. I can barely understand them sometimes."

Jane and the children settled in. Arthur and Katherine ran wild over the estate, climbing trees, fishing in the artificial ponds, helping the huge shaggy white dogs herd the sheep.

Their skin turned a deep nut brown from the sun. Dee worried that they were growing unfit for life in London, if they ever returned to London, and he took time out from his research to tutor them several days a week.

Once or twice Dee heard something clatter to the floor as Katherine passed. There was nothing uncanny about it, he told himself firmly; his daughter was growing, and still clumsy, like all young children.

One day Dee and Jane passed Magdalena in a corridor. "How did she get here?" Jane asked him.

"She followed me to Hungary, actually," Dee said. He had a brief thought of her as a young woman, but he thrust it away. "She wanted to be my servant."

"You're a good man, husband," Jane said.

"I hope so," he answered.

In May of 1586 a traveler brought Dee some bad news. King Rudolf had convinced the new pope, Sixtus V, to issue an edict banishing Dee from Prague. Dee had been charged with "necromancy and commerce with Satan."

"This is not as grave as it appears," Vilém said. "Rudolf does not know of your presence here—you're safe as long as you stay on my estate. And we can find ways to persuade Sixtus to rescind his edict."

"It's worrisome in one way, though," Dee said. "I'd hoped Rudolf had forgotten all about us."

"Perhaps he will, eventually," Vilém said. "I've never known him to keep his mind on one thing for long." He looked thoughtful. "Except for his grievances against Matthias, of course."

Dee smiled ruefully. "You don't comfort me, my friend."

A KNOCK CAME AT LOEW'S DOOR, AND A moment later he heard Pearl go answer it. Footsteps sounded down the corridor to his study, then Pearl put her head around the door and said, "Hanna wants to talk to you."

Hanna was Izak's mother. Sighing, Loew closed the book he had been studying. "Tell her to come in," he said.

Hanna took the chair on the other side of Loew's desk. She was a plain woman with a short-sighted squint, and mouse-colored hair tucked under a plain kerchief. Had she really once slept with Mordechai the peddler? She did not seem the sort to do anything so shocking.

She twisted her hands in her lap, her eyes lowered modestly. Finally Loew realized that she was waiting for him to speak first. "What can I help you with, my daughter?"

"It's Izak," she said.

Loew tried not to sigh. What had the young man done now? Sometimes he thought that Izak had caused him more trouble than the rest of the inhabitants of the Quarter combined.

"He's gone," Hanna said.

"Gone? I'm sorry to hear that. Still, he stayed here for nearly two years before he left—there's obviously something about this place that's important to him. Perhaps he'll come back."

"No, you don't understand," Hanna said. "I don't think he wanted to go."

"What do you mean?"

"I think someone took him."

"Someone—"

"He didn't take any of his clothes or other things. His—his letters from Sarah."

"Well, perhaps he left on impulse. How long has he been gone?"

"Four days. And there's another thing. Someone sent me a letter."

"A letter? What did it say?"

"I don't know. I can't read. Here."

She took a letter from her pocket and handed it to Loew. He adjusted his spectacles and read it quickly to himself.

"I have Izak," it said. "Tell Rabbi Loew that I will trade him for information on the thirty-sixth man. Tell him that he should leave the name of this man at the base of the statue on the southeast corner of the Cattle Market. Yours sincerely, Edward Kelley."

He looked up to find Hanna's eyes on him. She seemed stricken, as though she had read the bad news in his expression. "Yes, well," he said carefully. "It appears you're right. Someone took him."

"But why? What do they want with him?"

"They want to—to trade him for information."

"But that's good, isn't it? You can give this person the information he wants and get Izak back. Can't you?"

What could he tell her? That he didn't have the information, and he wouldn't give it to Kelley in any case? He couldn't bring himself to dishearten her further. "I'll take care of it. Try not to worry."

"What will you do?" She lowered her eyes again and smiled shyly. "Will you set the golem on him?"

"I'll see," Loew said.

After she left, he stood and began to pace his small study. This was all Izak's fault. If the boy hadn't gotten into the habit of wandering outside, away from the safety of the Quarter . . .

No. He couldn't let his anger with Izak cloud his judgment. It was Edward Kelley's fault. He would have to see what

Yossel could do. He headed down the hallway, went into his son's old room, and sat on the bed.

Yossel turned his strange clay-colored eyes toward him. "Good day," the golem said. His pronunciation had improved greatly over the months.

"Good day," Loew said. "I'm going to need your help again."

"Yes, I would like to help," Yossel said.

"I need you to find someone for me," Loew said. "Do you think you can do that?"

Yossel nodded slowly.

"Do you remember Izak?" The golem nodded again. "He's being held captive by a man named Edward Kelley. I'm going to need you to leave the Quarter and search for him. You'll have to go at night—I don't want you to frighten anyone, and I don't want Rudolf to hear about you. Do you think you can do that? Walk the streets in secret, looking for Izak or Kelley?"

Yossel nodded again.

"Start your search at the Cattle Market. He probably lives nearby, since that's where he told me to leave the information he wants."

The golem's expression did not change. Why was he explaining all of this? Loew wondered. Why was he treating Yossel as if he was a person, a member of the congregation?

"Yes," Yossel said finally. "I will do as you say. And then— then will you teach me all the things I want to know?"

"We'll see," Loew said. He stirred uneasily.

EVERY NIGHT, AS HE AND PEARL LAY IN BED, HE COULD HEAR the heavy tread of the golem as he walked down the hallway and stepped out the door. If Pearl was awake she would shiver and turn toward her husband. "I wish you could keep him somewhere else," she said once.

"Where would you have me put him?"

"I don't know. Away from us. What if he hurts one of the children? Or the grandchildren?"

"Don't worry. I'm very careful—he won't slip out of my control again."

"God willing," Pearl said.

Yossel always returned before they woke. After morning prayers Loew would go to his room and ask if he had discovered anything, but the answer was always the same—the golem had seen neither Izak nor Kelley.

Friday came, and Loew took the *shem* from Yossel's mouth. On Saturday evening, after the Sabbath, he put the paper back, and the golem shambled to the street to begin his rounds. The next day Loew went into his room and asked, "Did you see anything?"

He expected the usual answer, but to his surprise the golem said, "Yes."

"Yes? You found Izak? Or Kelley?"

"No."

"What then?"

"You asked me if I saw anything. I walked along the street of the silversmiths, heading to the gate that leads outside. I turned onto another street, and there ahead of me I saw a beautiful girl."

"A—a girl?" An evil picture came unbidden to Loew's mind, of the golem roughly handling a child, perhaps hurting or even killing her. "Who?" he asked harshly.

"Her name is Rivka."

Rivka, Loew thought uneasily. More of a young woman than a girl. She had long, dark hair, and an expression Loew thought too forthright for a woman. "Yes, I know Rivka."

"I asked her why she was awake when all the world was sleeping. She did not run away, or cry out—she did not seem afraid of me at all. She said that the moonlight woke her, and that she had to go outside and see how everything had been changed by the moon. She showed me how the moon turns the world its own color, that everything becomes the same silvery white. I had never noticed that before."

"What are you saying? That you didn't look for Izak or Kelley?"

"Oh, I looked for them. I only spent a few hours talking to the girl. But I knew after the first hour that I wanted to marry her."

"To marry!"

"Yes. Don't worry—I didn't say anything about it to her. I know I have to ask your permission first."

"It's impossible. You can't marry."

"Why not?"

"Because you're not a man. You don't have a soul. Because only men who are created in the image of God can marry."

"But I *am* created in the image of God. I look like men, and men look like God."

Loew had not thought the golem capable of such complex reasoning. "You're talking foolishness," he said, trying not to let his disquiet show. "Or blasphemy. Either way I don't want you to talk to that girl again. Do you understand me?"

Yossel said nothing.

A few mornings later Loew's fears were confirmed. "I saw Rivka again," Yossel said, even before Loew could ask him how his search had gone.

"I told you not to talk to her," Loew said.

"I couldn't help it. She looked so beautiful. She told me she had enjoyed our conversation, and hoped to see me again."

"She did, did she?"

"Yes. I asked her if she would marry me—"

"What!"

"I had to ask her myself, since you would not give your permission."

"And what did she say?" Loew asked, curious in spite of himself.

"She laughed. She said she was not ready to marry anyone. She gave me a peach. It was so soft—I never felt anything that soft. It was white in the moonlight. She told me to eat it, but I said that I had never eaten anything before, that you had never given me food. She laughed again and motioned to me to eat it anyway. It was astonishing. Why didn't you tell me there were such things in the world?"

For a moment Loew saw the scene before his eyes: the woman; the moon; the round white peach, a second moon. The golem, hulking over all. He would have to talk to Rivka, tell her to stay away from Yossel. "Never mind that," he said. "I told you I didn't want you talking to her again. Do you understand? You're to do as I tell you."

"But—"

Loew felt a thrill of fear. He had never imagined this, never expected that the golem would be so contrary. Dreadful pictures filled his mind, the golem rampaging through the Quarter, killing people, killing Pearl or one of the children. . . .

"Don't contradict me!" he said loudly. Too loudly: he felt helpless, without control. "I'm your creator—I tell you what to do. Your task is to listen and obey."

"Just as your creator tells you what to do. And you listen and obey."

"Exactly," Loew said, though he knew that to compare him to God was the worst sort of blasphemy. There was only one God. "Will you do that?"

The golem said nothing.

"Will you? Or do I have to keep you here with me at all times?"

There was still no answer from the golem. "Open your mouth," Loew said roughly.

"What?"

"Don't ask questions. Open it."

Yossel did as he said. Loew took the piece of paper from the golem's mouth. The light of intelligence went out of his eyes and his head fell slightly and came to rest on his shoulder. Loew watched him carefully, but he made no move after that.

Loew headed toward his study, deep in thought. What had he done? Had he been wrong to create the golem? He had not thought it through, had not considered all the consequences. And despite himself he could not help feeling sorry for Yossel. He had given the clay figure organs of generation just as men have, but only because he had wanted him to resemble a man in every respect. He had not thought of the effect this would have on Yossel himself.

Perhaps he should erase the *aleph* on his forehead, let the golem sink back into inert clay. But what if Rudolf attacked again?

And there was another reason to keep him alive, one that Loew could barely admit to himself. As far as he knew he was the first man in the world to create life from nothing. How could he destroy that creation? How could he give up this astonishing thing he had done?

He had gone as far as his study before he realized that he had another problem besides Yossel. If he did not animate the golem, there would be no one to help him search for Izak and Kelley. Loew would have to write to Dee for help. He had tried to keep his dilemma from Dee, had not wanted to burden the man with more problems than he already had, but now he saw that he had no choice, that he needed Dee's advice about Kelley. He sat heavily at his desk and took out pen and paper, inkwell and sand.

DEE WOKE SUDDENLY IN THE MIDDLE OF THE NIGHT, HIS HEART pounding loudly. Where was he? In Prague, in Poland, in Transylvania? He could see nothing.

Jane stirred beside him, and he remembered. Count Vilém, Trebona, alchemy. What had woken him? He strained to see, to hear. Then he heard it: someone was coming down the corridor toward his room.

The footsteps grew heavier. He sat up, struggling to throw off a blanket that seemed tied in knots. The footsteps came closer, then stopped in front of his door. Someone or something laughed maliciously.

Who was it? In the dark, horrible fancies filled his mind. It could be the demon; it could even be Erszébet, following him from Transylvania, ready to wreak some terrible vengeance. He had no shortage of enemies.

He listened intently but heard nothing else. Sweat covered his body; he felt ill, in the grip of some fever. Summoning all his courage, reciting the psalm against demons, he went to the door and opened it.

There was no one there. Dee took a candle from one of the sconces lining the wall and walked a little way down the corridor. He opened the door to the children's room and went inside.

All four were sleeping peacefully. He held the candle over each in turn and said their names silently, as though performing an incantation: "Arthur, Katherine, Rowland, Michael." Then he turned and went back to his room.

He woke what seemed a short time later. A terrible feeling of dread weighed upon him, a feeling he had thought he had left behind when he came to Trebona.

He listened hard. The same footsteps were heading down the corridor.

Once again the footsteps stopped at his door and he heard the malicious laugh. Once again he stumbled to the corridor and looked left and right down the hallway. Once again he visited his children's room, and once again he saw nothing amiss.

He did not go back to sleep, and so was awake when the

footsteps came again and the entire performance was repeated. And repeated again an hour later, though this time Dee could see the sky turning pale beyond his window and knew that dawn was near. Somewhere a cock crowed.

He lay still, watching the sky grow lighter. Objects emerged slowly out of the gloom, defining themselves: bed, wardrobe, chair. Their very ordinariness reassured him. When he heard servants bustling down the hall he dressed and went downstairs.

Count Vilém sat alone at a great oak table, breakfasting on bread and beer. "Good day, John!" he called to him. "Care to join me?"

Dee sat. His eyes felt stuffed with sand. Vilém gestured to a servant standing motionless by the table; the man left and returned with a platter of bread and beer. Dee stared at it, wishing he had some of that reviving drink Loew had once served him—what was it called? Coffee, that was it.

"John," Vilém said. "John, are you listening to me? A traveler brought some letters last night."

Dee forced himself to pay attention. "Letters. Yes."

"Listen to this," Vilém said, opening one of the envelopes in front of him. "It's from a friend of mine in Prague. 'I was recently introduced to a man who is fashioning a cup from a giant green stone,' he writes. 'He claims the stone is an emerald, though I have never seen or heard of one so large. He is a Jew, and says he is making the cup in anticipation of the coming of the Messiah. There are strange mystic currents in Prague. Everyone feels that something is about to happen soon, though no two people can agree on what it will be. You must leave Trebona, my friend, and come to the city—otherwise you will miss it.' "

Vilém looked up. "What do you think? Is something about to happen?" He saw Dee's expression and put his letter down. "What is wrong?"

"I heard something last night," Dee said. "Footsteps."

"Is that all? It was a servant, probably. One of the girls sneaking out to visit one of the stableboys."

"No. Loud footsteps. And a—a laugh. An evil laugh. I went out to the corridor but there was nothing there."

Vilém frowned. "I don't know what it could have been."

"No, but I do. I am—I have been haunted by a demon."

"A demon?"

"Yes. I have been running from it since I left England, but I can't escape it. I'm afraid it has followed me here, to your house."

"Well," Vilém said. "We'll post a guard outside your room. And I'll look in my library for something to banish it, some ritual or incantation."

Dee's heart sank. Vilém meant well, but he had no idea how to deal with the thing that haunted him. He was a hearty, pragmatic man, a man who thought that a practical solution could be found for everything. Dee had once believed that himself, before this thing had started to dog him. But even Loew, with all his learning, had not been able to help him. He was completely alone.

"Post the guard outside my children's room instead," he said.

Katherine came down the stairs. "Hello, child," he said. "Have some breakfast with us."

As she came closer he saw that she looked troubled. It was not a child's expression but an adult's, the face of someone with a problem too great to bear. The sight twisted his heart.

"What is it, sweetling?" he asked.

She put her arms up and he lifted her to his lap. She would soon grow too heavy for this, he thought, realizing to his surprise that she was already five years old. "I had a bad dream," she said.

He drew her close to him. His heart was pounding so loud

he thought she might be able to feel it against her skin. "What did you dream?"

"A—a thing. There was a bad thing. It came into my room. Then there was a light, and it ran away."

A light? Could that have been his candle? "What kind of bad thing?"

"I—I don't—"

To his horror she burst into tears. He cursed himself for asking her, for forcing her to think about the thing she most wanted to forget. Had her dream brought back memories of that night in his study? Even worse, what if it had not been a dream at all? What if the demon was stalking her again?

He had to do something, he thought. Surely there was a spell, a ritual. . . . He shuddered. Katherine must have felt something because she squirmed in his lap to face him. Her worried expression had returned.

"Everything will be fine," he said. "The bad thing will not bother you again."

A plate slipped across the table and smashed into a wall. Katherine cried louder. "What was that?" Vilém asked. His commanding expression had gone; he looked uncertain, almost afraid.

"It's the demon," Dee said, quietly, so Katherine wouldn't hear.

That night when he went to look in on the children he saw that Vilém had been as good as his word: a man in the count's livery stood in front of the door, his eyes alert. The guard nodded as Dee stepped inside.

The children slept peacefully. Rowland had thrown off his blanket; Dee covered him again and tucked him in.

The presence of the guard did not reassure Dee; he felt uneasy as he made his way back to the room he shared with Jane. His apprehension grew when he blew out his candle, plunging the room into darkness. He tossed on the bed, certain he would never get to sleep. Several times he thought he saw fantastic shapes in the dark, his mind creating phantoms where nothing existed, and he jerked awake, his heart pounding.

He fell into a troubled sleep. A scream woke him. He sat, then quickly spoke the spell for his glow-light. "What is it?" Jane asked, coming awake beside him.

"I don't know."

Together they ran into the corridor. A bright glare came from the children's room. At first Dee thought it was another glow-light, something the demon had summoned up. He woke fully, all his senses alert, prepared to do battle with whatever the demon had in store for him.

As he hurried closer he saw orange light flaming from the open door. Vilém came running down the corridor. The guard he had posted followed him, and other servants scurried around; the entire house seemed to have come awake.

Dee ran for the children's door. "No!" Vilém said.

Dee barely heard him. The fire was concentrated around the four children, playing around their bodies and caressing their faces. He rushed to the closest, Rowland, and saw to his relief that he was not burning; the fire illuminated and held him, nothing more. The children looked enchanted, as if they had lain under a spell for a hundred years, their faces glowing in the light.

He reached through the fire for Rowland. His hands and arms burned and sparks caught on his nightshirt, but he ignored everything and pulled his son out and laid him on the floor. Beside him he saw Jane doing the same to Katherine, and Vilém lifting out Arthur. He hurried to Michael and pulled him free.

As soon as the children were safe the mattresses and bed linen ignited. Dee heard an enormous *whoosh* and for the first time smelled fire and burning straw. Arthur came awake and started to scream; Katherine and Rowland heard him and woke as well, their cries joining his. Michael, remarkably, still slept.

Dee lifted Michael and shepherded the rest of the children outside. The ceiling gave way behind them, falling heavily on the beds and catching fire as well. Vilém called for water. A stream of servants ran downstairs to the well.

Dee did not join them. He hurried his family to his bedroom and crowded the children in the small bed, where he examined them carefully. They had fallen asleep again, understanding somehow that they were safe. None of them, miraculously, had been hurt.

"Husband," Jane said softly. He looked up at her. Amazingly, she was smiling. "Your beard is almost gone. And your eyebrows. . . ."

"Your eyebrows too," he said. He reached over and gently traced the nearly bare arcs over her eyes.

"Thank God the children are all right."

Dee frowned. "Not God," he said. "God was not responsible for any of this."

"No. It's that demon, isn't it? That thing Kelley called up in your study in England."

He looked at her, surprised. He had told her everything else, but he had been careful to keep this one thing from her, knowing how she would worry. "How do you know about that?"

"I see things, don't I? And hear things. I'm not stupid."

"No," he said. "Not stupid at all." He hesitated. Men ran up and down the stairs, shouting out orders. "I thought I had finally outrun it, but it's found us again. And it's toying with me. It could have killed the children, but instead it wanted to show me its power. It will kill me with worry one day."

"What are you going to do?"

"I think—I have an idea, but we'll talk about it tomorrow. I'm far too tired to decide now."

He made room for himself on the bed and fell into a deep, exhausted sleep.

He met Vilém in the corridor the next morning. The count was still dressed in his nightclothes. "Is the fire out?" Dee asked.

"Yes. The room's destroyed, though. Was that—was that your demon?"

"I'm afraid so."

Vilém said nothing. They walked to the children's room together. The count had not exaggerated; the room lay in ruins, the ceiling fallen, the floor awash with water. Servants came and went around them, sweeping and pulling debris from the room.

One of the servants hurried up to Vilém. "We received some letters this morning," he said.

Vilém glanced through the packet absently. He stopped at an envelope, his eyebrows raised, and then handed the letter to Dee. "You have some interesting friends," he said.

The letter was from Loew. As Dee reached for it he felt a sharp pain, and he noticed for the first time that his hands were red and raw, burned from last night's fire.

"Here, are you all right?" Vilém asked.

"Yes." He broke the seal and opened the letter quickly, wincing.

"I have some bad news about your associate Edward Kelley," Loew had written. "He has kidnapped the boy Izak and says he will exchange him for the name of the thirty-sixth man. I am at a loss to know what to do. I thought that since you were acquainted with the man you might have an idea or two. At least, I hope you will write telling me Kelley's address."

Dee looked up to see Vilém watching him closely. "What is it?" Vilém asked. "You look as if you've gotten bad news."

"Bad news, yes," Dee said. "Not for me, but for a friend of mine."

"What is it?"

"A young man I know has been kidnapped."

"Kidnapped? By who?"

By a man I once called my friend, Dee thought. If not for me this never would have happened. I bring evil to everything I touch.

He thought quickly. The demon had proved that it could find him no matter where he went, no matter how safe he thought himself. He had to stop running, had to turn and face it at last. "I'll have to leave here for a while," he said.

"What about your work on the Stone?"

"The Stone?" Dee asked absently, his thoughts still on his demon. "I wonder if perhaps the Stone is to be found somewhere besides workshops and studies, if the path to it lies outside, in the world."

"What do you mean?"

"Would you look after my family for me?" he asked.

"Yes, of course."

Dee went upstairs to pack. One last time, he thought. It was nearly a prayer. One last journey before we all return to England.

PEARL USHERED ONE OF LOEW'S STUDENTS INTO THE STUDY. "He says he has a letter," Pearl said.

Loew took the letter eagerly, hoping that it was from Dee. But one glance showed him that it couldn't be; there was no envelope, just a piece of paper folded in half. He opened it.

"I have not yet heard from you," the letter said. "My patience in this matter is not unlimited. The boy will die if I do not receive the information I want within seven days. Cattle Market, at the base of the statue. Yours sincerely, Edward Kelley."

"Who gave this to you?" Loew asked the boy. "Where did you get it?"

"A man came into the Quarter with it," the boy said.

"What did he look like? Did he say where he came from?" Loew remembered that Kelley had had his ears cut off for some offense. "Were his ears clipped?"

"I don't know. I don't remember. He looked like a man, that's all."

Loew tried not to become angry with the boy. Why should he have paid attention, after all? "Very well," he said. "You can go."

A knock came at the front door. Not now, Loew thought. I don't have time for this—I have to think. He heard Pearl speak to someone and then lead him down the hallway, heard them pass the student on his way out. The door to the study opened.

"Your friend is—" Pearl began.

"Doctor Dee!" Loew said, astonished. "I hadn't—this is— that is, you are very welcome. Now more than ever. My God, what happened to your beard?"

"The demon tried to burn my children," Dee said.

"My God," Loew said again. "Are they safe?"

"Now they are, yes. I'm the one it wants."

"But aren't you taking a risk by coming here?"

"It's worse than that. Somehow Rudolf got Pope Sixtus to banish me from Prague."

"Well, then, you mustn't stay—"

"I have to. It's my fault Kelley's after you. I was the one who led him to you, who told him about the thirty-sixth man. I have to make amends somehow. And Izak—is he in danger?"

Loew handed him the letter wordlessly. Dee read it

quickly, then looked up. "I know where Kelley lives," he said. "I'll show you. Come—we'll have the golem pay him a visit."

"I'm afraid I can't do that," Loew said. "I took the *shem* from Yossel's mouth. He's disobeyed me a number of times. I told him to search for Izak but he went his own way—he's been talking to a woman in the Quarter—"

"Well, we can't confront Kelley ourselves. He'll run to Rudolf as soon as he sees I'm in town, or he'll grab us both and torture us for information. God knows what he has in that house of his."

"The demon, you think?"

An expression passed fitfully across Dee's face; he looked like a haunted man, a man ridden by demons. He seemed to make an effort to cast away his evil thoughts. "Demons, yes," he said. "And other things, probably, by this time."

"That's another reason you shouldn't go. You can't face the demon—it's already done you enough harm."

"I'm done with running," Dee said. "And those seem to be my only choices—running or staying and facing this, whatever it is." He tried to smile, but it made little headway against the haunted look in his eyes. "But I would feel safer if the golem were the one to beard Kelley in his own den."

"Very well," Loew said. "If you think that's the right course. . . ."

"I do."

Dee followed Loew to Yossel's room. The rabbi reached into one of his pockets, pulled out a crumpled piece of paper, and placed it in the golem's mouth.

The strange clay-colored eyes opened and saw them. "Rabbi Loew," the golem said. "And Doctor Dee. It's good to see you both. And very good to be alive again."

He looked from one of them to the other. For a moment the clay features moved and Loew thought he saw an expression of resentment, almost of anger, pass over the golem's face. Then he smiled, and Loew shook his head. He had imagined it, that was all.

THEY MADE THEIR WAY THROUGH THE TINY STREETS AND alleyways of the Jewish Quarter. It was mid-afternoon; the summer sun burned hot, tarnishing the sky. Despite the heat, Loew had muffled the golem in huge shapeless clothing. The clothes were no disguise, though; Yossel's great height and shambling walk drew curious or terrified glances from nearly everyone they passed.

Once the golem stopped and gazed up at the window of one of the houses. "No," Loew said harshly. "Come along."

"What is it?" Dee asked. "Who lives there?"

"No one. A woman. I was going to tell her to stop talking to Yossel, but there's been no time. . . ."

What's happened in this town since I left? Dee thought. The tale sounded interesting, but he couldn't think about it; he had to concentrate all his attention on Kelley.

They received even more stares after they passed through the gate of the Quarter. The Jews had probably all seen Yossel before, Dee thought, but these people had never encountered anything like him. He looked at the golem's mismatched arms and wished for the hundredth time that he had had time to fix them.

They headed south through the Old Town and the New Town, the golem tirelessly, the two old men stopping to rest every so often. Living on Vilém's estate Dee had forgotten the bustling crowds of Prague, the priests and conjurers, gypsies and soldiers and madmen, traveling musicians and quack-salvers and mountebanks.

Finally they reached the Cattle Market. It was market day

today; cows and other livestock brayed and bellowed, and men selling their wares tried to make themselves heard over the clamor. Dee caught the mingled smells of hay and horseflesh and dung.

Loew pointed to a statue on the southeast side. "That's where I was supposed to leave a message," he said.

"You were, were you?" Dee said. His anger with his old colleague had grown on the long walk; he was furious with Kelley for playing with innocent lives to further his own ambition.

Then he remembered Kelley's familiar at the alchemists' tavern, the thing that had perfectly imitated a human except for its strange backwards hands, and he shivered in the summer heat. How could they confront something like that?

The sun seemed not to have moved at all in the sky, though they had walked a long way. Dee led Loew to Kelley's huge house. The rabbi motioned the golem forward. The two men hid themselves in the shadows of a coach entrance next door, close enough to overhear anything that might happen. Dee tried to catch his breath; the heat was suffocating.

They heard the golem knock, and then the door opened. "Yes?" someone said. It was Kelley's voice; to Dee's surprise he had answered the door himself.

"I've come for Izak," the golem said.

There was a long pause. Kelley was probably studying the golem, realizing that this was no ordinary visitor. "Ah," he said finally. "You're Loew's creation, aren't you?"

"Yes."

"I'm surprised he's let you out. From what I've heard he uses you as a slave, locking you away except when he needs you to do his bidding."

"God's devils!" Loew said. "He's trying to corrupt him." He moved forward.

"Stay here," Dee said. He put his hand on Loew's arm. He

could feel the muscles pull and strain, like taut rope. "We can't let him see us."

"I—I am not a slave," Yossel said finally.

"No? So Rabbi Loew allows you perfect freedom, the right to do whatever you want?"

There was another long pause. Loew took another step toward the street. Dee's grip tightened on his arm. "No," Yossel said.

"No? Tell me, what do you desire? What would you do if you were allowed anything at all, if you were free of him?"

"There's—there's a woman—"

"A woman, good. I can help you there, I think. I have potions, amulets, trinkets. . . . I can make her want you as much as you want her. Why don't you leave Rabbi Loew and come live here with me? I won't treat you as badly as he does, I promise."

"No. No, he is my creator. As God is your creator."

"Ah, but I have left God long ago. And you can leave Loew as well."

"No." Yossel's voice was louder, stronger. "I've come for Izak."

"What makes you think you'll find him here?"

"Rabbi Loew told me."

"And Rabbi Loew is always right, I suppose."

"Yes."

"I'm sorry to disabuse you, my friend. Izak is not here. It seems your precious Rabbi Loew was wrong."

"May I come in and look?"

"Of course not. There's a good deal in here I don't want anyone to see. Especially Loew."

"Loew isn't interested in anything but Izak."

"Oh, I doubt that. You tell your owner that he knows the terms of our bargain. He tells me the name I want, and I release Izak."

Dee heard a scuffle, and then a thump as something hit the floor. He stuck his head out cautiously. Kelley lay prone across the doorway. Yossel was nowhere to be seen.

"What is it?" Loew said intently.

"Yossel pushed past Kelley and went inside."

Nothing happened for long moments. Bells rang out somewhere in the city. A coach drove down the street and Dee and Loew ducked back into the shelter of the doorway. "Do you see anything?" Loew asked impatiently.

Just then Yossel ran from the house. He looked wildly up and down the street and rushed past them.

"Yossel!" Loew said. "Come here! Now! Yossel!"

The golem paused. Something had terrified him badly, Dee saw. How could a lump of clay have such a searing expression? The golem headed toward them reluctantly.

"What happened?" Loew asked. "What did you see?"

Yossel shook his head.

"What? What was it?"

"I can't—I can't say." The golem's voice was low, rasping.

"Tell me."

"No."

"Kelley's moving," Dee said. "He's going to wake up soon. We've got to go."

Without discussing it they headed around the market, anxious to put the noise and bustle between them and Kelley. "Tell me," Loew said urgently. "What did you see in Kelley's house?"

"Nothing can make me speak of it," Yossel said. "Not even if you were to promise me an immortal soul." And he said nothing else on the way back to Loew's house, though both Loew and Dee tried to draw him out.

Shadows were lengthening across the streets by the time they reached the Jewish Quarter, the evening finally bringing the promise of cooler weather. Someone had placed a bundle of rags against the wall near the gate. As they came closer the bundle moved and stood up, and Dee saw that it was Magdalena.

She had insisted on traveling to Prague with him but had gone her own way when the coach reached the city; she had not thought Loew would welcome her, and he had to admit that she was probably right. Now he nodded to her as she came toward them. "Good day, Doctor Dee," she said.

"Good evening, more like," Dee said.

Loew looked from Dee to Magdalena. For an instant Dee saw her as Loew did, a shapeless mass of soiled and ragged clothing, and he felt briefly embarrassed. Then he thrust the feeling away. Magdalena was a good person; he had no reason to be ashamed of her.

"This is Magdalena," he said to Loew. "She's been helping me with my investigations." He turned to Magdalena. "And this is Rabbi Loew."

Loew nodded without turning toward her. Dee felt annoyed at his rudeness; then he remembered that Loew did not look directly at any woman other than his wife.

"And who is this?" Magdalena asked, indicating the golem.

"My name is Yossel, lady." He held out his hand. Magdalena took it gravely.

"I have a great deal to tell you," Dee said. "Is there a place we can go to talk?"

"There's a tavern," Magdalena said.

"Good. Will you join us, Rabbi Loew?"

Loew hesitated. "Yes, very well. But I don't think they will look kindly on Yossel." He turned to the golem. "Yossel, go home. Go to your room. Do not talk to anyone on the way. Do you hear me?"

Yossel nodded and shuffled through the gate into the Quarter.

The tavern was like a border outpost, Dee saw as they went inside, a place that served Jews, Christians, and Saracens alike.

It reminded him of that other borderland he had visited, István's realm, with its confusion of different peoples and religions. The three of them, mismatched as they were, drew no stares from the other patrons.

As they went toward an empty table they passed a group of women seated together. One of them turned, and Dee recognized Marie.

"Doctor Dee!" she said. "You must—you must—"

The German defeated her. She spoke to one of her companions in French and the other woman translated.

"You must be careful," the woman said. "My friend Marie says she has seen the countess Erszébet in Prague."

"Erzsébet! Here?"

Marie spoke again. "Yes," her friend said. "There is—there is a door the countess wants to keep open. Do you understand what she means by that?"

"I'm afraid I do," Dee said. "Thank her for the warning. And ask her how she is, please. Has she found lodging in Prague?"

"Oh, yes," the woman said. "She is staying with me. She had a terrible scare in Transylvania, apparently, something so frightening she will not talk about it. Did it have something to do with this Hungarian woman?"

"Yes, it did. She'll have to tell you herself what it was, though."

"I understand. And meanwhile I will see that she is well taken care of."

Loew and Magdalena had found a table, he saw. He bid farewell to Marie and her friend and went toward them, deep in thought.

So Erzsébet was here, in Prague. Everyone was here, it seemed, everyone and anyone who would benefit from keeping the door open, or from closing it. Prague was the center, the place where all the lines crossed.

He had not come here accidently, he saw. He had been brought here, the demon chivvying him, harassing him, leading him every step of the way to the one spot in the world where it could come through the door the easiest.

Once again he remembered the old Yorkshireman's story about the farmer who had been tormented by a Boggart for years and who, in running away from it, had only managed to bring it with him. "We may as well turn back to the old house," the farmer had said, "as be tormented in another that's not so convenient."

If only they could somehow turn back to the old house. If only they could return to England, away from demons and fraudulent alchemists and women who bathed in blood.

But what if the demon wasn't the only one who had guided his steps? What if he was here for a purpose—to stop the demon, to close the door, to find the thirty-sixth?

He joined Loew and Magdalena and ordered mutton stew and some beer. Loew shook his head; he would not eat anything not prepared according to his dietary laws, Dee remembered. Magdalena declined food as well, but Dee understood in time that this was because she had no money to pay for it, and he ordered another stew for her. "Was that Marie?" she asked.

"Yes. She seems to have found friends here in Prague, for which God be thanked."

When their meals came she ate quickly, like a starving child. God knows when she had eaten last, Dee thought; it might not have been since they left Trebona. He would have to remember to ask her where she planned to stay the night.

"So," Magdalena said when she had finished. "What is it you wanted to tell me?"

"Well, for one thing Izak's been kidnapped," Dee said.

He was unprepared for her reaction. She put a hand to her mouth, an anxious look in her eyes. Now he remembered seeing her and Izak in the Jewish Quarter, and he wondered again about their unlikely friendship.

"Oh, no," she said. "What happened to him?"

He told her about the notes Kelley had sent and their visit to his house with the golem. By the time he finished she had regained her usual blunt confidence. "Well, then, we'll have to look around Master Kelley's house ourselves," she said.

"What!"

"No one else will do it. Even Yossel is afraid of him."

"We will not go into his house. You of all people should understand how dangerous it is to visit a sorcerer. Don't you remember Erzsébet?"

"I survived Erzsébet, didn't I?"

"With my help. And you can't count on that this time—I'm not going with you. I have no wish to meet whatever it was that frightened a golem."

"Fine. I'll go alone, then."

"No, you won't. I can't let you do that."

"How will you stop me?"

Loew stared at them, his brows raised, the proscription against looking at another woman forgotten. "Who's Erzsébet? What happened to you?" he asked.

"Erzsébet Báthory," Magdalena said, pronouncing the syllables with relish.

Loew's amazement deepened. "I—I've heard of her, of course," he said. He listened as they recounted their tale, taking turns: Erzsébet's rooms, Magdalena's transformation, the dead body.

"So you're twenty years old," he said to Magdalena when they had finished. "I wouldn't have guessed it."

She grinned, showing her few teeth, sharp and discolored as pebbles. "I'm glad," she said. "If you can't penetrate my disguise then it must be good indeed."

"But Erzsébet did," Dee said.

"Yes," said Loew. "That worries me too. What powers is she allied with?"

"Not godly ones, that's for certain," Dee said. "She told me she summons them by her bloodletting."

"I wonder—" Magdalena said. "Well, you both divide the world into two camps, God's and the demons'. But I wonder if there might be more than that. There are a good many powers that we know nothing about."

"Nonsense," Loew said. "There is God, and there are those opposing him."

"Every religion tells us that," Dee said. He remembered how exotic Loew's religion had once seemed to him. Now, allied with him against Magdalena's lunatic ideas, he realized that they were closer than he thought. "Whatever the differences between Loew and me, we both believe in a God that created heaven and earth."

"Every religion? Really?" She looked at each of them in turn, and he caught a glimpse of the forthright young woman hidden behind the blurred form of the crone. He could see that she was about to make one of her dreadful pronouncements, something blasphemous or obscene or both. "You've never asked how I perform the magic that transforms me into an old woman."

"Very well, how do you?" Dee asked.

"I pray."

"There, you see—"

"I pray to a woman. She's something like my mother, the way I remember her, and something like a statue I saw once in a Roman ruin."

"Well, of course the pagans believed in all sorts of errors—"

"Did they? How can you be sure they were errors? How can you know, absolutely *know*, that what you believe is true?

So many things exist that we can have no knowledge of—perhaps your gods are out there, somewhere, and mine too."

"Enough of this," Loew said. "What are we going to do about Izak?"

The discussion was making him uneasy, Dee saw; he had probably learned to tread carefully in matters of religion. And yet no one at the neighboring tables was paying them the slightest attention. In England people having these sorts of conversations had to look over their shoulders constantly; there were always spies eager to report heresies to the authorities for pay. Magdalena, at least, might have been arrested as a witch and possibly tortured. He felt a little shocked at the amount of freedom he seemed to have here.

"I told you," Magdalena said. "I'll get him from Kelley's house. We can do it tomorrow—I was at the alchemists' tavern earlier today, and they said he has an audience with Rudolf then."

"And I told you you're not going in there," Dee said.

"And I asked you how you were going to stop me."

Dee sat back in his chair, frustrated. She had become his responsibility, almost his daughter, he saw. Still, it was far better to think of her as a daughter than to remember her as the beautiful young woman she truly was. "The only way I know," he said. "I'll have to talk you out of it—show you just how foolish this idea of yours is." He turned to Loew. "Come, help me here. Even the golem was frightened by what he saw in Kelley's house."

"That's true," Loew said. "And Yossel is far stronger than all of us together. How could we survive something like that?"

Magdalena was silent a moment. Then she said, "When I was fourteen I became a prisoner of a man who used me very badly."

She did not seem to want to continue. Dee said, hoping to prompt her, "Did he—did he take liberties with you?"

Magdalena laughed harshly. "Oh, it was far worse than that. You are a wise man, Doctor Dee, but you know very little about some things. He raped me, and then he shared me with his friends. And after a while he gave me to strangers. At the end of the night he would tie me up and leave me in my room, and I would try to sleep. And then in the evening he would come back and give me supper—the only food I ate all day— and then his customers would arrive again."

Loew had gone very pale. "How did you get away?" he asked.

"One night he was drunk and didn't tie the ropes tightly enough. I worked my way loose, and when he came into the room I broke a chair over his head. I may have killed him—I didn't stay to find out. So you see, I know what it's like to be at the mercy of someone stronger than you, someone who wants to use you for his own ends. I'm going to find out what happened to Izak."

"But you don't even know him," Loew said.

"I know him better than you do."

"What? How?"

She laughed. "I know a good many people here in Prague. Not much goes on that I don't hear about."

"Very well," Dee said. "If I can't stop you, I'll have to go with you."

"And I," Loew said.

To Dee's surprise she began to laugh. "Wonderful," she said. "Two ancient men, tottering around after me as I try to move silently through Kelley's house."

"You can't go in there alone," Dee began, and Loew said, "You have no idea—"

She laughed again. "I need a protector, do I? You men could not have survived half the things I did."

"But you know very little magic," Dee said. "You said so yourself."

"That's true." She looked at each of them in turn. "You come with me, then, Doctor Dee. I won't need both of you."

"But—" Dee said. But he knew less magic than Loew. And he had been opposed to going into Kelley's house to begin with. But he couldn't say anything; he would sound the worst sort of coward if he did. "Very well. I'll meet you at the Cattle Market tomorrow at ten. Do you know where that is?"

"Of course."

Loew thanked them for the trouble they were taking for Izak, and the three of them separated. Dee walked toward the inn where he had left his worn and stained travel bags; he had decided not to stay with Doctor Hageck, who would doubtless attempt to talk him out of visiting Loew.

He climbed the steps to his room and opened the door. The heat of the day had not dissipated; the room was stuffy and close. It was only when he had unpacked and settled in that he realized he had never asked Magdalena where she planned to spend the night; he had been too shocked by her story to think of it.

He understood that what she said was true: he would probably not have survived the things she had had to endure.

12 DEE HAD HALF HOPED MAGDALENA WOULD change her mind, but as he neared the market he recognized her now-familiar shape; she looked like a bundle of rags propped up against a statue. As he came closer he saw that the statue was the one Kelley had mentioned in his letter, and he grimaced at the coincidence. The market was closed today; it seemed eerily silent, like a city hit by plague. Dung and hay and scraps of leather littered the ground, skittering in the mild wind. The sun had just started to burn off the clouds, promising another hot day.

She stood and they headed for Kelley's house, walking without discussion around to the back. The path brought them to a large courtyard. Dee studied the house closely, looking for the servant's entrance, and beside him he noticed Magdalena doing the same. Dee felt as if they were working in tandem, as if they had planned everything out beforehand. Well, that's not surprising, he thought. I should know her fairly well by this time.

He found a door; it opened when he turned the knob. Why wasn't it locked? What protection did Kelley have that he considered stronger than locks and bolts?

They went inside. Dee watched Magdalena carefully but she did not change shape. So Kelley's magic was of a different sort than Erzsébet's. Either that or it was weaker, but Dee did not think that was the case.

He looked around and saw that they had entered through the kitchen. The room was cold, a shock after the heat outside. Dim watery light came in through the unwashed windows. He smelled sour milk and cabbage. No doubt all Kelley's servants had fled long ago—that is, if he had managed to hire any in the first place.

As his eyes grew accustomed to the light, he saw that the kitchen was huge, as big as a cathedral nave. An open hearth lined with bricks gaped at one end. Tables stood against the walls, piled high with pots and plates and cooking knives. Ropes of old dried herbs hung from the ceiling, their scent making little headway against the stale kitchen smells.

They left the kitchen and came to a dining room furnished with a large oak table surrounded by at least a dozen chairs. He thought of Kelley sitting at the table, eating all alone in that vast space. Or would he be alone? Perhaps a different demon sat at each of the chairs, a hellish parliament.

He shook his head. He was allowing his imagination to paint terrifying pictures, to do Kelley's work of frightening for him. But so far, he reminded himself, they had seen nothing to be afraid of.

They walked on. The next rooms were empty, or had at most one piece of furniture in them, a stool or table or tapestry. Dee had brought a candle with him and he lit it at a guttering fire in one of the hearths, stopping longer than he should to warm his chilled bones.

Suddenly he heard Magdalena cry aloud behind him. He turned quickly. "Nothing," she said. "It was nothing. I thought I saw—"

"Yes? What did you think you saw?"

She shook her head.

"Tell me," Dee said. "What was it?"

"That man," she said.

"What man?"

She shook her head again. Dee opened his mouth to press her, but then suddenly he understood. She had seen the man who had once kept her prisoner. Now he noticed that she was trembling from head to foot.

"Let's go back," Dee said. "We don't have to do this."

"It was an illusion," she said. "Come—we have to find Izak."

They continued on through the vast house, opening doors and peering into empty rooms as they passed. Shadows thrown by his candle flickered on the walls. His ears began to fill in the silences; he thought he heard a chittering noise, and then the sound of small feet scrabbling across a floor overhead. He turned to Magdalena. "Did you hear that?" he asked.

"What?" she said. Her eyes were unfocused; she seemed to wander in a daze.

"Let's go back," he said.

"No."

Something moved ahead of him. He slipped back around the corner and motioned to Magdalena to stay where she was. His heart beat fast and strong, like a loose shutter banging in the wind. Sweat broke out on the back of his neck.

"Give me the gold," someone said.

"No," said another voice.

"We agreed to share it," the first man said. There was an unpleasant edge to his voice; he sounded aggrieved and menacing at the same time. "I told you when the master was away, and where the gold was hidden. If not for me—"

"Nonsense. I needed no help from you. And I don't recall any agreement."

The first man cried out in rage. Dee heard the ring of metal on metal, the sound of swords being drawn, and risked a look around the corner.

The two men fell upon each other. Their swords clashed in a ferocity unlike any Dee had ever seen. Then one man knocked the other's sword from his hand and the second man, heedless of the danger, moved closer, grabbed a handful of hair and pulled furiously. The first cried out and kneed the second in the groin.

The second man fell to the floor. The first bent over him and quickly stabbed him to the heart. But the second, incredibly, was still alive. He struggled up off the floor to a sitting position. The first backed away in horror.

What was it? What had the man seen? Dee moved for a closer look. "God," he said. The second man still lay sprawled on the floor, and yet somehow he was also sitting, then rising. No, Dee realized. It was his ghost that was rising.

The first man put his hand to his heart, a look of extreme terror on his face, and collapsed to the floor. Then his wraith rose as well, and the two ghosts grappled with each other. Back and forth they went, each trying to gain the advantage. One knocked the other into the wall and the second man passed straight through it. The first followed.

The hallway was clear now. Dee was about to motion Magdalena forward when the voices in front of him started up again. "Give me the gold," the first man said.

They were condemned to repeat their actions over and over again, Dee saw. Something in the house would not let them leave. He shuddered.

Magdalena had drawn up next to him and was watching the struggle in silence. When the two passed through the walls a second time he turned to her. "They'll probably do this until doomsday," he said. "We'll have to go another way."

"No," she said. She seemed more alert now, having been given a problem to work out. "If Kelley wanted to hide something he would put it here, past these men. He couldn't have better watchdogs."

She was right. Dee watched again as the two men repeated their meaningless ritual. How many times had they performed it? Now he noticed that their clothes looked decades if not centuries out of date, and that when they spoke their accents sounded wrong.

"How?" he asked.

"We'll wait until they become ghosts again," she said. "Then we'll be able to walk through them."

The picture made him shudder again. He studied the two men as they began their performance for what had to be the thousandth time. When the second man fell to the ground he edged forward, trying not to let his fear show. He did not want Magdalena to see him afraid.

He skirted the bodies on the floor. The ghostly battle swirled around him, and then somehow he was in the center, in the middle of the fighting, unable to see a clear path ahead. One of the wraiths passed through him and he felt all that man's feelings, fear and greed and anger and horrible frustration. His candle sparked blue where the wraith touched it.

"Move," Magdalena said urgently.

He tried to take a step but discovered he could not. The wraiths' emotions overwhelmed him. Now both the dead men occupied the space he did, pushing and shoving through him, and he felt the complex tangle of their obsessions.

"Move," Magdalena said again.

He took a step forward, then another. And then he was past them, rushing down the corridor, trying to shake off the loathsome touch of the dead men's souls.

"Wait," Magdalena said.

He turned and found he had gone past a closed door in his hurry. She edged it open. He joined her, holding his candle high. Something massive stood in the center of the room.

"It's a storehouse, I think," he said.

Someone moaned. "I told you—I don't know anything," a voice said. "I'm the last person Rabbi Loew would confide in. Please, I beg you, leave me alone."

"Izak?" Dee asked.

"What? Who are you?" the voice said.

"We're friends. Rabbi Loew sent us."

They moved forward into the room. The massive object was a bed, Dee saw. Izak was tied to one of the legs, his hands behind him.

"I've never seen a bed that big," Magdalena said. "An entire village could fuck on that bed."

"Magdalena!" Izak said.

She bent to untie the knots. "It's all right, Izak," she said. Dee had never heard her sound so tender. "We're here. We're going to help you."

Izak seemed dazed. Dee held the candle closer. Magdalena's ancient gnarled fingers found purchase in the knots. "Rabbi Loew sent us," he said.

"Why should Rabbi Loew help me?" Izak said. "He doesn't care if I live or die. It was Magdalena's idea, I'll wager."

Magdalena untied the last knot. Izak swung his arms slowly, wincing as feeling came back into them. "I don't—I don't know if I can stand," he said.

Magdalena gently lifted Izak's arm over her shoulder. The boy grimaced and stood when she did, painfully slowly. Together they made their way to the door, Izak hobbling, Magdalena steadying him.

"Let's go that way," Dee said, pointing away from the wraiths. "I don't want to meet those ghosts again."

"What?" Izak said. "What ghosts?"

Magdalena seemed to weigh the chance that they might find no way out against the certainty of having to pass through the ghosts. "Good," she said finally.

Dee indicated to her that she should go first; he did not want to hurry ahead and perhaps lose her, and he could keep an eye on their rear. She set off down the hallway, Izak leaning heavily against her rounded shoulders.

Their progress was painfully slow. They traversed a number of corridors, passing closed doors and empty rooms on both sides. Perhaps there was no way out, Dee thought. Perhaps they were doomed never to leave the vast house, to stay there forever, like the ghosts. Perhaps this was some rarely-visited corner of Rudolf's castle. . . .

Footsteps behind him jolted him out of his reverie. He turned quickly but could see nothing. He was about to hurry on when he heard a low laugh.

"Who's there?" he asked.

Silence. Magdalena and Izak were somewhere down the corridor now, a lumbering shadow like a four-legged monster, and he ran to catch up with them. Behind him someone called his name.

He stopped again, raised his candle, and peered into the gloom of the hallway. "Kelley?" he asked, though the voice had not sounded like Kelley's. "Where are you?"

He could hear nothing. No—was that another laugh? It sounded like Erzsébet. Was she here now? The laugh deepened; now it sounded like his demon. His heart sped until he thought he might faint.

He hurried forward, nearly bumping into Magdalena and Izak. "Move," he whispered urgently. "The demon's behind me."

"Are you certain?"

"Of course I'm certain, woman! Who else could it be?"

"Who indeed?" she asked.

What did she mean? He was about to answer angrily when she said, "I thought I saw a man, remember?"

"Yes," he said, understanding now. Kelley, or Kelley's house, was showing each of them what they feared the most. Magdalena had seen her captor; he had heard first Erzsébet and then the thing he had run a thousand miles to escape.

Think, he told himself frantically. So far the demon had only possessed those who had summoned it, or who had at least been in the room when it was summoned. It had grown stronger over the years, but he did not think it was strong enough yet to act of its own volition.

Another sound, this time of glass breaking. He jumped. Could he be certain of that? Kelley's house seemed to feed on the fear of those inside it. Perhaps this was not the demon, perhaps it was something worse, something called up by his own terror. And he was terrified, there was no hiding it. He remembered the repellant feeling of the demon crawling inside him and his fear grew by leaps and bounds.

"Quickly," he said to Magdalena.

She said something he could not hear. His heart pounded loudly. She was moving slowly, so slowly, Izak dragging her down. Why had she been the one to carry him, why didn't he? "Give me Izak," he said. "I can move faster."

She shook her head. "I'm stronger than you, old man," she said.

Something screamed behind them, an obscene sound, like a parody of a man. They went another few torturous steps down the corridor. He wanted to cry out in impatience.

Don't be afraid, he told himself. No fear, there must be no fear. Suddenly he remembered the psalm against demons and began to recite it aloud.

The thing behind them howled again. How much longer did they have to go?

"Light," Magdalena said abruptly.

It was true: something gleamed up ahead. "Could this be a trick?" he asked.

"I don't think so."

The light grew brighter. There was a final cacophony behind them—it sounded like bells falling from a cathedral roof—but it was muted, distant.

He saw an open door leading out to the courtyard. Izak moved free of Magdalena and together the three of them achieved one final burst of speed. They ran out into the heat of the courtyard, laughing.

"We can't stay here," Dee said. "Someone might see us."

They hurried through an alleyway away from the house and came out onto an unfamiliar street. Izak was limping badly, but at least, Dee thought, he could walk on his own. They went down a few streets and sat on a stone bench bordering a square.

"Who are you?" Izak asked Dee. "You talk about ghosts and demons as though you know them personally, you can find your way through that house of dreadful magic—"

"I told you," Dee said, still panting from his escape. "I'm a friend of Rabbi Loew's. My name is Doctor John Dee."

"Loew has no friends like you," Izak said. "And how do you know Magdalena?"

"Come," Dee said. "Let's take you home."

"I'll go with Magdalena," Izak said. "Not you." His rudeness was back; he seemed every so often to remember that he hated everyone and made haste to hide his real nature, the friendliness and openness of youth.

"She might not be strong enough," Dee said. "And what if Kelley comes after you?"

"Very well," Izak said, trying without success to give the impression that he didn't care one way or another.

The three of them made their way through the streets of Prague. Loew was waiting at the gate to the Jewish Quarter. "You found him," Loew said.

He attempted to clasp Izak to his chest but the boy twisted away and stalked off. Loew watched him go, an unreadable expression on his face. Magdalena hurried after him.

Loew turned toward Dee. He seemed to shake off his dark thoughts. "Thank you, my friend," he said. "Can you—can you tell me what you saw in Kelley's house? Or would you prefer not to speak of it?"

"The house shows you what frightens you most," Dee said. "I heard—I thought I heard my demon."

Loew was silent a moment, perhaps thinking of his own fears. "What frightens a golem, I wonder?" he asked.

"Nothingness, maybe. Uncreation."

"I doubt we'll ever know," Loew said.

Dee yawned.

"You're tired," Loew said. "And no wonder. Go home and rest. Do you have a place to stay? I'm sorry, I should have asked you before, but—"

"I'm at an inn—it's called At the Three Frogs. And tomorrow I suppose I'll go back to Trebona."

"Will you?" Loew asked. His eyes searched Dee's face shrewdly.

Dee laughed. "You know me too well. I should go home, go back to my family. I will. And yet something's about to happen here—everyone and everything says so. I don't want to miss it, whatever it is."

"Well, good day," Loew said. "Good day, and thank you. Our teachers tell us that when a person saves a life, it is as though he saved an entire world."

"I'm glad everything turned out well," Dee said.

He made his way to the inn and fell on the bed, still clothed. An hour later he woke to an urgent pounding at his door. He stumbled up and opened it. Rabbi Loew stood there, a stunned and hopeless expression on his face.

"What is it?" Dee said. "What's happened?"

"Yossel's gone," Loew said.

"What do you mean?"

"He's gone. I went to his room and he wasn't there. I was so disturbed after we visited Kelley's house yesterday that I forgot to take the *shem* out of his mouth. He sat on his bed for hours, not moving, drawing no attention to himself, waiting until the night, and then he left. I've only just discovered he's missing. He's disobeyed me, disobeyed a direct order—"

"Do you have any idea where he might be?"

"None. I looked at Rivka's house but he wasn't there. She hadn't seen him, she says."

"Who's Rivka?"

"A young woman in the Quarter. He says he's in love with her. I was sure that that's where he would go. . . . But I have no time for this—we must find him soon, before he does terrible harm. Will you help me?"

"Of course," Dee said. He smiled wryly. "It looks as if God doesn't intend for me to leave Prague after all."

For the second time that day he made his way to the Jewish Quarter. It was mid-afternoon, the day still hot and airless. He followed Loew to the town square and saw that the rabbi had gathered a group of men to help him. One after the other the men gave their reports: no one had seen anything, the golem was still missing.

Loew gave orders and the men fanned out away from the square. "You," he said to Dee. "I want you to go to the tavern we visited once, and the neighborhood around it. Yossel may have left the Quarter."

Dee headed back to the gate. How, he wondered, could the golem still be missing? Where could he hide? Surely someone had seen him; with his great height and misshapen features he would cause comment wherever he went.

At the tavern Dee questioned the customers, giving as vague a description as possible; he did not want to start a panic or draw suspicion to the Jewish Quarter. No one had seen him. Dee left and wandered the streets, keeping his eyes open and stopping a few passers-by. When the sun set he headed back, feeling hot and dirty and tired.

FOR THE REST OF THE DAY MAGDALENA SHOWED IZAK A PART of Prague he had never imagined. They went to alleyways behind taverns and picked out food from among the garbage; to a wealthy part of town where a woman never failed to leave out some bread and a saucer of milk, "for the fairies," Magdalena said; and finally to a dim alley with no exit, formed by the angles of several buildings.

"This is where I usually sleep," she said, showing him several dirty blankets piled in a nest. "Of course if you want to go home . . ."

"I have no home," he said. He felt dreadfully hungry despite all their scavenging, but he understood that this was the price he had to pay for his escape from the Quarter. He did not complain; it seemed a fair exchange.

She smiled at him, and he saw he had said the right thing.

She gave him half the blankets and they settled down to sleep.

The next day dawned hot and bright, and they rose and began their rounds again. Magdalena knocked on a door and a woman came out and handed them some cold meat.

Izak marveled at how she had made a life for herself in the forgotten parts of the city. "Won't Doctor Dee give you food?" he asked.

She laughed. "He does when he remembers. He worries about me, but he's very impractical."

"But—but that's terrible. He has so much, and you have so little. Why aren't you angry with him?"

"I don't know. It's no good to be angry about things you can't change."

Izak thought about that for a moment. He couldn't change his bastardy, yet he could not help but be furious at Loew's pronouncements, and at the casual way the peddler had used his mother. Perhaps when he was as old as Magdalena he would be more accepting. "How long have you lived on the streets?" he asked.

"Oh, a long time," she said.

"Where are we going now?"

They went to an inn where merchants and aristocrats drove up in expensive coaches. He followed her around to the back. Piles of half-eaten food littered the alleyway; he was amazed at how much people threw out. They picked out what they wanted and Magdalena set off for their next destination.

The day had grown hotter; the heat seemed almost a tangible thing, someone walking along with them and screaming at the top of his lungs. "How long did it take you to find all this?" he asked.

"A long time," she said.

It was the same answer she had given before. He wished she would be more open with him. "But where did—"

"Hush," she said. "Listen."

They stood still a moment. "I don't hear anything," Izak said.

She shook her head and they continued along the street. A moment later she held up her hand and stopped again. "Someone's following us," she said.

"I don't—"

"You can only hear it when we're moving." She turned, and to Izak's horror she headed back the way they had come. He hurried after her.

There was no one there; the heavy heat kept most people inside. But Magdalena continued down the street, peering into doorways as she passed. Finally she stopped and laughed. "Izak," she said. "Come look at this."

He went toward her, his heart pounding, wondering what this strange woman found amusing. Yossel stood in the doorway, hunched over, trying to hide his tremendous height.

"He thought we wouldn't notice if he followed us," she said, still laughing.

"It's not funny," Izak said. "He tried to destroy the Quarter once. You didn't see it—it was terrible. And look—he's gotten free of Loew. Who knows what he'll do now?"

"My master forgot to work his usual magic," the golem said. "So I walked away. I deserve to be free too."

"That's true, you do," Magdalena said. "Don't you see, Izak—we're all outcasts, all at the mercy of people who think they have a right to control us. We should stick together."

Suddenly Izak saw the golem from her point of view. It was true—both he and the golem had managed to escape Rabbi Loew and his harsh edicts. He felt a surge of sympathy for the creature, as though they were brothers with Loew as their terrible father.

"What do you want?" Magdalena asked him. "Do you need some of our food?"

"No. I want to be safe from my master. He is searching for me."

"Well, come on, then. We'll show you our hiding place."

She led them back to the alleyway, and they settled down among Magdalena's blankets. "So you've run away from Rabbi Loew," she said. "That was brave of you. He's a powerful man."

"Yes." Yossel paused; Izak sensed that he was working out a complex thought. "But I have to leave him. All children must leave their parents and find their own way eventually."

"He's more than a father, though, isn't he?" Magdalena said, thoughtfully nibbling a rind of bread. "He's your creator. The only man I know of who ever created life. I think he envies women and the life that grows inside them—that's why he made you. He has to have mastery over everything, your Rabbi Loew, even birth."

"He made me to protect the Quarter," Yossel said. "And there was something about a thirty-sixth man. . . ."

"The thirty-sixth man, yes," Magdalena said. "He and Doctor Dee were looking for him."

"What man?" Izak said, looking from one to the other. "Why does everyone know about this but me?"

"You mean he never told you?" Magdalena said. "That's why Edward Kelley kidnapped you, to force them to share what information they had with him. You went through all of that, and no one explained to you what it was about?"

"No one tells me anything."

Yossel and Magdalena repeated what they knew: the thirty-six men, Rudolf's interest in the search, the various lists. Izak sat amazed, forgetting even to eat. So that was what had happened. He had been a pawn, a piece to be moved back and forth on a board. "You're right," he said to Magdalena. "They don't care at all, these great men of the world. They're too busy with their plans to think about us."

"Let's go away," Yossel said. "I want to see the world, to learn more. We can make our own way, our own rules."

It sounded wonderful, Izak thought. The three of them, traveling together, having adventures. Yossel would protect them, and Magdalena would find them food. . . . But he had to stay, at least for a while; there was something he had to do in the Quarter first.

"I can't leave just yet," Izak said. "I have to revenge myself on the man who used my mother so badly. That peddler, Mordechai."

"I don't understand," Yossel said. "What do you mean by revenge? Why do you hate him so much?"

"He's my father. He used my mother and then left her. He—"

The golem's deep voice rode over his. "The peddler is not your father," he said.

"He's not?" Izak said. "How do you know? Who's my father then?"

"I know because I wander the Quarter and I hear things. People do not think I have any understanding, you know. They will say anything in front of me."

"But who is my father?" Izak said impatiently.

"A neighbor of yours. The butcher, Baruch. His wife was the one who started the rumor about the peddler. She never knew for certain about her husband, of course, but she wanted to throw suspicion onto someone else. I heard her screaming at him one night, berating him about his faithlessness, telling him all she had done to protect him."

"My—my neighbor? My mother and Baruch? But she hates him. She crosses the street when she sees him coming."

"It was not lovingly done," Yossel said. "It was rape."

"No wonder," Izak said softly. "No wonder she never told me. She must have been so ashamed. . . ."

"Will you come with me, then?" Yossel asked.

"That's enough," a voice said. It was Rabbi Loew.

Suddenly the alleyway was crowded with people, Loew and Dee and several strong men from the Quarter.

"How long have you been standing there listening to us?" Magdalena asked.

"Long enough," Loew said. "Yossel, come with me."

The golem looked at him. A complex expression passed over his face, affection mingled with resentment. "Ah," he said. "My creator." He sounded almost mocking.

"Get out of there," Loew said.

"Why should he?" Magdalena asked. "What does he owe to you?"

"He owes everything to me. I created him, after all."

"Yes, that's true," Yossel said. To Izak's horror the golem stood up.

"Don't go," Izak said. "Stay here with us. After all you've said—"

"I would like to," Yossel said. "But I can't disobey." He stood and walked toward Loew. The other man grasped him by his thick wrist.

"Why not?" Izak called after them. He heard the despair in his voice. "Break away—you're stronger than he is. Don't leave—"

Neither Loew nor the golem answered.

BY THE TIME LOEW RETURNED TO THE SQUARE MANY OF THE men had come back for the midday meal. Women bustled around, handing them food and drink. People cried out and backed away as Loew led Yossel docilely into the square, and he saw the expressions he had grown used to, fear and astonishment.

"Where was he?" someone called.

Loew ignored him. He raised his voice and said to the townspeople, "Don't worry—he won't escape again. Thank you, everyone. You're free to go."

Dee walked with Loew and the golem to the rabbi's house. Loew led Yossel to his room, then reached into his mouth and removed the *shem*.

As soon as the light of intelligence left the golem's eyes Loew said, "It worries me that Izak and Magdalena have become such friends."

"They seem to feel they have something in common, that they're both outcasts," Dee said. "And something in common with the golem as well."

"Yes, I heard that. They want to travel the world together, they said. Well, at least Yossel will not be able to go with them."

"What will you do now?"

"I should, I suppose, unmake him completely—that's what the people here want me to do—"

"But you find that difficult. He's your creation, after all."

"Yes, exactly. It is a blasphemous thought, but I cannot help but wonder if God had this much difficulty with his creation. And then I realize that he did, that the first man and woman disobeyed him as Yossel disobeys me." He sighed. "Well, it will soon be time for evening prayers. Perhaps God will tell me what he wants me to do next."

"Farewell, then," Dee said.

"You're leaving. Of course. Thank you for your help, and I sincerely hope I will not have to trouble you with our problems again."

Dee laughed. "Perhaps the next time I will trouble you with mine."

LOEW FOUND IT HARD TO CONCENTRATE ON THE EVENING prayers; he thought again and again of Yossel, of how he had found him in the company of vagabonds. This was not what he had planned for his creation, not at all. The golem had come with him obediently enough, but Loew sensed his growing restlessness, even anger. And Izak—what was he to do with Izak? Why didn't the boy stay in the Quarter where he belonged?

A distant sound disturbed his reverie, a faint rhythmic noise that insinuated itself into the chanting of the prayers. Footsteps marching, heading toward the synagogue. Soldiers?

The sound grew louder. The door to the synagogue burst open, and ten or twelve men in Rudolf's uniform pushed their way inside. The king had finally decided to move against him, Loew realized with horror, and the golem was no longer there to protect him.

Everyone quieted. The soldiers squinted, trying to see in the dim light from the high windows and hanging lamps.

"Where is Rabbi Loew?" the soldier in front called out. "Give us Loew and we'll go away."

"There he is!" another said, pointing to the chief rabbi standing at the front of the synagogue.

Before Loew could say anything the soldiers made their way down the narrow aisle. The people in the synagogue stood and watched as they passed, beginning to mutter to each other. One of the soldiers brushed a hanging bronze lamp and the shadows swayed back and forth, throwing fantastic pictures on the wall.

The leader reached the chief rabbi. The old man stood without moving, his eyes blinking rapidly as if he were trying to block out the events in front of him. In one fluid movement the leader wrenched the rabbi's arm behind him and put his sword to the other man's throat. The rest of the soldiers formed a ring around him.

"I'm not the man you're looking for!" the rabbi said,

breaking from his paralysis and trying to twist away from the sword. "I'm not Judah Loew!"

"Where is he, then?" the soldier asked.

"I don't know. I don't see him—he didn't come to prayers tonight."

Loew did not dare move. From the corner of his eye he could see other men standing still as well, as still as the benches behind them. The bronze lamp rocked back and forth, slowing, its rusty squeaks loud in the silence.

"I don't believe you," the soldier said. "We hear he's a pious man, very pious. Not the kind of man to miss his prayers."

"I'm telling you the truth!" the rabbi said. "I don't know where he is."

The leader looked out over the congregation. "Is this true?" he asked.

There were nods among the men. A few of them said, "Yes," quietly, as if they did not want to provoke the leader any further.

"Then where is he? Where is Judah Loew?"

No one said anything. Loew found that he was looking at the dark stain on the synagogue wall, the blood of martyrs.

"I will kill this man if you do not tell me where Loew is," the soldier said. "And then I will kill another, and another, for as long as I have to. And finally the answer will not matter, because you will all be dead. Now, I ask you again. Where is Rabbi Loew? Is he among you?"

Loew stepped toward the aisle. It was one thing to hide among other men, another to allow those men to die for him.

Someone else called out something; Loew could not hear it over his own panic. The man standing next to Loew grabbed him by the wrist.

"It's me!" a voice shouted. "I'm Rabbi Loew!"

It was the peddler, Mordechai. Izak's father, if the rumors could be believed. Mordechai walked calmly toward the front of the synagogue, one hand raised slightly in surrender. He was still wearing his long shapeless cloak, and he held a staff in his other hand.

Loew moved forward. The man next to him held on firmly to his wrist. "Let him go," the man whispered. "You're worth more to us than he is."

Loew shook him off, but by that time the soldiers were marching back down the aisle, their captive held firmly between two of them.

Loew watched them, uncertain. Should he say something? Should he let Mordechai go, let Rudolf discover the soldiers' mistake? But what would Rudolf do then?

The soldiers left the synagogue. It's over, Loew thought. I can't do anything. But something he said to Dee came back to him — "When a person saves a life, it is as though he saved an entire world" — and he felt deeply ashamed. He was not worth more than Mordechai, not in God's eyes.

THE NEXT MORNING DEE HEARD POUNDING AT HIS DOOR once again. He went to answer it, certain he knew who it must be. And there, just as he expected, stood Rabbi Loew.

Dee laughed wryly. Loew scowled a moment, seeming to wonder what was so amusing, and then he too laughed. "It doesn't look as if I'll ever leave Prague," Dee said.

To his surprise Loew spat several times and said something in Hebrew; Dee caught the words "*ayin ha-ra*," the evil eye. "You must not say such things," Loew said. "You don't know who might be listening."

"You're probably right," Dee said. "But come, my friend — what's happened? What brings you here?"

Loew told him about Rudolf's soldiers, about the peddler who had gone off with them in Loew's place. "Why would Mordechai of all people play the hero?" Loew asked. "I never thought him capable of something like that. On the contrary, he seemed the worst sort of coward, a man who would seduce women and then leave them with child."

For a moment Dee did not understand what Loew was talking about. Then he realized that Loew had not listened as closely as he had to the conversation in the alleyway, that the other man had missed something important. "I don't know that Mordechai *is* Izak's father," he said. "The golem said he overheard some people talking, and that he thinks Izak's father is someone else, a man named Baruch."

"Baruch? Izak's neighbor, you mean? But then why does everyone assume it's Mordechai?"

"Because—" Dee struggled to remember the conversation. He had not paid much attention; he had been more interested in capturing Yossel. "Baruch's wife was the one who spread the rumor. She wanted to draw suspicion away from her husband."

"Then Mordechai—"

"—is not a bad man."

"Traveler, Jewish Quarter!" Loew said suddenly.

"What are you saying? That he's one of the thirty-six?"

"It's possible. He risked his life for me. And he visits us about once a month—once every thirty-six days, I'll bet. And in that case—"

Dee finished his thought for him. "In that case, the thirty-sixth man is in Rudolf's hands."

IZAK WOKE AND WONDERED WHERE HE was. He stared up at the square of light above him and after a moment realized that it was formed by buildings hemming him in. Then he turned over and saw Magdalena, sleeping in a nest of blankets beside him.

Suddenly all the strange events of the day before came back to him: the conversation with the man of clay; the revelation, wrenching his life out of its accustomed shape, that the peddler was not his father as everyone had supposed. And Rabbi Loew, interfering once again, coming to take the golem away.

Magdalena opened one eye and brushed her wiry gray hair away from her face. "Well," she said, "are you ready to go out into the city?"

"Of course," he said, and they set off on their rounds again.

A few hours later they returned to their hiding place, carrying the spoils of their search. "Isn't it dangerous for a woman to live on the street the way you do?" Izak asked. "How long have you been doing this?"

"Oh, many years," she said.

"That's what you said the last time. Do you still want to travel together, the way the golem said? Because if we do, we're going to have to know things about each other. I can tell you all about my life, but there isn't much to say. But you— you've been places, seen things. . . ."

Magdalena sat still a moment. She wasn't ignoring his question, Izak saw, but thinking about the best way to answer it. "I haven't been on the streets as many years as you suppose," she said slowly.

"No? But—"

She lifted her hand. "Hush," she said. Suddenly her hair became a light brown, her eyes clear blue. She straightened from her bent crone's shape.

Izak scuttled back against the wall, his heart beating rapidly. Was this witchcraft? Sorcery? Was she an old woman who had magicked herself into a beautiful young girl, or had she always been the girl, and the woman was the illusion? "What—" he said, barely able to speak. "What—"

"Hush," she said again. Her voice calmed him. "This is my true shape. I took the other to protect myself. No one ever notices an old woman."

He reached out toward her. She moved back, so quickly he didn't see her go. "I once vowed that no man would ever touch me without my consent," she said. "If you do that again I'll turn you into a toad."

To his own surprise he laughed. "If you could turn people into toads you'd have done it long before this. You don't need to threaten me. I'll never harm you, never touch you unless you give your permission."

"You'll never touch me, then," she said fiercely. "I've been . . . hurt at the hands of men. No one will ever do that to me again."

"I would never harm you, in any case," he said softly. "Not all men are monsters. But I understand that you have to learn that for yourself."

NEITHER LOEW NOR DEE SPOKE FOR SEVERAL MOMENTS, silenced by the idea that Rudolf might have the thirty-sixth man. "We have to get him back," Dee said finally.

"How?" Loew said. "Go back to Rudolf's dungeons? Do you really want to risk that again?"

"There's no other choice. We can't let Rudolf learn what he's got—"

"We don't know for certain that Rudolf has anything. Mordechai could be the thirty-sixth, I grant you that—"

"We can't take the chance that he isn't." Dee thought back to his notes. "We know it's not Anna or Jaroslav or Samuel. That leaves five people, that's a gamble of one in five. We have to—"

"How? The two of us against the might of the Holy Roman Empire?"

"We have the golem—"

"Oh, no. I'm not putting the *shem* in Yossel's mouth ever again. You just said that he overheard some people talking about Izak, that he has a whole life I know nothing about. I won't let him out of my control."

"Well, what else? That's why you created the golem, isn't it—for protection? And as you say, we can't do anything by ourselves."

"I don't know." Loew began to pace the narrow hallway in front of Dee's room. "You're right—we can't leave him there. I don't know."

"Let's free him, just this once. We can keep watch over him, make certain he does nothing but what we tell him to do. And afterward you can put him back to sleep, or unmake him. . . ."

"Very well," Loew said. He seemed to decide all at once. "Let's go."

Together they set out for the Jewish Quarter. "Where do you think Rudolf is keeping Mordechai?" Dee asked.

"The same place he kept us," Loew said. "The Daliborka."

At Loew's house they headed toward Yossel's room. "Judah, what are you doing?" Pearl asked, following them down the hall. "Are you freeing that monster again?"

"Yes," Loew said.

"Why? He's destroyed things—you know that. Maybe the

next time he'll even kill someone. And the townspeople—they don't want him. They're afraid of him. Of you."

"I can't help that," Loew said.

"Judah, for God's sake, you can't do this. Do you know what they say about you, the things I've had to hear? They say you dabble in witchcraft, that you speak to demons—"

"Don't listen to them, then."

Loew and Dee stepped into the golem's room. Pearl stayed at the threshold, one hand at her mouth. Loew took out the piece of paper and put it in Yossel's mouth.

The golem opened his eyes. "What do you want?" he asked. There was a harshness in his voice that Dee had not heard before.

"We need your strength again," Loew said. He seemed unworried by the golem's truculence.

"Why should I help you? When I obeyed you the last time you put me to sleep."

"You know why. Because I'm your creator. I made you from nothing. You must do as I say."

The golem bowed his head for a moment. "It's true, you made me," he said finally. "Very well. But this time after I carry out your commands I want to stay awake. I want to be taught the same things that other people learn, how to read, how to pray. And I want to marry Rivka."

"I won't bargain with you."

"At least teach me something. I want to learn. I know nothing about the world—"

"We'll discuss this later. Right now I want you to break into the Daliborka and free the man Rudolf's imprisoned there. Do you know where that is?"

"Yes, I do."

Loew's mouth twisted. "And yet you say you know nothing about the world. When did you learn about the tower?"

"When I was free to walk about in the world. When you told me to search for Izak."

"I told you to go to the Cattle Market. The Daliborka is in the opposite direction. You continue to disobey me—do you see why I can't trust you?"

"I only wanted—"

"Never mind. I won't argue with you. You'll do as I say. And this time I'll go with you, to make certain of that."

The three of them walked to the river. Yesterday's heat had dissipated; the day was cooler, and pleasant wind ruffled the surface of the water. Clangorous traffic plied back and forth across the bridge. In the rare moments of silence the wheeling birds screeched overhead.

They crossed on the side of the bridge reserved for travelers on foot and came to what Dee now knew was called the Lesser Quarter. A poor name, he thought; the opulence nearly overwhelmed him. He had been away for so long, traveling in distant lands, that he had almost forgotten the richness of Rudolf's kingdom.

The golem began the climb up to the castle. Beside him Dee heard Loew labor for breath, and he stopped too, already tired. "Wait," he said to the golem.

Yossel looked from one to the other, a puzzled expression on his face. For a moment it seemed as if he would disobey; then Loew repeated Dee's command to wait, and the golem stopped.

"Why do you puff like that?" Yossel asked. "Why don't we continue?"

Loew glared at the golem, but Dee, taking pity on him, said, "Because we're old."

"Oh," Yossel said. "Will I become old too?"

Loew continued to say nothing. "I don't know," Dee said. "You're the only one of your kind in the world."

"The only one . . ." Yossel said, breathing the words. Another expression passed across his face. Was it loneliness?

When they were rested they continued up the hill. Dalibor Tower was at the eastern end of the castle outbuildings. They skirted the castle walls carefully, keeping watch for guards or servants or guests of the emperor, but the few people they saw ignored them and went about their business. Probably the folks in the castle had grown used to strange visitors.

As they approached the tower Dee heard a commotion up ahead, what sounded like two men arguing. "Wait," he said. This time the golem obeyed him. He motioned the other two around a corner of one of the outbuildings.

"What is it?" Loew asked.

"Hush. Listen."

One of the voices grew louder. "I delivered him to the tower like you told me to," the first said.

"And then what?" the second man said. "He flew out the window?" He laughed loudly at his own wit.

"I don't know what happened to him." The first man's tone had grown wheedling. "All I know is, I left him in the tower. I don't know how he got out."

"He got out because you forgot to lock the door."

"No. No, I swear—"

"Well, the only other explanation is that you let him go. How much did he pay you?"

"He didn't pay me a penny. I swear to you—"

"Not a penny? You let him go for nothing, then?" More laughter. "I'd confine you to barracks, but unfortunately I need you to help search the grounds. But you're sticking close to me, do you understand? I'm not going to lose him again."

The first man muttered something Dee couldn't hear. "What was that?" the second man asked.

"He's—he's a great magician, they say. What if he's disappeared? What if he turns us into toads?"

The second man laughed. "He's not, though. He claimed

to be this fellow Rabbi Loew, but rest assured that King Rudolf knows what Loew looks like. The man's just a peddler."

Dee heard Loew gasp beside him. How had Rudolf gotten that information? Had Mordechai been tortured?

"A peddler?" the first man said. "All right, then—I'm ready!"

The two men headed away from the tower, their footsteps growing fainter as they went. "Where could he have gone?" Dee asked. "Does he know any magic?"

"No. I don't think so, anyway. None of the thirty-six do, as far as I know. I'm supposed to protect them."

Something screeched in the tower room, a sound horribly like the demons in Kelley's house. Dee spun around. The raised center of the tower—the circle that he had puzzled over—was lifting. It rose higher as he watched, and then someone pushed it over to the side, and the peddler's head came into view.

They hurried toward him. "Who—who are you?" the peddler said, fear evident in his voice.

"Is that where you hid?" Loew asked, and at the same time Dee asked, "What's down there?"

"Rabbi Loew?" Mordechai asked. "What are you doing here? It isn't safe for you. And is that your golem behind you?"

"It isn't safe for you either," Loew said. "Come, we have to—"

"Hush," Dee said. "I think they're coming back."

No one spoke. Footsteps headed toward them, two men by the sound.

"Quickly," Mordechai said. "There's a ladder."

He began to lower himself. Dee hurried to the circle and looked inside. He could just make out the first rung in the light from the open door.

He followed Mordechai. The ladder went down into pitch darkness. "What is this place?" he asked. "How do you know about it?"

"It's a dungeon," the peddler said. Loew and the golem came down the steps after Dee. Mordechai went back up and muscled the circle back into place. The dark was absolute now; Dee felt as if he'd gone blind. The air was chilly and smelled of mold and damp earth and something else, iron perhaps. Or old blood? He shook his head; he was being fanciful.

He recited a spell and a small light bloomed outward around them. The shadows fell back; Dee made out the wavering forms of Loew and Mordechai. The golem remained in shadow, a dark looming shape.

Dee had not noticed what Mordechai looked like earlier. Now he saw that he was shorter than either Dee or Loew, with a sun-browned face. His white hair was thinning on top; what remained curled around the sides of his head like sheep's wool. His beard, also white, was trimmed close to his face. He had brought a candle out of one of the voluminous pockets of his dark shapeless cloak; he put it back when he saw Dee's glow-light.

"I know because I hear things," Mordechai said. The fear Dee had heard earlier was gone. "People tell me things when I travel. I daresay even Rudolf's forgotten about it, though."

An animal chittered from somewhere, and another animal answered. Five or six of them ran at once, their paws skittering over the floor. Rats, Dee thought.

"Someone just told me an intriguing story, in fact," Mordechai said. "Apparently there's a man in Prague who's making boots to give to the Messiah when he comes. Boots made of the finest, softest leather in the world. They say he's been working on them for five years."

"Never mind that," Loew said. "Why did you tell the soldiers you were me?"

"They were about to arrest you."

"And you preferred them to arrest you instead? What did they do when they found out you weren't me?"

Mordechai laughed. "Their hospitality leaves something to be desired, it's true," he said.

"Did they torture you?"

"Come, Rabbi Loew," Mordechai said. "I'm far younger than you. Isn't it better this way?"

"But why did you do it?"

"Do you have any children?" Dee asked abruptly.

Mordechai was silent for a moment, clearly surprised by the question. "My wife and I have two, a boy and a girl," he said. "I visit them as often as I can."

"Just two?"

"What odd questions," Mordechai said mildly. "Why do you ask?"

"There's a rumor you're Izak's father."

"Izak? Oh, yes, Hanna's boy. A nice kid—I wouldn't mind having him for a son. But I always thought his father was Baruch the butcher."

"How often do you visit Prague?" Loew asked.

"Every thirty-six days, if I can. Now would you mind telling me what all this is about?"

Dee heard Loew take a deep breath. "Do you know the story of the thirty-six righteous men?" Loew asked, watching the peddler intently.

"No. Wait—yes, I remember something. They're supposed to uphold the world, is that right? Keep the world from ending, something like that?"

"Yes."

"I don't understand."

"We think—we have reason to believe that you're one of these men."

Mordechai laughed. "Me?" he said. "No, that's impossible. I'm just an ordinary man, trying to make his way in the world."

"You probably wouldn't know if you were, though."

"I daresay no one thinks he's righteous enough. So by your reasoning anyone alive could be the man you seek."

"You appeared on a list."

"A list, was it? My name was on a list?"

"Not your name," Loew said reluctantly. "It said 'Traveler, Jewish Quarter.'"

Mordechai laughed again. "And I'm the only one who travels to the Quarter, is that what you're saying?"

"No, of course not. Come—let's leave this place and talk in the light. Surely the guards have gone by now."

"Certainly."

Mordechai climbed the ladder, cautiously lifted the covering, and pushed it out of the way. Dee winced at the loud groan it made, then winced again as the strong sunlight poured in. He spoke a few words and his light went out.

Mordechai pulled himself up to the floor of the tower. Dee went next; Mordechai gave him his hand to help him climb. Loew came after him, and the golem at the end.

They hurried away from the castle, all of them casting quick backwards glances as they ran. No one seemed to be following them. They went as fast as they could into the Lesser Quarter, the golem and Mordechai in front, Dee and Loew lagging behind.

They made their way past the outsized manor homes, nearly castles in their own right, that Rudolf's nobles had built for themselves. Dee slowed to a walk, struggling to keep Mordechai in sight as he headed in the direction of the river.

Suddenly Mordechai stopped. As Dee caught up with him he saw a group of men fanned out across the road, blocking their way. One of them, Dee saw with dread, was Kelley.

"Stop there," Kelley said. He pointed to Mordechai. "That's the one, the thirty-sixth. Bring him to me. Bring the rest of them as well."

TWO MEN MOVED FORWARD AND GRABBED Dee roughly by the arms. "So you found him," Kelley said. "The thirty-sixth. I don't suppose you were ever going to tell Rudolf."

"How do you know who he is?" Dee asked.

"I saw him in the glass."

"I thought you couldn't use the glass."

"Yes, well, I've grown more adept since we last met. And I've gotten help."

Now Dee saw something odd behind Kelley, some kind of distortion in the air. It looked as if a poorly-made pane of glass hung there; some of the men behind it seemed stretched to nine feet tall, others pinched to the size of gnomes. As Dee watched the disturbance swelled and grew and began to mold itself into the shape of a man.

"Your demon," Kelley said, following his gaze. "I've managed to make him visible in this world. And did you like what I had him do in Trebona?"

"He's not my demon," Dee said hotly. "You summoned him."

"Come now, doctor. He's yours, bought and paid for. Who was it who said knowledge is worth any price paid for it? That is what you said, isn't it? You didn't say, 'Any price except trafficking with spirits,' did you?"

"I didn't call him up, I—"

"Well, it doesn't matter now. You were the one who brought him to Prague, anyway. You thought you were running away, but in fact he was leading you here step by step.

The door opens here, you know. This is where he's the strongest."

Yes, of course, Dee thought. I already know that. But Kelley wanted to talk, wanted to show his old master what he had accomplished by himself. And the more he talked, the more chance they had that something might happen. That, maybe, Mordechai might escape.

"So you weren't the one to make him visible, as you claimed," Dee said, cutting off whatever Kelley had been saying. "It would have happened anyway, as the door opened wider and he became stronger."

"Nonsense," Kelley said. "I learned the spells, I spoke them—"

Kelley turned, somewhat nervously, to look at his demon. He's not in complete control of it, Dee thought. That's interesting.

The demon had become more solid as they spoke. Dee glimpsed a face for a moment: red eyes, scaly skin, two great fangs jutting upward from the bottom row of its teeth. Then the shape wavered and became a bundle of bones loosely tied together. The bones were thin as twigs and the color of ebony, sucking in all the light around them.

Suddenly Dee remembered his visit to Kelley's house, how he had had to face what he feared most in the world, his night-terrors. He tried frantically to think of something pleasant, something to banish the evil. Jane.

The shape distorted again, and he saw a hellish mix of fangs and scales and Jane's lovely eyes and hair. It was the worst sight yet, so terrible that he cried aloud.

Everything turned black. The demon moved within him. He felt himself, his soul, his spark of awareness, sink down and nearly gutter out, smothered by the demon's presence. It feeds on fear, he thought. It knew I was afraid. It was behind everything that happened in Kelley's house. His heart pounded so heavily he was afraid he would die.

The demon forced his eyes open, then worked his legs, turning him in a small circle. The two men holding him had apparently run away. His muscles moved without his volition; it felt as though snakes crawled inside him.

A crowd had started to form, drawn by the noise, or perhaps the scent of magic. Everyone stood still, looks of horror on their faces. He saw Magdalena and Izak and Mamugna. And was that Erzsébet next to them? The demon turned him again and he caught a blur of motion at the corner of his eye; someone or something stood high up in a tower overlooking the street, someone familiar.

"Not the best body I could have chosen," the demon said. It laughed horribly, contorting Dee's face into an unfamiliar grimace. "An old one, about to die. I'll have to choose someone else. Who will it be, I wonder."

The demon turned him again. It stopped when it came to Magdalena. Dee realized with shock that the demon saw Magdalena as she really was, a young healthy woman.

As Dee continued to look at Magdalena, unable to turn away, he felt himself growing aroused. Horrible pictures filled his mind. He saw himself forcing her to the ground and tearing off her clothes, saw her scream and try to push him away. In his vision her cries only served to madden him further and he fell on her and thrust himself into her, a lecherous old goat defiling a beautiful maiden.

It's the demon, he thought. The demon is putting these dreadful pictures in my mind. It's jealous of us, of our flesh, of the things we feel with our bodies.

The demon laughed again. It had read Dee's thoughts, insinuating itself into all the secret places of his mind, ferreting out all those things he kept hidden from the world.

Someone was speaking. He strained to hear it over the

pounding of his heart, the song of blood in his ears. Hebrew, he thought. Someone saying something in Hebrew. Loew, chanting the psalm against demons.

He had forgotten Loew in his terror. "He shall cover thee with his feathers, and under his wings shalt thou trust," Loew recited. "His truth shall be thy shield and buckler."

Nothing happened. The demon continued to stare at Magdalena. Dee's tongue protruded and licked at his lips, sinuous as a snake. "Yes, I like that one," the demon said. "I think I'll have her."

Magdalena stared back at the demon, her head high. She looked proud, unafraid, but Dee wondered if she was remembering the man who had used her and then given her to others, the last time someone had taken control over her body. And then another thought came, one that Dee would have banished immediately if he had been in his right mind. Take it away, he thought. Let it possess someone else, even Magdalena if it has to. Just get it out of me, give me my body again.

"I will be with him in trouble. I will deliver him and honor him," Loew said. He sounded frantic. He had come nearly to the end of the psalm and the demon had not left Dee's body.

Magdalena continued to gaze steadily at the demon, showing it herself, her unswerving truth. Dee waited, not daring to hope for anything. Suddenly he understood what she was doing. Fear drew the demon—and she had gone through fear and come out on the other side. There was nothing more anyone could do to hurt her.

He willed himself to be calm, to follow her example. His heart still pounded horribly, but he was able to make a clear space in his mind. At that moment he was able to understand something. Fear drew the demon, yes, but so did lies.

And he had lied, to the demon and to himself. The pictures in his head had not been put there by anyone; they had been there all along. He had admired Magdalena, had thought her young body beautiful, had entertained, though never for more than a second at a time, thoughts of taking her to his bed and having her for himself.

He collapsed to the ground. The demon was gone. He drew a shaky breath, barely in control of his own body.

Then he remembered the demon's last words. No, he thought, horror filling him. I've failed her like everyone else. He twisted to look at Magdalena.

One of Kelley's men laughed; Dee realized with relief that the demon had taken over him instead. Kelley's other men scattered, understanding finally that it could come for any one of them. Mordechai was free now, but he made no move to leave.

Dee sat up. There was a sharp pain in his forehead. He put a hand up and it came away covered with blood. He must have hit the cobblestones when he fell.

More people were joining the crowd, taking the place of Kelley's men. Some he recognized from the alchemists' tavern, Sendivogius and László and others. Mamugna's dogs whined at the edges of the crowd, their tails down. Erzsébet stood at a distance, biting her fingernails.

He remembered the movement he had seen in the tower. He glanced up and flinched in pain, but not before he had recognized the man. King Rudolf stood there, staring down at the street. The magic had drawn him too.

"This one is not very interesting either," the demon said, its deep voice coming from the mouth of Kelley's man. "Who else is there? Who wants to be next?"

Another man jerked an arm. His eyes grew wide with terror. Then the woman next to him did a horrible wrenching dance. A man began to pull out his hair. One of the dogs growled and snapped at Mamugna, its lips drawn back in a snarl.

The demon was working its way around the circle, taking

over each person or animal in turn. Three people stood between Mordechai and the demon, then two. The man next to Mordechai thrust a finger in his eye and screamed in pain.

Dee held his breath. What would happen when the demon took control of Mordechai? It had promised to kill the thirty-sixth man and remake the world according to its desires.

But Mordechai stood unmoving. A woman on his other side chewed on her fingers, drawing blood. Some people were impervious, then. Mordechai and Magdalena, and who else? Rabbi Loew was next in the circle.

As Dee watched, horrified, Loew threw back his head and laughed a deep gravelly laugh.

LOEW BRACED HIMSELF, WAITING FOR THE DEMON TO TAKE over his body completely. Nightmarish pictures filled his mind, the man destroying his eye, the woman biting her fingers. Then these were replaced by worse things, horrors drawn from his own imagination.

But to his surprise nothing more happened, though he felt the demon's presence in his mind. He wondered why. Could it be because he was a good man, even a righteous man? Could that make him somehow safe, able to withstand possession? Because he was a good man, he knew that—better than almost everyone in the Quarter, better even than the chief rabbi.

Then why wasn't he chief rabbi? Why did the folks of the Quarter withhold that honor from him? He could do so much good for the townspeople. He could—if Mordechai were gone he could remake the town the way he wanted, could finally put his ideas into practice, could see to it that all the laws were obeyed the way they should be.

The demon looked at Izak with Loew's eyes. Izak, for example, he thought. If he had control of the Quarter and everyone in it he would see to it that Izak never left, that he stayed in the town and lived his life out unmarried and repentant, content with his lot. He saw that Izak and Magdalena were standing near each other. He would put an end to that immediately; Izak must not be allowed to become familiar with such a woman, someone who, according to her own words, had lived on the streets, a plaything for any man to come along.

Mastery, he thought. That was what he wanted, what he needed. Now he saw other pictures: Rivka looking downcast, as a woman should, her usual bold expression gone; Baruch the butcher confessing his sins; the golem docile and following his every command. He saw everyone in the Quarter filing into the streets and crowding the synagogue, saw himself preaching, telling them what they were and were not permitted to do. And if everyone listened to him, if they followed all of God's commands, perhaps the Messiah would even come. . . .

All this could be his, the control, the mastery he had always wanted. He had only to get rid of Mordechai, to—to kill—

He came to himself with a start. What had he been thinking? How could he even contemplate killing a man, especially this man? The demon had tempted him, had put these dreadful ideas into his mind.

Though it had been a pleasant picture. If anyone were to be given control over the Quarter it should be him; he had always known that. He had had a vision of how things ought to be done for a long time.

A long time, he thought. The demon had not given him these ideas, then; they had always been there, at the edges of his mind, growing stronger as time passed. He was no better than Rudolf, really; he too wanted to remake the world in his own image. Perhaps that was what had prompted him to create the golem in the first place.

He shuddered. The action seemed to push the demon

from him. He fell back against a wall, unable to move, chastened by what he had discovered about himself.

DEE WATCHED AS THE DEMON LEFT LOEW'S BODY. THE CROWD had thinned, leaving only Mordechai, Izak, Magdalena, Erzsébet, and a few others. And Rudolf, Dee saw with a start. The king had come down from his tower.

The demon circled the crowd again, taking over one person after another. A strange green fire began to spiral upward, crackling loudly, lifting hair and loose clothing into its vortex. Kelley was speaking something, and so was Magdalena, praying to her pagan goddess, Dee supposed. Loew recited the psalm against demons again. Dee felt the crosscurrents of magic grow thicker as other powers made themselves felt within the circle.

Suddenly Rudolf giggled. Everyone turned to look in his direction; shock came into their eyes, one by one, as they recognized him. A silence fell over the crowd as they slowly stopped reciting their spells.

"Oh, I like this body," the demon said with Rudolf's mouth. "I liked it the last time I had it, and I like it even more now. I would certainly enjoy being one of the most powerful men in the world. And my first command as king—kill that man. The thirty-sixth, the one who claimed to be Loew."

No one moved, not even Mordechai. Why doesn't he run, Dee thought. Is he staying here to—to somehow help us? Is that what being righteous means?

Loew began to recite again. His voice sounded hopeless, as if he knew what he did was futile. The psalm had once caused the demon to leave Rudolf's body, Dee remembered, but he knew it would not be effective a second time. The demon had grown too strong.

"For my second command—bring me all the gold in the world. Bring me everything. I want to collect everything, to own it all, to contain the world within my castle. I want all the women in the world as well. A different woman each night, for as long as I live. And I want to live forever."

Suddenly Dee understood, horrified, what would happen next. The demon would feed Rudolf's appetites while it continued to give its own orders. No one in the crowd would obey it, but sooner or later it would make its way back to the castle, and everyone there would simply assume it was Rudolf. None of them would be convinced of the demon's real nature; the story sounded fantastic, even to Dee. And it would have at its beck and call the entire might of the Holy Roman Empire.

Rudolf fell to the ground, writhing. His arms and legs shot out at strange angles; his head knocked against the ground several times, drawing blood. The green flame circled him and then jumped the gap between them to sizzle along his skin. Rudolf jerked and gasped.

Dee could not allow the demon to keep Rudolf's body. He had once drawn the demon to himself, in Rudolf's castle. He closed his eyes to brace himself and reached out.

The familiar blackness engulfed him, and the familiar loathsome feeling as the demon took control over his movements. "I want Rudolf back," it said petulantly. It stared with Dee's eyes as the king continued to twist in spasms on the ground. "Give me Rudolf!"

Rudolf began to mutter. Drool flecked his lips. "I want all the flowers," the king said. "All the trees, all the stones, all the lakes and rivers and oceans. Everyone and everything in the world must swear fealty to me. All the angels, all the demons. God himself."

He's no longer frightened, Dee thought. His mind has gone, has fled from the horrible thing happening to him. The demon's lost its hold. That's why it was so easy to call it to me.

He quickly hid the thought from the demon, sending it to the clear space he had made in his mind. The demon must not know why it could no longer take over Rudolf; it might think of a way around his madness, a way back in.

The demon raged within Dee, desperately trying to return to Rudolf. The green fire arced toward him, striking him unpredictably and then jumping back, scorching his already raw hands and arms and face. The sparks maddened him but he could not move to protect himself.

Other powers flew within the circle as well: a thin silver stream that strengthened as Rabbi Loew spoke, a gold shimmer that came from Magdalena. Mamugna was saying something, and Sendivogius and even Kelley; the babel confused him, made it hard to concentrate.

Pictures came into his mind, and this time Dee knew that they came from the demon, because he could never conjure up anything so terrible. He saw his daughter Katherine taken by the demon; saw her grow up within his house, an obscene parody of his beloved child; saw the demon relinquish control just enough for Katherine to understand what was happening to her before it finally quenched her immortal soul. He saw it move from Jane to Arthur to Michael, mimicking their behavior perfectly, then saw it reveal itself to him, leaving him shocked and despairing to realize that he had, all unknowing, spoken to it, eaten with it, made love to it.

"Give me back Rudolf!" the demon said. "Give him back or I will torment you like this forever, I swear it!"

Why did the demon think he could return it to Rudolf? He could only summon it to him, nothing else.

Or was there more? Could he have more power over the demon than he thought? Why didn't Kelley control it? Kelley had been the one to summon it, after all.

Had he, though? There must be no more lies, Dee had learned that much. Kelley had summoned it, but then, as Kelley had just reminded him, Dee himself had said that knowledge was worth any price paid for it. And in offering to pay the price Dee had invited the demon in, had allowed it to bridge the gap between the worlds. Suddenly he knew what he had to do next.

He wrested control from the demon—*his* demon—and began to chant. He spoke psalms in Hebrew, prayers in Latin, hymns in English. If Magdalena was right and all beliefs were equally true—and judging from the jangle of light and noise coming from all parts of the circle it seemed that she was—then it didn't matter what he said. He could recite nonsense syllables if he wanted to. It was important only that he concentrate, keep his goal firmly in mind, and pray sincerely to his god.

Someone spoke loudly over him and he faltered, forgetting what he had been about to say. It was Kelley, chanting to the demon, working to strengthen it so that it could possess him fully again. He felt the demon well up within him like a contaminated tide, pulling him under, drowning him.

No. Concentrate. Nonsense syllables. Suddenly he remembered his son Arthur, playing at his feet. "I can speak Czech," Arthur had said. "Listen."

"*Strč prst skrz krk!*" he shouted triumphantly.

To his amazement the demon's hold weakened. He took control of it quickly and sent it into the body of the golem.

Yossel opened his eyes very wide. "I like this body," the demon said with Yossel's mouth. "It's very strong, stronger than any of these others."

The green fire hovered over Yossel. Everyone had gone quiet; all the prayers to all the various gods were silenced.

Yossel's arms flexed. His legs moved. "I don't need Rudolf after all," he said. He scowled, the anger clear on his face for anyone to read. "This body is strong enough to take care of the thirty-sixth with no help from anyone. This is the one I want."

The golem stood still. Dee watched it closely. He hoped

that the demon was spreading itself throughout the body, taking on substance, melding itself with the clay man. It had wanted the world of the senses, of feeling, and what better way to explore the world than with a body more powerful than any other?

Yossel began to change; he seemed stronger, more confident. His malevolent expression deepened. "I'll be able to study now, and to pray. To marry Rivka. To do anything I like, really, marry anyone I like. I'll keep Loew locked in a room, just as he kept me, and I'll visit him whenever I have a question about my studies."

The golem looked around the circle. "No, what am I saying? I won't need to pray. I'll be king, god. Everyone will pray to me. I'll make others like me—no one will ever treat me harshly or laugh at me again. I'll never be alone. All I have to do is kill this man here. A fair bargain, eh, peddler?"

He took a step toward Mordechai. Mordechai stood still, his gaze steady.

"No!" Loew said. "No, don't! I command you!"

The golem stopped. Emotions passed quickly over his face: hatred, desire, fear, longing, uncertainty. Finally he looked at Loew with something like love. His uncertainty returned. He moved toward his creator, went back to Mordechai. He shuffled to a spot midway between the two, in front of Dee, then bowed his head to Loew, his mouth open, his expression unreadable.

Dee reached up quickly into his mouth and took out the *shem*.

The golem fell inert to the ground. Dee looked around the circle, not daring to breathe. Would the demon leave its new body and possess another one? Or had it put too much of its essence into the golem, had it died along with the golem's body?

The green flame guttered out. No one screamed or cried

out or hurt themselves. No one moved. Rabbi Loew bent to the clay body sprawled out on the cobblestones and rubbed at the first letter on its forehead. The *aleph* disappeared; now the word spelled *met*, or "dead."

Loew stood up carefully. "It's over," he said.

"Not yet," Dee said. "We have to close the door. We need to make certain that nothing like this comes through to our world ever again."

"Do you?" Erzsébet said. He had nearly forgotten she was there. "You know what will happen then. No more magic. No more wonders, no more alchemy. Are you ready to sacrifice all that?"

He ignored her. "Quickly!" he said. "The demon was one of the things holding the door open. We must do it now, before something else comes through."

"I've learned a bit about you, Doctor Dee," Erzsébet said. "You desire knowledge more than anything in the world. What will happen when you can no longer look into your scrying glass and converse with angels, when you cannot understand the mind of God? How much will you be able to learn on your own, with no one and nothing to help you?"

"The scrying glass?" Dee laughed harshly. "I learned nothing from the glass. And at least my intentions were good—as you said, I wanted knowledge of God. You only wanted to bathe in blood and stay young forever."

"What is wrong with that?"

"Quiet!" he said. He reached out and felt the door standing open between the worlds. Cold wind and darkness and glittering stars swirled behind it. "Help me," he said to Loew.

They pushed together. The door resisted. Erzsébet smiled mockingly at them and chewed her fingernail. "I bathed in blood today, Doctor," she said. "I'm as strong as I'll ever be. I won't let you close the door."

"Push!" Dee said. He thought of his children, of Katherine taken over by the demon. He could not let anything like that happen again, not to anyone he loved.

Something behind the door pushed back. Something or several things: the demons were rousing in anger at the closing of their doorway to Prague. A tentacle snaked out and crept along the cobblestones. He kicked at it frantically and it retreated. Erzsébet laughed.

Great mouths filled with teeth appeared in the doorway. He strained with his last bit of strength; he could feel Loew laboring beside him. And someone else was helping them; he recognized Magdalena.

Suddenly something gave. He made one last effort. A resounding slam echoed out into the streets.

"God damn you, Doctor Dee!" Erzsébet said. She turned and ran.

"No," Dee said, looking after her. "No, I don't think I'm the one who's damned."

"Come," Loew said. "We still have to get rid of the golem's body."

"Oh God," Dee said. He leaned against the side of a building. "Oh God, I'm so tired."

"As well you should be. We did good work here today." He looked around him and saw Mordechai. "Mordechai, will you help us carry the body?"

Dee had never heard him sound so deferent. Well, Mordechai was the thirty-sixth man, after all, a righteous man, one of those on whom the world depended.

"Certainly," Mordechai said.

"Where are we going?" Dee asked.

"The synagogue."

"The synagogue? What will you—"

"Don't worry. We'll take him upstairs and put him in the attic. And there let him rest for all the long centuries to come. I will destroy all my notes, and if we are fortunate no one will ever learn what I have done."

 THE CROWD BEGAN TO DISPERSE. IZAK and Magdalena walked away, Magdalena wearing her true shape, the young woman. Dee realized that she would never be able to change again, that the magic she had used was gone from the world. But she seemed for the first time to inhabit her body: still wary and suspicious, but no longer fearing men and what they might do to her in their lusts. She had faced something far worse, and had triumphed.

He saw, horrified, that the king still writhed on the ground, muttering something softly to himself. He bent to listen.

"I want you all killed," Rudolf said petulantly. "All of you. Why does no one obey me? I am your king, your emperor. I want that one killed first."

To Dee's surprise the king pointed at Kelley. "You did not tell me you found the thirty-sixth, did you, Master Kelley? What were you going to do with him? Do you think you're strong enough or wise enough to rule the world yourself? I'm sick of your betrayals."

Kelley turned and fled. "Bring him to me," Rudolf said.

Only Dee and Loew and Mordechai and Sendivogius were left. No one moved. The king threw back his head and howled like a wild animal, then slammed his head against the ground. "Bring him to me, I said! You are all dead, all dead men!"

Chills broke out along Dee's arms. "I think he's gone mad for good this time," he said.

"He wasn't strong enough," Loew said. "The demon's possession, the currents of magic flowing around him—it was all too much for him."

"You," Dee said to Sendivogius. "Help him back to the castle. If he recovers his wits I'm sure you'll be rewarded handsomely. Money, patronage, whatever you want."

Sendivogius bent to Rudolf and hoisted the king's arm over his shoulder. "What are you doing?" Rudolf asked. "I said I wanted you killed. Stop! Where are you taking me?"

Sendivogius headed toward the castle. The anger seemed to leave the king; he walked quietly, leaning heavily on the other man. Suddenly he stopped and howled aloud. Sendivogius spoke soft words to him, urging him to continue.

Dee watched them until they were out of sight. Then he and the others positioned themselves around the golem, Mordechai at his head and Dee and Loew at his feet. Mordechai called out, "One, two, three!" and they all lifted the body together. It was surprisingly light. Because Mordechai, the thirty-sixth righteous man, was helping them?

Perhaps, Dee thought, it was because he himself suddenly felt wonderfully renewed, as if he could carry the golem with no help from anyone. He had not backed down. He had finally faced his demon.

They began the long walk to the Jewish Quarter. Mordechai was in the lead, walking backwards and every so often craning around to see the road. "The golem—" Loew said.

"Yes?"

"At the end, when he looked at me. Do you think he sacrificed himself knowingly? That he obeyed me to save my life?"

"I don't know. Maybe. Maybe he did."

They walked for a while in silence. "What was that you recited?" Loew asked.

"I—it was something my son taught me. It means—"

"I know what it means." He sounded amused. "I wondered why you said it."

"I don't know. It popped into my head just then. No, wait. I said it because—because the goal of the alchemist is the union of opposites. Man and woman, sun and moon. And Englishman and Bohemian, I suppose. Or Christian and Jew."

"What are you saying? That an old tongue twister is really an alchemical formula?"

Dee laughed. "Well, no, not really. I think what I mean is that there is something to be said for unions, for meetings, for traveling. That two separate things, or ideas, or countrymen, can combine into one thing, something different, maybe something better. Me, for example. I feel as if I've changed a great deal since I came here." He laughed again. "I told Vilém that I could best pursue the goal of alchemy outside the study. It's not about making gold, not really. That's what Kelley never understood."

"I don't think I follow you."

"Don't you? But you learned something too, didn't you? I saw your face change when the demon possessed you."

"I did, yes."

They had been keeping their eyes on Mordechai ahead of them, but now they turned and looked at each other. Dee opened his mouth, and then Loew, but neither said anything. They had been about to trade confidences, Dee knew, to say what they had learned from the demon, but each of them had changed his mind at the end. It was too personal to speak of.

"Anyway, there will be no more alchemy, if Erzsébet was right," Dee said. "The door is closed now." He spoke the words to summon his glow-light, but nothing happened. "Magic is gone from the world."

"But there is still learning," Loew said. "Learning, and the meeting of opposites."

"Yes," Dee said. "That's true."

As they walked Dee noticed people stop and stare at them, then hurry away. A few crossed themselves, something Dee had rarely seen since the reign of Catholic Queen Mary thirty years ago. Everyone, it seemed, was aware that something strange had happened, something uncanny, and no one wanted to linger very long in the presence of magic.

Finally they came to the bridge across the river. Mordechai looked behind him and maneuvered the clay body through the archway. Drivers swore at them as they veered out in front of the coaches, then fell silent when they saw the great body of the golem.

At the other bank Dee at last felt a dull pain in his arms and called a halt. They set their burden down. "What will happen to Magdalena, I wonder?" he said when he got his breath back. He rubbed his arms. "And Izak, too. I saw them leave together."

Loew scowled. "Izak should not have gone away with that woman," he said. "He—" He shook his head. "Well, I suppose it's out of my hands now."

He *has* learned something, Dee thought. "Perhaps they'll be happy together," he said. "We can wish that for them, anyway."

Loew looked doubtful; he hadn't learned as much as Dee had hoped. They picked up the body and continued on. At the synagogue they stopped two men cleaning the bronze lamps and asked for their help. The men backed away, clearly unwilling to touch the golem. "It's not alive," Loew said. "It can't hurt you."

The men still looked uncertain. "It's dead," Dee said. It was not dead, not in the sense that he understood the word, but the men seemed mollified.

The five of them carried the golem up the narrow staircase to the attic. Light came in through high windows, illuminating a slow stream of dust. Dee saw a few torn prayer books, a broken chair, a branched candelabra. The climb had tired him and he nearly dropped the body, but the others managed to catch it and set it down gently.

Dee stood back. What would future generations make of the clay body in their attic? Would someone try to make it live again? Or would it gradually fall apart, join the dust around it and become forgotten?

They left the room. There was a key in the lock, and Loew turned it and put it in his pocket before heading downstairs.

"Well, my friend," Loew said. "I think this is finally good-bye."

"Not yet," Dee said. "I have one more thing to do before I go." He turned to Mordechai. "Can I have use of your flint and a candle? If Erzsébet is right, I have no magic left."

HE LEFT THE JEWISH QUARTER AND HEADED SOUTH. IT HAD been dawn when Loew had come to his door to tell him about Mordechai's arrest and now, somehow, it was nearly evening. Several times as he walked he glimpsed the river through the maze of buildings on his right, and saw the sun flashing off the water as it began to set.

The journey he had to make was a long one and he rested twice, once in a manicured park and once by a fountain in the shape of a centaur, the water pouring from its mouth. The streets were nearly empty; he wondered if everyone in the city had somehow felt the magic he and the others had unleashed and fled indoors until it passed.

Finally he arrived at Kelley's manor house. It seemed deserted; no lights shone in the windows and no smoke curled from the chimneys. He went to the front door and knocked boldly, waited a moment and knocked again.

As he expected, no one came to answer the door. Kelley could be cowering somewhere in his chilly house, too fearful to even light a fire, but Dee did not think so. He knew the other man too well by now. When Kelley had heard Rudolf pronounce sentence on him he had run as fast and far as he could; he was almost certainly on one of the roads leading out of Prague.

Dee tried the door, and it opened to his touch. He imagined the house responding to the surge of magic rushing through the city, imagined the ghosts rousing and the old terrors growing stronger.

He stopped on the threshold and lit Mordechai's candle, then stepped inside. He braced himself for more of the house's phantoms but nothing happened; he caught only the faintest shudder of wind and a few quiet voices muttering to themselves. Holding the candle out in front of him like a talisman he headed farther into the house.

The stairs were where he remembered them and he mounted to the next floor. The candle flame flickered, casting long shadows on the walls; the cold marble carvings seemed to move in the dim light.

He reached Kelley's study and went inside. As he had hoped, all his equipment was still there. He brought his candle closer and saw what he had come for, the gray velvet bag containing the showstone. Kelley had taken it back from Rudolf.

He held it in his hands, feeling the chill ball of glass through the cloth, turning it around and around in his long fingers. He grasped the bag by the neck and lifted it high in the air, intending to shatter it against the floor. And then, for no reason he understood, at that time or later, he changed his mind and carried it out of the house.

It was very late by the time he returned to his inn. A clock somewhere was striking the hours, on and on, but he was too tired to keep an accurate count. The stars dazzled, as if someone had thrown all the emperor's jewels into the sky. He climbed the stairs to his room and fell on the bed.

He woke to the sun in his eyes. He stood up carefully, feeling every muscle protest. And he realized he was ravenous;

with a shock he remembered that he had had nothing to eat the day before.

An hour later, fed and dressed and blinking in the sunlight, he made his way to the Jewish Quarter. A clock rang once; the sound seemed to shimmer in the bright air. Was it truly one o'clock? Had he slept as long as that?

When he got to Loew's house he saw that a group of people stood at the door, arguing fiercely. "Where is it, then?" someone asked, and someone else shouted, "Yes, what have you done with it?"

"He's gone," Loew said. Dee could not see him over the heads of the crowd, but his voice carried loudly into the street. "He won't trouble you any more."

"How do we know you're telling the truth?"

"Yes, show him to us. Or is he still hiding in your house, about to run wild, to kill and maim like he did the last time?"

"He never killed or maimed anyone," Loew said. "You know that as well as—"

"He's in the synagogue," someone said, cutting Loew off. "In the attic. My brother and I helped put him there yesterday."

"Are you certain?"

"Of course I am."

"Which synagogue?"

The crowd began to disperse, following the man who had spoken. Loew stood at his door, watching them go. "Well, it can't be helped," he said. "I should have known something like this couldn't be kept quiet."

"Don't worry—they don't know how to restore it to life," Dee said.

Loew looked up, seeming to see Dee for the first time. He smiled wryly. "Let's hope not, anyway."

"This time I've truly come to say goodbye," Dee said. "I'm going back to Trebona, to my wife and family."

"Goodbye, my friend. I hope you can visit me here once or twice. I don't think Rudolf will bother us any further."

"Of course I will," Dee said.

They stood a while, unsure what to say. Dee moved forward awkwardly and embraced the other man. Loew stiffened for a moment and then returned the embrace. Unions, Dee thought. Meetings. Never one in the whole history of the world as strange as this.

He returned to his inn to pack, and took a coach to Trebona.

HE STAYED WITH HIS FAMILY AT COUNT VILÉM'S HOUSE FOR two more years, visiting Loew in Prague several times. A year after he returned he learned of the death of King István, and he wondered what would happen to Erzsébet without her protector.

Jane bore him another son in March of 1588, whom they christened Theodore. In the fall of that year they began to hear news of a great sea battle that had taken place between the English navy and the powerful Armada of Spain. Early rumors said that England had triumphed over Spain, but Dee thought that that could not be true, that England could not possibly overcome the might of the Armada.

And yet it was; in the next few weeks they received several letters confirming it. (He had almost grown unused to the luxury of letters; he had traveled so much that letters had followed him across Europe like flocks of birds, always landing one address behind him.) He drank into the night with Count Vilém in celebration, giddy with joy.

England now began to occupy his thoughts more and more. He wanted to go back, to see his people again, and his queen. He had saved a good deal of Vilém's allowance, and he spent an entire day adding and subtracting, realizing finally that they could indeed afford to return home.

The family set off in a magnificent train: three new coaches drawn by four young Hungarian horses each, three wagons for their furniture and clothing and books, and three riding horses. They made their way back slowly; he could not help but contrast this journey with their hasty and terrified flight outward, and he saw a good many things—castles and churches, people and libraries—that he had missed before.

They stopped for a long time in Bremen, putting their riding horses to pasture in the town meadow. He presented the twelve coach horses to the Landgrave of Hesse, who had given him protection as he moved through the landgrave's territories. From Bremen they sailed on to England.

They reached his house at Mortlake near Christmas, where they found a number of unpleasant surprises waiting for them. His precious library had indeed been plundered and burned as Kelley had prophesied, and his financial affairs, which he had left in the hands of Jane's brother Nicholas Fromond, lay in ruins.

For the next few years he lived quietly, studying and visiting his neighbors and attempting to replace his lost books. He thought about his time in Bohemia a great deal. Kelley had been right about the library burning, and he had seen Mordechai in the glass. Could some of the other things he claimed be true as well? Did his wondrous angels really exist? He tried to make contact with them but could not: Because he had never been able to see them? Because Kelley had lied? Because the doors between the worlds had closed for good? He continued to write to Judah Loew, of course, and Loew told him the same thing: that he was unable to see or hear spirits and could no longer do the simplest magic.

But no matter how much Dee experimented he could not

bring himself to look in the showstone; over the years he lost track of it and finally came to consider it lost.

More children were born. In a fit of nostalgia for the wonders Kelley had shown him he named one daughter Madimia, after the child-angel. Perhaps there really was a Madimi, somewhere out there in that realm of angels that was now closed to him. He regretted this flight of fancy when a third daughter was born, and he gave her the prosaic name of Frances.

The large family put a great strain on his finances. He tried several times to win patronage, but to no avail. Finally, at the end of 1592, he began work on a document which he called *The Compendious Rehearsal of John Dee*, a list of the many things he had learned and written and would write in the future, "if God grant me health and life." He meant to send the manuscript to Queen Elizabeth, to show her how deserving he was of her patronage.

He spent a good deal of time on this document, pottering about the house, picking up books and putting them down. He explained in the manuscript itself that he wrote about things almost at random, as they came "out of diverse chests and bags wherein they lay." He looked for his diary, hoping to resolve some of his questions about when and where certain things had happened, but he seemed to have lost that somewhere between Bohemia and England as well.

One day he found a chest in a corner of the attic that he had completely forgotten. He pried out the nails that held it shut and opened it. Suddenly something transported him back to Bohemia, a chance smell emanating from the chest or the feel of a fabric.

Inside he found the fur he had bought in Transylvania; it looked barbaric in the cold light of England and moths had been busily at work eating holes in it. There was the brooch he had bought for Jane but never given her, and some Bohemian glasses, several of them cracked, and a button made of horn, and a few tarnished Hungarian coins. There was a stack of letters, most of them from Loew, and some moldy books—so *that* was where that ephemeris had gone to—and at the very bottom a mouse gray velvet bag, also moth-eaten, with something heavy inside it. The showstone.

He opened the bag and took out the stone. And then, as he wrote later, "I had sight in the Crystal offered me, and I saw."

Dark shapes swam upward from the depths, cities and houses and people. Then one face emerged out of the confusion and resolved itself. Kelley. He jerked back in alarm.

He had not had any contact with Kelley over the long years, did not even know if the man was alive or dead. Curious, he peered into the glass again. He saw that Kelley had returned to Prague, that he had somehow convinced Rudolf he knew the secrets of alchemy. For this he was granted a knighthood; Dee watched the ceremony with a combination of amusement and dismay. And Kelley had married: his new wife was a wealthy Bohemian noblewoman, and with her money he purchased a brewery, a mill, and several houses.

He saw Kelley sitting at his desk, busily writing in a book. As the scene became clearer Dee realized with shock that the book was his own diary. He read all sorts of nonsense over Kelley's shoulder: how the two of them, Dee and Kelley, succeeded together in finding the Philosopher's Stone; how they sent an ingot of pure gold to the queen; how Arthur played with toys transformed into gold. Kelley mimicked his script, something he had done a number of times before; he was a perfect forger, whether of handwriting or gold. These lies were all that posterity would know of him, Dee realized, and his old anger, which had never completely left him, returned.

The scene shifted again; Dee understood somehow that he was peering into the future. He saw Rudolf's madness return, saw the king grow impatient and demand the Philosopher's

Stone. And when Kelley was unable to give it to him he had his new-made knight arrested and thrown into a tower at one of his hunting lodges.

Kelley would remain there for years, Dee saw, while his wife went heavily into debt petitioning Rudolf and his counselors. Finally he would bribe a guard for a rope and lower himself from the window. But the rope would break, and Kelley would be found the next morning unconscious and suffering from a broken leg. Dee watched, his earlier anger now replaced by compassion, as the leg was amputated, as Rudolf, taking pity on his old counselor, brought him back to Prague.

Kelley would spend the next few years in poverty, trying desperately to get back into the king's good graces. He would be locked up again, this time for debt, attempt escape again, and finally swallow a poisoned drink smuggled in to him by his wife.

Next Dee had a sight of Rudolf, his face contorted in madness. He saw that in a few years what the king had long feared would come to pass: after a good deal of intrigue his brother Matthias would take over his throne. "You have arrived at the conclusion that you must abandon God altogether," Matthias would say, accusing his brother. "You consort with witches, alchemists, Kabbalistic intrigues and similar things. . . ." Rudolf would die, alone, insane, and with no legitimate heirs, within the year.

That picture faded and was replaced by a swirl of other images—and these scenes too, Dee realized, portrayed the future. A procession of dark-clad men walked up the center aisle of Judah Loew's synagogue, investing him with the title of Chief Rabbi of Prague. Erzsébet Báthory sat on trial for the deaths of 650 young women; he saw her found guilty, saw men wall her up in a room in her castle; her food was passed to her through a small slit in the door but otherwise she had no contact with the outside world until her death a year later.

More shapes swam in the glass. Izak and Magdalena moved toward each other carefully; he put his arms around her, and she trembled but did not back away. Then he caught a brief glimpse of them a few years later, sitting by a hearth-fire, surrounded by a great number of cats. They had a ballad sheet spread out on a table before them; Izak was taking the tenor part and Magdalena the soprano. And though they didn't harmonize completely, Dee could hear that they were satisfied with the music they made.

That sight passed quickly, though the music remained. A young child dressed in a gown of red and green silk appeared in the glass, dancing before him. Her gown changed color as she moved. His skin prickled; he realized that this, at long last, was the angel Madimi. She curtseyed gravely to him, her eyes kind. He understood that this was all he would be granted. But he thought it would be enough.